San Francesca

THE UNBEATEN TRACK PART 1

JJ Williams

authorHOUSE®

AuthorHouse™ UK Ltd.
500 Avebury Boulevard
Central Milton Keynes, MK9 2BE
www.authorhouse.co.uk
Phone: 08001974150

First published by AuthorHouse 11/26/2007

ISBN: 978-1-4259-7926-3 (sc)

Printed in the United States of America
Bloomington, Indiana

This book is printed on acid-free paper.

SAN FRANCISCO, 3 SEPTEMBER 2003

God I hate flying. I should have taken all the three valiums instead of just the one, as I only managed to get two hours sleep. And I should have just washed it down with water and not with half the bottle of Jamesons that I bought at Heathrow.

Now I feel like fucking shit. It's as if I have just woken up with a banging hangover. I wouldn't have minded if I got a decent sleep. But I couldn't could I. I kept getting woken up by this old chap, who had been to San Francisco a thousand times before, would go at the same time of year and on the same flight. The old fella wouldn't shut the fuck up. Respect the aged I do, but after a valium and downing half a bottle of Ireland's finest, one's patience start to wear a tad thin. In the end I told the old timer to be quiet and save his chronicles for someone who gave a shit. Mind you this was only after he mentioned that he was a retired teacher from Harrow School for Boys. So he probably deserved a bit of abuse. I reckon he was one of those perverted, multitasked teachers who doubled as the Rugby coach, just

1

so he could instigate some towel flicking in the showers.

I suppose two hours sleep is better than none at all, even with a hang over, and at least I haven't woken up in my one bedroom, London flat next to some slapper after a Friday night on the lash.

I am in the golden state of California and to add to my delight my backpack is one of the first to arrive onto the baggage claim carrousel.

It is a stark contrast to when I arrived in Thailand last April. Then, my backpack didn't arrive at all! And I was only compensated with a cotton British Airways t-shirt and shorts combo to wear. I was so fucked off that I ended up getting pissed up on vodka and red bull flavoured ephedrine at a Bangkok massage parlour come sports bar with the taxi driver that picked me up at the airport. I spent the night watching Arsenal away at Villa on a large screen, while these two petite, Thai birds numbered 9 and 27 gave me an all over massage complete with body slide.

Arsenal won 2-1; Pires scored a blinder; getting on the end of a long cross field Ljungberg pass, coolly flicking the ball over the pursuing Boateng and then lobbing a volley over our old nemesis, Schmeichel in the Villa goal.

Here in San Francisco, I have my backpack and I'm good to go. I clear Customs and Immigration with minimal hassle and decide on this occasion not to take a taxi to my hotel, as I normally would when travelling. For once, I will take advantage of the local San Francisco transport system. First, I need to buy a cheeseburger and a bottle of water in order to wash away this thumping hangover.

San Francisco airport is not situated in the dog arse end of town like so many big city airports. It is located in a picturesque area with the backdrop of magnificent mountains for a view.

I still have not decided where I will be staying; it's either going to be the Union Area or Fisherman's Wharf.

I approach an overweight, female airport officer, and by the time I get to her, I have decided that I will be staying in Fisherman's Wharf. She tells me to take the Number 9 subway to Powell Street, get off and catch the tram all the way to Fisherman's Wharf.

"The tram!" I say with enthusiasm.

"Yes baby, that will take you all the way. And where dya' get that cute little accent?" I tell her I am from London.

"Oh yes you are. Yes you are." She continues as I smile and head for the subway. "You take care now, and you have yourself a good day, because I'm sure you will."

That security officer made me feel great. The Yanks get so much bad press, in light of their handling of the recent conflicts in Iraq and Afghanistan, that it is almost becoming compulsory to hate Americans these days, but from this moment on that's yesterday's news.

This subway is no dark, dingy Bakerloo Line and it certainly isn't the delay-ridden Northern Line. This has got me thinking back to some nightmare tube journeys to work as the clean, airy train arrives bang on time. All of these good vibes are making up for that tiresome flight and aiding my hangover to disappear. After three stops, I arrive at Powell Street in Union. I did not know what tram to catch, but what did catch my eye was an attractive, Hispanic looking, girl with long, dark, wavy hair.

I approach her. Nearly losing my footing in the process, she grows more striking the closer I get. When I get within talking distance, I do my best not to look at her pert, full breasts and focus on her hazel eyes. I ask her politely which tram I should take to get to Fisherman's Wharf. The Latino beauty did not quite catch what I said, so I reiterated, but this time a little slower and not in so much of a deep cockney accent. This time she smiles and tells me to take the next tram. She is curious as to why I called her "love". I can't pick her accent, she is definitely Hispanic but it seems her accent has become very Americanised and she doesn't have that Mexican twang.

After finishing giving her a brief access lesson in Cockney, the tram pulls in. It turns out that the pretty Latina is going in the same direction as I am. As she climbs the couple of steps into the tram, I gaze admirably at her shiny, shapely calves. I do not follow her to the back of the tram, I go to an innocuous position at the front, but making sure I keep her in my peripheral vision.

I have visions of the film "Bullet" and "The streets of San Francisco" as the tram passes through China Town at the top speed of around ten miles an hour. I cannot resist the temptation, and sneak a cheeky look at the lovely Latina. Who is wearing a summer dress that slots perfectly over her curves. My eyes are soon fixed back onto the surroundings of China Town.

Back home, I would get a Chinese takeaway from my local 'Chop Stix' at least twice a week. Here you have more traditional, authentic meals to choose from. At Chop Stix on Ladbroke Grove, it would be chicken in black bean sauce, a number 61 or crispy duck in at number 20. Here I see for starters I could have "Lo Bok Go" *(turnip cake)*. Then I could move on to "Lot jui ha" *(pan-fried shrimp stuffed in pepper quarters)* and then finish simply with "Dan Todd" *(Custard Egg Tart)*. I just manage to catch the name of the restaurant as we continue down Powell Street.

> **The Lichee Garden**
> 1416 Powell Street,
> China Town
> 415-397-2290
> No Reservations
> Relaxed local joint,
> pleasant décor and
> cheap

The tram takes a left on Washington, then a right into the very steep, art deco, Hyde Street. The tram has emptied a little, as a few tourists have disembarked in China Town. In my peripheral vision, I notice that the Latina is still on board and for the first time I catch sight of her whole body, and it is a masterpiece. I again wonder where she is from. With those legs, it could be Argentina, but with that arse, it could easily be Brazil, and as for the breasts, well let's face it, you can find good tits all over the world.

My focus is switched back on to the tram ride; it feels as if I am on a slow-paced rollercoaster as we continue down Hyde Street. I can now see the sparkling blue bay at the bottom of the Art deco Street. I hate being a tourist; however, on this occasion I join the Japs, and get my camera out. I take a couple of pictures of the bay and of the colossal Golden Gate Bridge that has now come into play.

The tram guard shouts "Fisherman's Wharf". He has done a grand job getting us here. I make sure to get off before the Latina, in order for me to track her movements.

> **San Francisco Cable Car Tickets About £6 Powell street Tram, the Best ride in town**

I am already asking the Latina for directions to my hotel before she has even stepped onto the sidewalk.

"Oh hello Love!" she surprises me with her best cockney accent. I smile in appreciation of her humour.

I manage to keep my cool and focus on those hazel eyes. She tells me that there is a Marriott Courtyard Hotel a few blocks away. She asks what I am doing here. I tell that I'm taking a long trip from San Francisco to Acapulco. I can tell she is impressed. She then asks me if I have a pen. I naively hand her one from the side pocket of my backpack, not knowing why she wants one.

"Well if you're in town for a few days, London boy we should grab a coffee, and I could maybe show you around town." She writes down her name and number on her tram ticket and hands it to me, with my pen.

I gaze at the number in a silent amazement. Then disaster strikes. I feel a tingle between my legs. It is the start of an erection. I purposely drop the pen on the floor and squat down to gather it, disguising my boner in the process.

While I'm down there I quickly picture myself waiting for a 52 bus in Ladbroke Grove on a rainy Wednesday morning. The morning after Arsenal have again been knocked out of the Champions League at an early stage.

I rise to a standing position as my member has decreased to a disguisable semi.

I tell her that I'll call her Later, she laughs. "Hey senor! Aren't you even going to tell me your name, love?" I introduce myself in full, "Richard James, pleased to meet you love," while I look at hers on the ticket. Her name is 'Francesca'. We say our goodbyes and I float down Beach Street on Cloud Nine. A block later, I'm at my hotel.

I am staying at a Courtyard Marriott, using the last of my Marriott Reward points that I have collected over the years. It's a box standard room with a huge TV, basic furniture and a humongous bed.

I watch the TV for a while, but I soon get bored of the Californian Governors race, which is currently led by action movie legend, Arnold Schwarzenegger, with Hustler Porn mogul, Larry Flint and Gary Coleman (little Arnold from Different Strokes) in hot pursuit. I could not imagine the mayor for London race being led by an Austrian body-builder with a porn King and a bankrupt, black midget in contention. I shake my head and lightly chuckle to my self "Welcome to California".

I pull myself away from the TV and turn my attention to the view outside of the window. As I look at the spectacular vista of the bay. I think to myself that I had better enjoy my stay here, because after I leave this hotel, it's going to be smelly backpackers, hostels and guesthouses. I continue to look at the bay. To my right I can see Alcatraz Island in San Francisco Bay and to my left is the awe-inspiring Golden Gate Bridge beaming over the Pacific. In between them, I look down and see the tram ticket with Francesca's number on it.

Jet lag is kicking in big time and I slump onto the gigantic bed. It is now 7:00 pm. I decide not to go out for a walk just yet; instead, first I order a pizza. I order a Mexicana with chicken to replace the pepperoni. I give the deliveryman a tip when he hands me the pizza, which is as big as the TV. The pizza is washed down with a Jamesons and diet coke. Now I feel charged and revitalised and can now take that walk and then maybe I can call Francesca. Yea, I'll do just that when this episode of *Seinfeld* has finished. After watching for ten minutes I am getting increasingly tired, that jet lag just won't let go. The humour of Jerry, Elaine, George and the outrageous Kramer is not enough to stop my eyes from shutting.

My eyes blink open. But they now see Mr Miyagi and Daniel going through a martial arts routine. I laugh as I realise I'm watching "*The Karate Kid*". I must have slept through the *Seinfeld* marathon. It is now 3:00 am! So much for my stroll and I guess I'll have to call Francesca tomorrow. I decide to go back to sleep, even though I am not feeling that tired anymore. So, the bottle of Jamesons is polished off to aid me.

Three hours later, I am awake again. 6:00 a.m. isn't a bad time to arise.

I step out of the hotel in the midst of the famous San Francisco fog and head toward the bay and decide to turn left at the start of the Embarcadero, which is the Sea Front or the promenade if you like. I get as far as Pier 39 when I hear an oinking noise. I approached the noise and discover that it is a colony of seals that have taken up residence on an island jetty.

The oinking noise Combined with a whiff in the air that you would normally associate with the camel house in London Zoo, I think is an interesting place to kill some time before breakfast.

There must be at least a hundred seals here. I get my camcorder out to take some footage of the scene. After about a minute of filming, an old white-haired fisherman gets in the picture. He smiles and says howdy once he notices that he is on camera. He's in his sixties, probably retired. I sense that he comes here a lot, because he has named certain seals.

"That's Wilma over there. The one that's been bitten, that's Dorothy. And yep, that's Mary right up on top there, ho, ho."

"So how did you get to name them?" I ask inquisitively confused.

"Well, you know, I just give them the names of all my ex wives. They behave just like them too, Ho, Ho. Wilma is a greedy seal and always goes with the male with the most fish. Dorothy is aggressive and cunning, she waits to see which male has the best home, seduces him then aggressively chases him out. And Mary, oh Mary, she's new to town and acts all shy, but truly is a little hussy. Look at her; she just sleeps with just about everyone, ho ho."

He introduces himself as Joe. He is a retired fisherman. A three-time divorced retired fisherman. I could have spoken to Joe for a lot longer but hunger has kicked in big time. Breakfast time! Joe sends me in the direction of a café that he knows well.

"Yea you'll get a great feed there son," he says. The café is called Francesci's.

Outside I check out the menu and decide on corned beef, hash browns and two fried eggs. An Asian-American woman greets me. I hope that is the accurate description for her Ethnic group. I do not want to upset anyone. There are so many categories these days. I recently met this bird in Queensway, West London. She was working at the juice bar at the Whitleys Shopping Mall. We got chatting and progressed to the point where we could ask each other where we were from. She told me she was from South Africa. I thought that I would impress her, by saying, "Oh you must be a Cape Coloured," as she had caramel coloured skin.

She corrected me angrily with, "It's Cape Malay, actually!"

The waitress brings me coffee and continues to top it up while I collect my thoughts. I think about what I have left behind and what I will miss. I think of my mother and family, my friends, London nights and Arsenal. I feel a little emotional as my food arrives. It is a decent spread, and hmm! It tastes great. It makes me think of London again, boring Wednesdays, countless boring, reality, celebrity television shows, working all week at a boring, limited job, wishing I was somewhere else- like here, and then spunking the wages that I should be saving for an overpriced mortgage that

I will never ever afford to pay back on overpriced drinks at ponsey wine bars, where birds only chat to you if you've got a bit of gear for them. Do I miss London, do I fuck.

As I continue to tuck into my food, I look around the café and at the old, black and white pictures of fishermen of days gone by, on the wall. I am looking at an old picture on the door of the golden age of the fishing industry when the door opens. Joe the retired, multi-divorced fisherman walks in.

"Hey my man from England, how's the breakfast going? Ha ho!" he slaps my back.

"Yea it's lovely, thanks for the recommendation."

He then takes off his coat and kisses the Asian waitress. This must be a close-knit kind of breakfast cafe. I bet these guys have been coming here for years. I think its great, a real old, traditional local fisherman's joint. Then Joe walks into the kitchen. Ok, Joe is an employee of the café. Why not, I think to myself, why not recommend your place of work to a tourist?

Actually, it turns out that Joe is the owner of the café, and the waitress is his wife. She hails from the Philippines. So that makes her Philippine-American, actually! I pay for my food, say my goodbyes, and head out. I do not feel as if I have been shafted, because the food was top draw. In fact I feel privileged to have been asked by Joe, (albeit slightly indirectly) into his café.

I'm a big fan of the family business. I am also a big fan of Joe. It looks like he has found happiness in his fourth marriage, going the Asian way with his young Pilipino wife. I am a great fan of an interracial marriage and why not! Im chuffed for him. There's fuck all wrong with going on holiday and bringing a native girl back home. Nor is there anything wrong with ordering a Thai bride off the Internet.

Maybe I am stereotyping here. Just because you see a middle-aged white man with a young Asian girl, it does not mean he got her off www.Asianbrides.com does it?

> **Francesci's**
> **Beach Street**
> **Between Hyde St and Larkin St**
> **Fisherman's Wharf**
> **Get there early enough and have breaky with some real fishermen and maybe the owner.**

After that, I feel like furthering my stroll, in order to lose those extra pounds I have amassed from that corn beef breakfast.

I look into the distance and see the stunning, Golden Gate Bridge, now looking even more outstanding as the sun starts to break through the morning mist. I continue south down the wharf, but nothing is really much to look at here, this early in the morning. Apparently, these streets of Fisherman Wharf were once a thriving fishing and shipping harbour and the heart and soul of San Francisco.

I see that the shipping and fishing industries has long since gone and been replaced with tacky tourist traps. For example, across the street we have that fucking *Ripley's Believe It Or Not!* Well believe it or not, I'm definitely not going in there when it opens for business. Then you have that Waxwork Museum. Who in their right mind comes to San Francisco and wants to see life-sized models of Donny & Marie Osmond for fuck sake?

They could do so much more with this place; maybe restoring some of the old flavour of the shipping and fishing industries, or adding a fish market selling local and international fish or hold an Annual Fishing competition or festival. You know, give something back to the old fisherman, like my man Joe, the likes of whom you can still see, but only few and far between and only in the morning between 5 a.m. and 7 a.m., when they are unloading their catch. I say more tasty catch and less tasteless kitsch!

I work my way through the art deco streets around the marina. I love these houses, they remind me of *Mrs. Doubtfire.* I walk aimlessly in a daze until I get to a massive park called The Presidio, the gateway to the Golden Gate Bridge. I find out from the high school group I have infiltrated, who are getting a history lecture from their teacher, that it is a historic Spanish outpost. Actually, this was the most northern out post of the Conquistadores.

Two high school chicks spot me. With the exuberance of youth, they make their way over to me and are now standing about two metres to the right from where I am absorbing the history lesson. The two chicks start flirting with me in a high school, girly, giggling fashion. One of them is sturdy, pretty and blonde, the type of which we have become very familiar with over the years in teenage high school flicks from *Porky's* to *American Pie*. The other is a Jewish or Italian looking brunette with a tidy round arse. She kind reminds me of Stockard Channing (Rizzo from Grease). This triggers me to carry on with my walk.

Fort Point
Marine Drive (556 1683)
Bus 28 or 29
Open 10 am-5 pm
Admission: Free
A brick fortress on the southern edge of the Golden Bridge and the northern-most point of The Presido. For Civil War performances check local guides.

I set off leaving the young teens to their lecture on the Northern Conquistadores of 1776.

Arguably, the greatest British artist to cross the pond is Alfred Hitchcock. I am a big fan of his work. One of my favourite films would have to be *Vertigo*, and I am now standing at Fort Point, the exact spot where the beautiful Kim Novak dramatically faked a suicide attempt in order to delude the great Jimmy Stewart.

I am almost on the bridge, but before I set off on my pursuit, I spend a minute gazing at it. Suddenly I hear familiar girlie giggles. It is the high school chicks and their school party. They must be here for some sort of historic performance.

As the girls continue to giggle, I wave goodbye to them and start my pursuit of the bridge.

When I think of bridges, I think of Lambeth, Vauxhall or Waterloo, and walking over them in no more than five minutes to get to the ugly south of London, full of villains, sprawling 1950's council estates and shit football teams like Palace, Charlton and Millwall. To compare those pint-sized crossings of the Thames to this immense suspension bridge is like comparing a pyramid to a coffin.

I cannot believe how big this bridge really is. It's so big that it makes me feel lonely, as I make short inroads into the crossing. I am not lonely for long, as I can hear footsteps coming behind me. They do not past me when I expect them to; instead, there is a tap on my shoulder. The two high school chicks have wandered from their lecture.

"Shouldn't you girls be at that civil war lecture?" I ask them.

"Not really," says the blonde.

"OK, then aren't you a little young to be following a strange man across a bridge?"

"Who says we were following you mister?" says the young brunette.

"And who says we're young?" adds the blonde.

"Well for starters you're on a high school trip."

"Ha ha, well that's where you are wrong, Mr. Accent. We are actually on a teachers training program," says the brunette.

"Yea we are on a kind of work experience before we start college," adds the blonde.

"College," I say doubtfully. It is all a load of bullocks, of course, but I go along with it for the ride, as the three of us continue across the bridge.

"So what you doing later, Mister?" asks the blonde.

"Later? Nothing. No, actually I have to meet an old friend from London."

"Well, what about tomorrow afternoon?"

"What about tomorrow?"

"Tomorrow there is a free outdoor concert at Golden Gate Park. D'ya wanna come with us?" I pause for a while and then agree to meet with them tomorrow.

The blonde writes down her number then together they run back to join their school party. Maybe I am biting off more than I can chew with these two young birds. But it's always good to keep your options open. Francesca is a stunner, but apart from death and Tottenham Hotspur never winning the premiership in my lifetime, there are no guarantees in this world. In any case, those two young birds will be good fun if nothing else.

I am now more than half way across the bridge, and the end is in sight.

It is a glorious day. The sun has now completely burned through the clouds and the view of the bay is breathtaking. A few wind surfers, and I think you call the other lot kitesurfers, have taken advantage of the breezy conditions. Beyond them is the island of Alcatraz. In the sky, a helicopter has joined the postcard setting. First it flies over the bridge and then underneath it for good measure.

I am finally there; the colossus bridge has been crossed. I'm fucking knackered in much need of a glass of water and maybe a Diet Coke to quench my thirst. While I'm guzzling them down I look over at a group of cyclists, also having a breather. I notice that one of the bikes has been left unattended. One of the cyclists must be taking a piss.

The rest of the group abandon their bikes and take time out to get their drinks, and then pose for a group photo. I have no choice; well that's a lie. I have three choices; I could walk back over the bridge, call a cab, or "borrow" one of these mountain bikes. I take the third option, but I question myself with a bit of moral decency.

It's not fair that I steal one of these bikes, is it? One of these cyclists will have to walk back to wherever they are staying. Maybe the bike that I borrow belongs to someone that is just as tired as I am.

I am half way across the bridge on a decent spec mountain bike. The fresh wind is caressing my face. This is absolutely fucking fantastic, why didn't I think of hiring a bike myself? I complete the rest of the bridge and make my way through the cycle route of The Presidio.

Now I'm not a thief, but I was desperate, there was no way I could have made it back across the bridge on foot. That cycle group must have some sort of insurance policy that caters for this type of situation. Surely the bike hire company will send a car to pick him or her up. But then he or she would have missed out on half a day of great cycling. To appease my bugging conscience, I decide to return it to the bike hire shop and not just dump it on the street as I did in Oxford once.

Oxford many years earlier

I got off the Coach at Gloucester Green bus terminal in the centre of Oxford. I was late as usual to meet my girlfriend, Andrea. Not having any cash to get a taxi, I grabbed myself a half-decent unchained bike from the rack and rode it all the way to the "Wheatly" area of town.

Andrea's parents were lecturers at one of the universities. That day they were due home in less than an hour. In that time I had to reacquaint myself with Andrea and then get her into bed for some teenage kicks. I was only seventeen at the time so sex didn't last long and I was far too young to worry about satisfying her.

After twenty minutes of trying to persuade her with some heavy petting, I was fucking her in the missionary position like a rabbit on speed for all of two minutes. That left almost half an hour, enough time for us to watch *Blockbusters* and chat over a cup of tea and a slither of fruitcake, that her mother used to make.

With five minutes to spare, I got back on my borrowed bike, rode it back into town and left it exactly where I found it.

There must have been an unwritten law in Oxford back then, on the "borrowing" of bikes. It's all changed now though, probably 90 percent of the bikes there are chained and locked.

SAN FRANCISCO,
4 September 2003

The address of the bike hire company is engraved onto the bike lock. It's on Columbus Avenue, which is not far from my hotel.

Once on Columbus, I see the bike hire shop, but the staff can't see me. I'm waiting for the opportune moment to run in and drop the bike off. There is only one member of staff working at the moment. As soon as she goes to the back of the store, I run in, lean the bike against the counter, and then scamper out unnoticed.

Exhausted I get back into my hotel room at around 2:00 pm. That whole expedition has taken me over six hours, but it was well worth it. On the bridge, I saw a world icon and I met two young college chicks in the process, whom I might meet up with tomorrow.

Blazing Saddles Bike Store
1095 Columbus Avenue
North Beach
415 202-8888
www.blazingsaddlessanfransisco.com
$7 per Hour or $28 per day
Cycling is a great and safe way to see the city. Marked cycle routes lead to most attractions. Always lock you bike when left unattended!

Now I am nervous, as it's time to call Francesca. First I need a drink.

To save cash I have bought a bottle of single malt Scotch (Glenmorangie), and a bag of nachos from a liquor store.

I pour myself a glass on the rocks with a dash of dry ginger ale. Unreal, I cannot tell you how good that tastes. I am soon on to my second glass.

I pick up the phone and call Francesca. She answers, and the conversation is flowing immediately. I add some wit along the way. We arrange to meet tonight at a bar on Broadway called Sake Lab at 7:00 pm.

When I hang up the phone I jump on the bed and celebrate. I still have some pizza left over from last night, but I do not have a microwave or a bottle of salad cream to make it edible. I have to make do with the nachos that I bought from the liquor store.

Sitting on the bed flicking through the thousands of channels on cable I settle for the California Governor's race for about five minutes, but I soon start flicking again as I sip my twelve year old scotch, soaking it up with nachos. Incredibly, I manage to find the Fox Sports Channel, who are showing a highlights package of last weekend Premiership games. I should be pissed off as they are showing Tottenham's home game against Fulham, but on this occasion, I am loving it. Our old boy Luis Boa Morte has just scored Fulham's third in a 3-0 win. I can hardly contain myself, as there is nothing better than watching Spurs lose at home, especially when the camera focuses on their long-suffering home fans.

All of a sudden, the whole building shakes.

"What the fuck?" The TV and the alarm clock have reset itself and my glass of scotch has spilled onto the carpet. Fuck this, I'm calling reception.

"Hello and good afternoon Mr James How can we help you this afternoon, sir?"

"Err, just to let you know, the err...room just shook."

"Welcome to California, Mr. James."

"Oh so it was an earthquake?"

"Yes, just a small one, sir. Is there anything else we can help you with Mr James?"

"No thanks."

I discover that it was in fact only a small earthquake, as it is immediately announced on news flash on TV. It read 3.9 on the Richter scale, which is nothing compared to the 1989 earthquake that devastated the Bay area. However I am completely overwhelmed and shaken all the same. It's a good job I have already called Francesca. I pour myself another drink, a stiffer one this time and try to compose myself for the next set of games on extended highlights package.

The first game is Arsenals very first appearance at the City of Manchester Stadium against Man City. I remember watching our last game at Maine Road, Manchester last February in a strip joint in the East End that showed live games on a Saturday. We spanked them 5-1, with an exhilarating display of attacking football.

This season however it was looking a completely different story. After only 10 minutes, Lauren miss controlled a long cross-field pass and deflected the ball past the wrong-footed Lehmann and into the net. It wasn't the best piece of play by the Cameroon fullback, but to be fair to Ralph, he did get a push in the back from Sinclair, that Graham "Arsehole" Poll somehow missed. Mr. Poll of Hertfordshire is the original Arsenal-hating ref, and he hates Vieira in particular. I would like to know the ratio of Arsenal away-games we have lost when that arsehole from Tring has been adjudicating.

Seaman has just settled into the goal for the second half, and is getting a rapturous reception from the travelling Gooners. I have seen Michael Thomas play against us for Liverpool, likewise Ian Wright for West Ham, Petit for Chelsea and even Rocastle for Leeds. However, watching Seaman in goal against us is like seeing your dad stick up for your opponent in a playground school fight.

The adulation, applause and songs for Seaman had not died down by the time Wiltord blasted in our equalizer to become the first Arsenal player to score past the pony tailed one since our Icelandic bit part player, Siggi Johnson put one past Spunker in 1990 whilst playing for QPR.

Sipping this scotch is giving me more trivial, geeky thoughts. In fact, the last Arsenal player to score past Seaman was Edu last season, home against Blackburn when he inexplicably looped in an own-goal over Seaman in a shocking 2-1 home defeat. One for the Arsenal trivia books or pub quizzes surely.

The game was won for us by Ljungberg, who scored one of the easiest goals of his career, from close range, after a mix up in the City defence. Freddie Ljungberg, the Highbury favourite runs towards and celebrates with the travelling Arsenal fans for hugs and adulation, but it's all too much for that wanker Poll who shows the super Swede a yellow card for unsporting behaviour.

It is now 6:50 and I'm sitting in the Sake Lab waiting for Francesca.

When you are in a bar alone it is always a good idea to sit at the bar and make small talk with the bar tender, especially when you're an out of Towner.

The bar tender is a quite attractive girl in her twenties, with a warm smile. It is still happy hour and she hands me the drink and the cocktail menu. True to form, I order a scotch and dry, but thinking of my budget, I get a shot of Red Label instead of Glenmorangie. Commercial Hip Hop is being played in the background. 50 Cent states, *"I don't know what you've heard about me, cause I'm a mother fucking P-I-M-P."*

The Sake Lab is new and futuristic looking in a trendy way. It has a classy restaurant area, where I reckon Francesca and I will eat later. The bar has a real mixed-crowd feeling about it. Young city

25

types with loose ties, adventurous tourist and funky students with rich parents gather to sample the various sakes on offer. I need another drink. "Why don't you try one of our sake cocktails?" suggests the bartender.

I agree, and from the handy sake chart for novices, I order a Junmai Surprise. It actually turns out that I order two sakes: my first and my last! I think I'll go back to Red Label and dry.

It is now 8:00 pm and there's no sign of Francesca. I am feeling a little peckish, not good as I am downing these scotches pretty fast. As the music continues, I wonder to myself how many times I am going to hear *"California Love"* by TuPac featuring Dr. Dre during my stay in the Golden state.

I look to my left and notice that a smartly dressed, well-groomed guy has taken the stool at the bar next to me. He has ordered the fanciest sake cocktail on the menu: The Daiginjo. He is staring at me intermittently, after a while in order to bring to a close the uncomfortable feeling I turn and face him.

"How's it going mate?" I ask in my deepest cockney accent.

He grins with intent, "Oh fine, thanks for asking. How are yooooou?"

"Not bad, just enjoying the local cocktails."

"Well I have many 'cock-tales' to tell if you know what I mean, ha ha ha," I laugh, but decline to hear about his "cock-tales."

He tells me his name is Malcolm. Camp as they come, Malcolm is a film animator, originally from some small, insignificant town in Washington State. "Hey, are you here alone?" he inquires.

"Not exactly Malc, I'm meeting a friend."

"Oh Tiger! You gotta date? How long have you been here?"

"Ahh, about two days."

"Woo, just two days and you've got a date already? You little tiger you!"

"No, I was just lucky, in the right place at the right time, you know."

"Woo, just luck huh! Is it a boy or girl?"

I pause for a second. "Oh no no, it's a girl, it's a girl," I say, setting the record straight.

"Oh my 'gay-dar' was wrong, it must need some tweaking."

I ask him what he is doing here alone. He tells me that he comes here most Fridays to pick up "gay strays." He avoids the more conventional gay clubs.

"Those clubs are full of gay trash, just not my scene anymore. Hey man d'ya wanna join me for dinner?"

"Err no thanks Malc, I'm gonna eat later. I've got a date, remember?"

"Ok, no problem. So what d'ya like as a straight guy: good tits or good ass?" he asks randomly.

I pause while I think. I do like a good peachy, sturdy arse. But maybe this is the start of one of Malcolm's psychological mind tricks, where he tries gets me to question my sexuality. Therefore, arse might be the wrong answer. So I tell him that I'm a breast man.

One sake cocktail and two scotches later, it's about 9:00pm Looks like Francesca has stood me up. I finish my drink and slap my hand on Malcolm's leg. "So Malc, how about that dinner?"

"Yea?" he replies excitedly.

"Yea, come on lets go. I'm 'Ank Marvin."

"Ank Marvin? What ever baby, me too."

We get a table by the window in the retro-futuristic restaurant. I am feeling a little tipsy, but I have my wits about me and am well aware of Malcolm's "gay-dar."

Our conversation is flowing as we order matching cocktails. Then our waiter makes himself known to us; his name is Julian. Another gay boy but more effeminate than what Malcolm is.

"There you go Malc, there's one for you," I suggest.

"No way Ritchie that is just too easy man."

Just before our drinks arrive, I ask Malcolm what kind of guy he likes. I could have asked him whether he prefers giving or receiving but I don't know him that well yet.

"Actually I prefer straight men. There nothing more sexually satisfying than turning a straight guy to the camp side and just watch him suck my cock."

I'd better watch myself here, and watch my drink. I don't want Malc to slip a date rape pill into my sake! This is going to be my last drink for now. The food I order will absorb the sake and scotch, and I should be OK.

I order from the Robata grill. I go for the *Combo Robata (two skewers of Asparagus with prosciutto, chicken and scallions, scallops without the bacon wrap, chicken wings and two pieces of pacific oysters)* Malcolm goes for an aphrodisiac option of a fancy sushi dish.

"Oh sushi is so sexy, don't ya think Richie?"

"Er yea, I guess so," I reply.

Ahh man, still no sign of Francesca. I've been well and truly stood up. I suppose it was wishful thinking, that I would bag a bird like Francesca. I mean really, what was I thinking? Mind you, I did not think I would end up with a couple of San Francisco benders for my troubles.

Malcolm is now talking to the young, effeminate waiter.

"Hey Richie babe, d'ya wanna go to a club? Me and Julian here are going to 'The Stud.' It's in the SoMo area, its not far."

"The Stud," I say.

"Yea it's not far from here. Come on, Richie."

I look at Malcolm who now has his arm around Julian's waist. "Look man, she's not going turn up man, just deal with it."

"Who?" Julian speaks!

"Richard has been stood up by his new girlfriend."

"No way!" Julian speaks again!

"Hey, Richard if you don't want get stood up, get gay," Malcolm's says, rhythmically. He continues, "No gay guy in the right mind would stand you up," I grimace and then agree to tag along.

We tally up our bills together, pay and then head for the exit. We are outside waiting for Julian who is getting his pay cheque and getting dressed for the night ahead. Julian appears in a very tight t-shirt that's slightly low cut, a pair of hipster jeans and flip-flops.

"Wooo look at you! How sexy is that?" says Malcolm as, Julian gives us a very camp twirl, then advances towards us. Julian does not speak much. Dare I say he has been getting by on looks alone. He looks like a male, gay version of Paris Hilton. Malcolm cannot resist him. He grabs Julian buy the hip and French kisses him. Ahh! for fuck sake! That is one sight that we straight men just can't come to terms with no matter how un-homophobic we claim to be. I turn away, look down the street, and hail down a taxi.

> The Sake Lounge
> 498 Broadway (at Kearny)
> San Francisco 94133
> 415 8370228
> Happy hour 6-8 pm,
> Late night sushi Fri & Sat
> 6 - 1:30 am.
> Your movements may be
> tracked on "gay-dar!"

I think of Francesca's no show and feel like going back to my hotel alone, but fuck it, loneliness is such a drag as Jimi Hendrix said in "*1983*." Not the year 1983 the song on 'Electric Lady Land' released in 1968.

In the taxi, I am in the front leaving Malcolm and Julian in the back to do whatever.

"This is going to be a great night. I've already picked up, two boys," says Malcolm. The taxi driver gives me an uncomfortable look. "Oh no," I say to him, "I'm not ga....Oh never mind."

I think all us straight guys, no matter of how much we try, we all have or have had some sort homophobia in our lifetime. Should it really matter to me, that he thought I was gay? I am after all very comfortable with my sexuality. I feel homophobia in men is with those who have a fear that they are actually homosexual themselves.

We reach our destination and are outside the Stud Club. If the queue is anything to go by this is going to be an interesting eye opener of a night. Outside the club there are six-foot tall plus drag queens, plenty of trendy gay guys, a few lesbians (the butch and lipstick variety) and a few straights, I presume. I follow Malcolm and his new boy-toy, Julian to the front of the queue, where the Door Bitch awaits. Door Bitches! I fucking hate Door Bitches, bloody stuck up cows. They fucking do my head in. As usual this Door Bitch, like all the others is devastatingly attractive. Her only flaw, presumably, will be her attitude.

"Hey Malcolm baby, how are you?" says the door Bitch greeting Malcolm.

"Fine Trinity. Look at yooooou! That dress is amazing!" replies Malcolm.

They pretentiously kiss each other on both cheeks and talk while Julian and I look on. Moments later Julian and I get the nod. We are in thanks to Malcolm's popularity.

Once inside Malcolm takes the opportunity to show off his new accessory (Julian). While this is taking place, I make for the bar. I order a scotch, and turn to face the uninhibited crowd on the dance floor. The music blaring out of the hanging speakers, I would describe as sexy, Balearic House. It is accompanied by some equally sexy dancing from the freaky crowd. I notice a beautiful brunette through the dancing crowd. She looks very familiar. She is Latin looking and….its, its… Francesca!

My nerves and my heart jump out of my body, run off and leave me at the bar. I am momentarily frozen. I watch her work her way through the dance floor alone, but she seems to be making herself known to many of the revellers. I retrieve my nerves and heart, get myself together, down my scotch and start to approach her. My nerves and my heart may be back in their rightful place but I am still nervous like a young Impala alone in the Serengeti, as I can now smell her. Oh well, here goes…

"Hello Francesca." She jumps and freezes with her hands over mouth. Her hands then leave her mouth and end up around me in a tight grasp.

"Hey Richard! Thank God you're here."

I don't quite know how to answer that but I do anyway. "What happened to you at the Sake Lounge?"

"I'm so sorry I got called in to work."

"Work!"

"Yea I couldn't turn it down and I didn't have anyway of contacting you. But I am just so glad you made it here. Actually what are you doing here? I can't believe it."

I fill her in on my evening thus far. She is amused when I tell her about my new friends (Malcolm and his mute accessory). She says I look great. I'm wearing a lemon coloured Fred Perry polo shirt with navy trimmings, slightly faded Evisu jeans and pair of Navy Adidas Gazelles(in my opinion the greatest ever trainers, sneakers or whatever people call them, ever made).

Francesca ushers me to the bar, where she buys us drinks. I notice that the buff bartender doesn't ask for any money for these drinks. I think nothing of it as I am now over the moon with reacquainting myself with Francesca. She is looking sexier than yesterday, wearing a turquoise, satin top that wraps across her torso, her pert breasts sit perfectly underneath each of the crossing straps and it is cut low enough to expose her pierced naval. She is also wearing black pedal pushers, the kind that Bananarama made famous in the early Eighties. Her arse looks magnificent in them as they fit her like the skin of a grape.

After a brief bit of useless first date chit chat, she tells me to hang loose while she works for another couple of hours. I agree and don't even bother to ask what kind of work she does here.

The bar man pours me another Scotch, it's on the house. He asks who I am and how I know Fran. He tells me he's a student from Kentucky, well sort of. He dropped out of The University of San Francisco last year, got into the club scene and ended up dating the owner of the club, and now wants to be an actor!

Seems like Mr Buff has gotten caught up in the bright gay big city lights. I think he will regret it one day, probably one day soon, as there are thousands of young gay men who pass through this city every year. I know I am generalising here, but homosexuals aren't known for their lack promiscuousness or their fidelity.

I wonder what Francesca does here. Maybe, she is just one of those people who are employed by the club to make it look good. You know, for quality control purposes. Not everybody can be cool and gorgeous. You could not fill a club of this magnitude every night of the week with the just the cream of San Francisco. Therefore, they let the average Joes and Joanna's pay their way into the establishment and the likes of Francesca get in for free to uphold the 'glamour.' Hold on, but isn't this suppose to be a gay club in the most liberal city in the States, a city where anything goes?

A perspiring fag hag comes to the bar for a drink. She gets a glass of water and downs it in one shot.

"Hey man, having a freaky time?" she says in a trippy fashion.

"Yea I'm having a trip of a lifetime," I reply, "and its just begun."

"Just begun? Hey man, you gotta catch up. Have you had a pill tonight, man?" She tells me that the pill she has taken tonight is the best she has ever had and insists that I should take one.

"Hey man, there she is!" She says pointing at the dance floor.

"Who?"

"The girl who's got the pills, man."

"That's Francesca!"

"You know her, man?"

> **The Stud Club**
> 399 9th street
> San Francisco
> 415 863 6623
> Anything goes, with your dance style, your clothes or your sexual preference.

Francesca comes and leans at the bar next to me and the Fag Hag.

"So you know," she says folding her arms looking at the dance floor.

"Well I'm not going to judge you," I reply.

"No time for that we gotta get out of here. I'll explain later."

She insists that we go to my hotel. We leave the club through a back exit that she knows. We pass through a narrow alley and emerge into the 9th Street.

I hear a voice shout, "Hey man!" It's the same cab driver that I drove me and the girls from the Sake Lounge. Fran and I sit in the back in a complete silence. After a while the cab driver decides to speak.

"You know what? Earlier when I picked you up, you judged me man. You judged me, because you actually thought that I wasn't gay. And baby, I'm as gay as the city of San Francisco."

I grimace as Francesca gives me bemused, disappointed look.

In my hotel room, I pour Francesca, who is sitting on my grand bed, a scotch. I fix myself one too and sit beside her. "Hmm," she says with appreciation, when she takes her first sip. Then she hits me with it. She tells me that she has been selling ecstasy and coke for about six months. It all started one morning after a big night out. She woke up and discovered that she had a few wraps of cocaine in her bag, left over from the night before. She has never been a big drug taker so she decided to sell the stash at a club the following night. She made around $200. Getting so much money for doing so little became addictive as taking the drug itself. Francesca became friends with a few dealers on the scene, and started working for a local legend called Creole. She was working for him for the first two months, making an earning on what she sold for him. Then when she got enough money, she went it alone. Same old story!

"So what was all that about tonight?" I ask.

"Well I am no longer selling for Creole, but that was his club, and he would have killed me if I was in there not selling his drugs."

"Fucking hell! First the earthquake and now this! Not to mention being stood up then being pulled by Malcolm."

After the pause. Francesca breaks the silence, "Must have been some experience for you, that quake, huh."

I smirk, get up and then get myself another drink. Francesca joins me at the window, pours herself a drink and clicks on the TV. She flicks through to Channel 66, MTV. Christina Aguilera sings *"You are beautiful no matter what they say."*

"Hey, Richard I'm sorry about tonight, you know everything, standing you up, the drug thing, and getting you to jet out of the club like that."

"It's been a great day," I reply, "I couldn't have dreamt having a better day than this. Look it's been great just seeing you tonight."

Francesca puts her drink down, steps towards me and gives me a kiss. I react by grabbing the back of her head. As we kiss, I run my hand down her neck, slowly diagonally down her lean back and then onto her rear. Francesca softly nibbles my bottom lip at intervals. She can feel my hard-on and presses against it.

My right hand has moved to her left breast. It is firmer than I thought. I run my fingers over her erect nipple, as if I was playing a harp. Francesca surprises me as she runs her hand over the bulge in my pants, and then slips her hand inside my jeans and into my boxers.

It is that great feeling you get, just before you know you are going to have sex with a stunner for the first time (a fresh kill). There is nothing like it. I wonder how a girl feels at this moment. I wonder how Francesca feels. How can I describe it? For me it is as if we are locked in deadlock at Highbury; Bergkamp has just threaded a slide rule pass into your path now you only have the keeper to beat.

I take Francesca by the hand and usher her to the bed. I get straight on top of her as we continue kissing. I stylishly remove her turquoise satin top to reveal her C cup-sized perky breasts. I kiss, lick and suck them as Francesca groans with pleasure. It's now time for those tight Bananarama pedal pushers to come off. These are piss easy as they have an elastic waist. They are soon off and the G-string follows. I slither down her as if I were giving her a Thai body slide.

Her pussy has been waxed. Her flower is not a fleshy one; it sports a fine line and looks like an empty hamburger bun, classic camel toe! To pry it open, I run my tongue slowly from her clit down her bridge and then concentrate totally on the clit. My aim is to get her to orgasm then I can slip my shaft into her and then go to town. I do indeed get her to cum. My cock is ready to take off like Apollo 13. I shag her firstly missionary, deep and slow. Thank fuck I'm tanked up on scotch and sake, otherwise I would have shot my load by now.

"No stop! No stop!" she yells. Her accent has switched back to her native Hispanic tongue. She turns around, and offers herself to me on all fours, arches her back and sticks her arse out. You would have to be at a Brazilian "Rear of Year" show to see this one topped. After some slow deep strokes and then some up-tempo pounding, we cum together, this time Francesca squirts. I do not know how many of you have witnessed female ejaculation, but when you do, all else will seem eclipsed.

I awake the next morning to the sound of the shower. Francesca steps out of the bathroom wrapped in a white fluffy towel.

"Hey baby sorry about this but I'm in a rush. I gotta get back home and get changed for work."

"Work!" I reply surprised.

"Yea, baby, real work. I work in a coffee shop in Union. Believe me, I wish I could stay."

I wish that too. "So you've got a real, day job to supplement that job night job of yours?"

"My student visa only allows me to work twenty hours a week."

"So you're a foreign student? Where are you from?"

"Don't you think you should have asked me that before you fucked me? I am from Argentina, baby."

"But you speak perfect English… and that American accent…"

"I went to drama school for almost five years in Buenos Aries."

I look at her firm, slender legs. "So you're an Argentine eh!"

"And you're English eh!"

Francesca gets dressed, kisses me on the forehead and leaves.

I am back where I started alone in my hotel room, watching the Californian Governors race. However, it is not as if nothing has happened. Arnie may still be winning but I feel as if I have already won. I'm not saying I'm the gov'na, but after last night, who would argue.

I leave the hotel at around 1:00 pm and head to Golden Gate Park, where the college chicks told me to go. The Annual 9-11 Power to the Peaceful free anti-war concert is taking place headlined by protest music icon Michael Franti and his band Spearhead.

It's not going to be an epic walk today, as the Golden Gate Park is a lot further than the bridge itself and last night was a long one. Therefore, I jump in a cab. Once there I get out and follow the huge crowd, first through the Japanese tea garden, then past the National AIDS Memorial Grove.

In the music arena, anti-war and anti-Bush flags are for sale at one stall and Ché Guevara, Marxist and Ghandi T-shirts at another. Another stall sells essential homeopathic massage oils that can apparently get you as high as a skunkweed joint.

I soon notice the familiar faces of the college chicks; they are giving out leaflets. They are actually not leaflets; they are fake, left wing propaganda dollar bills. Both girls are wearing ankle-length, sequin skirts complimented with tight sleeveless tops. Both sets of tits look inviting, as I read the slogans on their T-shirts. The blonde's top reads "NO WAR FOR OIL," while the Jewish-looking brunette's simply reads "WHAT IS IT GOOD FOR?" Enough said, I suppose.

Amy, the blonde, has a massive Maori tattoo that goes from her shoulder to her wrist. I gaze at it while they brag that Michael Franti is a good friend of theirs. They also tell me they are from Santa Cruz and that I should join them there in a few days for a reggae concert. Maria, the Jewish-looking girl, writes down a phone number. I might just take them up on this offer.

"Enjoy the concert, Mr. Accent," shouts the blonde as I walk away. "See you soon."

I look at the number on the paper Maria handed me that is beautifully encapsulated in a heart. Before I left London my confidence was a bit low on the pulling front, I thought that old Richard the Lion Heart lover had lost his touch. I turn around; look at the two college chicks, and smile. Lost my touch? Bollocks have I!

This is a typical anti-war, left wing gathering; hippies, Rastafarians and punks wait in anticipation for the local acts to perform. I purchase a Ghandi T-shirt in order to blend in. There is a huge roar as Franti and Spearhead take the stage. They proceed with funky/reggae beats complimented with anti-establishment rap lyrics. In fact, every song seems to have the same anti-war/ Anti-fascist and of course anti-Bush edge to them.

President Bush certainly isn't a popular figure in these circles. The consensus around here is that they liken Bushes seizure of the White House to that of Hitler announcing himself ruler of Germany in 1933, while the German Reichstag mysteriously burned.

Back home we are pumped with newsreels that insinuate America is a racially divided nation; with war mongering, right wing, red necks on one side and blacks and Hispanics on the other. However, today at Golden Gate Park it is a different tale all together. Blacks and whites, hippies and punks, skinheads and Afros dance together in appreciation of anarchic lyrics and beats.

It's the media that racially divides a country. Well, they play a big part in anyway. Whenever there is what I would call a minor racial incident or even if the incident is just a disagreement between a white person and a black person, the media, backed by the government, always have to blow it out of proportion and make it a national race issue, which then gets us talking, and then, if by magic, guides us into taking sides, which will then lead to a disagreement that's a racial difference of opinion. Then, hey presto, the nation is divided racially! Meanwhile the powers that be are raising taxes, introducing tolls, congestion charges, raising fuel prices and then adding extra zero's to their salaries.

The Hip Hop Poet KRS1 said on one of his records *"If Blacks and Whites didn't argue the most, we will see that the Government is screwing us both."*

I decide to buy an organic veggie burger at one of the food stalls. As I pay, the white Rastafarian stallholder recommends that I buy the special "Free Your Mind Cake" for dessert. I do just that and wash it down with a corona. As Franti and co continues their peaceful rage against the machine, I start to feel a little light-headed.

> **Annual 911 Power to the Peaceful Festival**
> **Speedway Meadow, Golden Gate Park San Francisco, CA**
> **http://www. powertothepeaceful.org/**
> **If you're in this neck of the woods at this time of year this concert is not to be missed, whatever your political preference. However far Right Wingers are advised to remain inconspicuous.**

I wake up the following morning with a hangover and a monged out feeling as a result of the hash cake and a nightcap of three scotches.

Memories of the concert are extremely hazy. All I have to jolt my mind are left wing, anti-war, Marxist leaflets, one of which has the college chicks' number.

The Sunday sun shines down on San Francisco Bay and its time for a walk to clear my banging head. As I am leaving the hotel, the bellboy hands me a message from Francesca. It reads:

"Hi ya, 'Love'. Really miss you. I'll be at a bar called "Pier 23" around 5pm. If you feel like it, I'll see you there."

I get to Pier 23 early at around 4:30, head straight to the bar and order myself a white wine, which for my reckoning, is the best "hair of the dog" drink money can buy.

A wide screen, plasma TV above the bar is showing a live screening The San Francisco 49ers opening game of the 2003 season against the Chicago Bears. They are being roared on by a decent crowd who have assembled to support the local team.

Next to me is a huge Canadian named Ray, wearing a huge baggy ice hockey jersey that could probably fit three of me into it.

He is also a huge rugby fan. We discuss the impending Rugby World Cup and make a bet, as he is cock-sure that New Zealand are going to win. The bet is simple, if the Kiwis win, I pay him

$1000, and if England win, he pays me $1000. For now, he buys me a drink.

Behind us, three girls are sitting at a table; one of them has huge, obscene fake tits.

"Those are 'California Specials'," says Ray. He tells me he prefers small ones. Yea, he's probably another middle-aged white man one who has turned to Asian girls.

He asks me if I like the silicon California Specials. I tell him that they wouldn't put me off but I do prefer large, real big ones, or a small handful, or whatever comes my way really.

"Me, my friend," says the big Canadian, putting his arm around my shoulders, "I love cute little Asian girls; you know Thai, Pilipino, Malaysian…"

A group of African American men walk in, two of them are wearing French berets. Anyone else would look like a bunch twats with those on their nuts! Nevertheless, these guys along with their shades have pulled it off. One of them is wearing a yellow top, which looks like an English Football shirt. I take a second look and see that the manufacturer is Reebok and the emblem is of a sheep lying down holding a flag, its one that I recognise, but one that I can't put a name on. Got it! Fuck me! It's a Preston North End away shirt! I just have to talk to this geezer he must be a northerner. This will be the first English person I have met since I've been here.

It turns out that his name is Larry, from Oakland and is married to an English girl, a Lancashire lass, whom he met in England while playing American football. The best way to describe him is Puff Daddy wearing a Preston North End away top.

"Yea baby, I spent two years up there," reveals Larry. "I worked the door at a night club in Blackpool called the Waterfront when I wasn't playing football. My girl came back here with me to visit my folks, and she didn't want us to go back man." He insists on buying me a drink.

Such a friendly place is San Francisco. It makes me think of how unfriendly my hometown can be. I try to think of the last time I was in a bar in London and a stranger bought me a drink. To be honest I can't remember it ever happening. I'm in this joint all of ten minutes and I have already had two beverages bought for me by two guys I didn't know from Adam.

Larry tells me that the kids in Preston were wild and out of control.

I'm afraid that is a common occurrence in the ASBO (Anti Social Behaviour Order) streets of our inner cities today. It is as if the youth of today has taken over, and it's only going to get worse unless the problem is seriously addressed.

I blame the government; first Thatcher's money hungry Tory tenure, because that's the era most of the parents grew up in, and now the similar Blair government.

When I was a kid in growing up in West London, I was part of a local gang who used to wreak havoc in the streets of Notting Hill. However, there is a huge gulf between us, and the hooded youths of today's Britain. Back then, we were fearful of our local park keeper, who we called Tom the Parky. He used to put us in line if we stepped out of it. I'm sad to say that the days of the strict, regimental "Parky" are long gone. 'Law' and 'order' are just two words in the dictionary or another American drama, as far of the youths of Inner City Britain are concerned. An ASBO to a Youth is like an MBE to a model citizen. I'm sure that in some teenage gangs you can only be accepted if you have the letters, A.S.B.O after your name. I would say bring back the uniformed park keeper, but what good would that fucking do in the present climate? I can't imagine youths in inner city London, Birmingham or Manchester being fearful of a park keeper. I'm afraid to say that we would wake up reading the headline, "Park keeper stabbed to death by hooded youth after a row over swings."

It is the little things you take away that can change the shape of a country.

Thatcher doing away with free milk during school breaks is another factor. I don't think school was ever the same for me. The nourishment of milk was replaced with a tuck shop containing liquorish, Sherbet Dip Dab and Bazooka Joes. At the time I loved it. The 10p my mum gave me to buy sweets was well spent back then. However, wasn't it just another one of Thatcher's ploys to divide the country into the "haves" and the "have-nots?" The boys and girls at private, public and grammar schools, of course, had the choice of nourishing milk while the under-funded, government school kids bought cheap sweets full of E numbers and additives in order to fuck us up! Yes, I'm afraid, I am one of Thatcher's poisoned youth!

I envy Larry and the future his children have, just look where they're going to grow up. I know America and indeed California have their social and economical problems but there is one thing that they have here in abundance, and that is hope.

Pier 23 on a Sunday has a resident band and they are being announced by the cool looking lead singer, wearing a three piece suite.

"On drums, we have Woody Johnston!" The audience cheers and applauds in high spirits as the impressive 49ers have thrashed the woeful Chicago Bears in their opening game of the season.

"On bass we have the local legend, Charlie "Coops" Cooper, yes that's Coops!" Coops looks like the black version of Sigmund, from Sigmund and Roy.

"And on lead guitar is Wacko Jacko, Steve Jackson, right over there! And on piano is me, yes me. I'll be Bob, yeah just call me Bob." Bob!

Fucking Bob! I was waiting for some cool, smooth, bluesy name. But no, we get to call him Bob.

After a few blues covers, Francesca walks in, looking stunning as ever wearing skin tight Levis and yet another tight vest top. She is with another girl, who looks a bit older but equally as stunning, who wears a white, flowery, knee-length frock that fits perfectly over her curves. Francesca sees me but the two of them ignore me and head straight for the bar. Moments later Francesca is handing me a scotch and dry. Fuck! If she wasn't a dodgy drug dealer she would be a 10/10 for sure!

At the bar, I get chummier with Larry and his friends. Fran is impressed with the fact I have made friends with the locals. She whispers in my ear, "Don't mention anything to my friend, about what happened last night, you know, between you and me."

Her friend, Gabrielle, is a dancer from Cirque de Soleil. "So I hear you had a good night the other night. I hear it was your first night on the town," starts Gabrielle.

"Yea, it was some night, and Francesca is some girl." Francesca looks at me out of the corner of her eye, as she sips her glass of white wine.

Larry comes over and puts his arm around me. "Hey man, you wanna come to party tonight, man?" Francesca gives me another cold stare. I tell Larry that I would be happy to come along if Francesca and Gabrielle can come too.

"Yea man, all you guys are all welcome."

"So where's this party?" asks Francesca with crossed arms.

"It's up in Oakland, baby."

"Oakland! I'm not going to the hood tonight honey, no offence man."

"No offence taken baby. So what about you my man, you wanna come party in Oak Town?"

I look at Francesca's beautiful face. "I would love to come mate, but I'm having a night with the lady, you know what I mean."

"Hey man no problem, here's the address anyway." The jive-talking, Preston North End away top-wearing brother heads back to the deck, where the band are playing a decent, lively blues set. Their rendition of Led Zeppelins "Bring It on Home" is particularly good.

The band dramatically switches genres from blues to a kind of salsa/Bosanova set, which prompts a few couples to step onto the dance floor. Francesca whispers in my ear, "Would you like a dance?" I agree and she leads me onto the wooden dance floor. Francesca, is an Argy, so of course she wipes the dance floor with any one else on it. I just follow her lead. She is very seductive with her moves, wrapping her legs around the back of my knees, tango style.

She whispers in my ear again, "I told you not to say anything." I whisper back that I did not say a thing. She then tells me that she had a great night last night, as I become more confident with her lead.

Her attention is now focused on the entrance. I look and see that a Latino homeboy has just walked in. Francesca unravels her arms and legs from my body hastily and scurries to the hombre.

I am left alone on the dance floor in the middle of dancing couples, with a feeling of perplexity.

Gabrielle then takes over where Francesca left off and whispers in my ear, "I know what happened with you and Fran last night. She hasn't told me, but I know." She too wraps her leg around the back of my knees, tango style. She tells me that the hombre is Francesca's boyfriend, well sort of. Creole is the small-time drug dealer Francesca works for. Well I knew it was too good to true, fucking lying, drug dealer. Who wants to be with a pusher anyway?

Gabrielle tells me that Francesca has been a naughty girl and recently she has been selling a potent new ecstasy pill, which is mixed with Ketamine, a drug which is also infamously dubbed the "date rape pill." To some drug users, it is the ultimate high because apparently it produces a total out of body experience. While on this drug, your heart is the only bodily function you can feel; your very breath caresses it. It is the highest you can get with oral drugs. The drug community of San Francisco love it, as they can totally escape their minds without the fear of being infected with AIDS or any other of the diseases you can get from using contaminated needles.

Creole and Francesca are having a very intense heated argument, while Gabrielle still has her limbs wrapped around me.

"She has a lot going on in her life, you don't wanna get involved," Gabrielle says, hinting that I should forget about Francesca. "You had your time the other night, you got what you wanted. It must have been a hell of a night with her, believe me I've had hands-on experience," she says with a mischievous raised-eyebrow look.

Francesca storms out of the bar with Creole in hot pursuit. I unravel Gabrielle's arms and legs from my body and make for the door.

"Don't even go there," Gabrielle says, as she claws me back. "Look, believe me, she doesn't even know you're here right now."

I agree and continue with my un-complicated salsa steps. After one more drink, my mind is totally Francesca-free and I am ready to party. Gabrielle and I jump into a cab and head over the Bay Bridge to Oakland.

I get out of the cab and open the door for Gabrielle. We are now in Oakland, or Oak Town, as it is known to the homies!

> **Pier 23**
> **San Francisco Waterfront**
> **415 262-5125**
> **"Tween the Tracks and the Tugs"**
> **Catch a big Sunday American football game, a cool and eclectic band and jive talking, Preston North End top-wearing brothers on a Sunday.**
> **A great place to pick up single straight females who claim that all the good men are either taken or gay.**

The heavy bass Hip Hop music coming from the art deco terraced house is making the whole street vibrate. I for one do not know what to expect from this. I also don't know what to expect from Gabrielle. What am I doing with Gabrielle? Who the fuck is Gabrielle? I don't even know this girl. Mind you, I don't know Francesca either, do I?

Gabrielle is about 30, she has a very muscular upper body, her trapiezius and deltoids could belong to Madonna, but she does not have as much tit as the one time Material Girl, now Kabbalah spokeswomen. Her legs though, are curvy and shapely like most other Argy birds. She kind of reminds me of a young Cher.

She takes my hand as we walk towards the house party. "Don't worry yourself with Fran. You don't want that hassle. Her life is very, very complicated. Why get involved? You're just a tourist for Christ sakes!" You've been here, what, all of three days? Just have a good time man."

I see lots of sense in what Gabrielle has told me, although she is becoming repetitive.

Inside the party, Larry, still standing proud in his Preston North End away top, welcomes us.

Preston North End, a sleeping giant, were the first English Football team to go an entire league season unbeaten. Imagine Arsenal unbeaten for a whole season; huh! like fuck. Last season we fucking threw our title away in typical Arsenal title defence fashion and literally gave it to Man UTD. In my lifetime thus far, I have yet to witness

Arsenal win back-to-back championships. Not since the Herbert Chapman team of the 1930s has an Arsenal team been able to do retain their title. Last season we had a golden opportunity to do so, but some lack-lustre away performances at Bolton and then Blackburn put paid to that.

The party has a well blended, mixed crowd; Caucasian, Hispanic, a few Asians–probably Vietnamese. African Americans, however, dominate the party, which is typical for Oakland. In fact, Bobby Seale and Huey Newton started the militant Black Panthers here in 1966. They were famous for wearing black berets, so that could explain why some of Larry's mates were sporting them. Maybe. Larry hands Gabrielle and I a bottle of Budweiser. He says that he can't stay and talk as he is next up on the turntables.

I am left with Gabrielle. I ask her how long she has known Francesca.

"Just over a year. I met her at one of these Argentinean social clubs, they have here. You know, we are around the same age and like any other race, when you're away from home you normally latch onto to somebody from your home country."

I ask her if she has really slept with Francesca. "Yea sure, it was just one drunken night, when her boyfriend, that punk Creole, was messing with her."

"What, was it full on sex?" I ask, my interest piqued.

"Yea, full on oral, I instigated it all. I guess she was a bit taken back by my advances at first."

"So are you bisexual, Gabrielle?"

"Who isn't?" she replies shrugging her shoulders. "I don't know. Sometimes, I prefer men, but I think having sex with a women is very erotic and sensual, even more so when it's a threesome with a guy."

"So would you and Francesca…maybe repeat that?"

"Don't even think about it Richard." She smiles, takes my hand and leads me to the front room where the Larry is mixing on the turntables. The multi-racial crowd are bumping and grinding to the heavy bass sounds that is has the chandeliers shaking in unison with the beat.

After one more Budweiser, I am over the edge even more so now that Gabrielle is rubbing her firm body against mine. I have a massive boner, but this time I am not going to think of Arsenal being knocked out of Europe to soften the stiffy.

I ask her if she wants to go somewhere quieter. She smiles and says maybe. In my eagerness, I suggest the garden shed or the toilet and then a bedroom upstairs.

"No not here. Let's go to my place, I live this side of the Bay Bridge," Gabrielle insists. Probably the best idea as not many gardens in the state of California have sheds.

In the back of the taxi Gabrielle runs her hand up the inside of my leg from my calf to my hard crotch. I follow suit. She has calves like a ballerina, firm and shapely. I run my hands all the way up to her panties, which are soaking wet. I put two fingers inside her and work on her clit. She pulls out my throbbing shaft and begins to tug away, as we kiss passionately with complete disregard of the taxi driver's presence.

The cab stops outside of Gabrielle's apartment but the driver doesn't bother tell us, as he is watching the performance in the rear view mirror. I am on the verge of a climax when I here a knock on the window. Both Gabrielle and I take about 10 seconds to look and see that it's Francesca!

She yanks the back door open. "How could you? You two!" she screams. Gabrielle and I just sit there like two naughty school kids as she releases my cock and I pull my hand out of her knickers.

Francesca continues to yell. "Gabrielle, what the fuck are you doing? I thought you are my best friend! And Richard, what the fuck is this? You British bastard! What was the other night all about? I thought it meant something."

Both Gabrielle and I get out of the cab for the summons. "Look I'm sorry Fran, we got drunk at the party and…" pleads Gabrielle.

Francesca continues tearfully, "I came here for some comfort. You know I'm having a tough time at the moment."

The taxi driver shouts, "I got a meter here guys, I gotta get paid for the ride."

"I think you've had your money's worth mister," replies Gabrielle.

I apologise to Francesca, telling her that it has been a terrible mistake, and say goodnight to Gabrielle. I jump back in the cab and tell the driver to take me to Fisherman's Wharf, Marriott Courtyard.

Back at my hotel, I am sobering up myself with a special fried rice and prawn crackers I bought at the Liche Gardens in China Town. Tomorrow I will catch the bus to Santa Cruz. I think it's a good time to leave.

It's funny that two nights ago I was lost in Francesca's world. I still am if the truth be told. However, I was ready to jump Gabrielle's bones without a care. It's a man thing, a cick thing. It would not be a women thing or a pussy thing, would it? On the other hand, maybe it is! Women like sex just as much as men don't they?

I am wide awake at 3:00 am. My body clock is still on London time. An Oasis "Then and Now" Rockamentuary is on VH1. I find it hilarious that they need to add subtitles when either of the Gallagher brothers speaks. The Americans just can't cope with that MAD-Chester accent.

As Liam is going off on an F-word frenzy and talking about "'aving it with his dad," I am startled by a knock on the door. I look through the spy hole, and then open the door. It is Francesca.

She walks in and asks for a drink. Again, I feel like a guilty schoolboy as I pour her a scotch.

Then she hits me with it. "I've had a crazy night, and I'm not gonna bullshit you anymore. On my part, yes, I am a drug dealer, and yes Creole is...well was my kind of boyfriend, and I am sorry for not giving you the full picture. I had to face the music tonight. Not only for the drugs but also over you."

"Over me?" I ask, stunned.

"Yea I told him all about you."

Why would she do that? Now I'm feeling guilty for what happened with Gabrielle.

"I don't blame you for what happened with Gabrielle, I know her too well. She's a complete nymph. Nobody can refuse her, not even me. I guess she told you about that."

Funny isn't it. The difference between men and the fairer sex. We men would re-mortgage our homes and bankrupt ourselves to see Mariah Carey or Beyoncé naked on all fours getting eaten out by a naked Madonna. Or Charlotte Johansson and Jennifer Lopez naked, clit to clit in the scissors position. But how many women would even want watch Brad Pitt and David Beckham grappling in an uncompromising position?

Francesca lies on the bed. "Can you stroke me?" she asks. I lie behind her in a kind of spoon position and start to stroke slowly up her side. Inevitably, her curvaceous hips and firm thighs give me a hard on. She spins around, takes out my rock hard manhood and gives me the perfect blowjob. I cum in her mouth, she swallows then licks her lips. "Now get some sleep," she insists.

I am woken the next morning by Francesca who has ordered breakfast in bed, which consists of a pot of coffee, a rack of toast, and a basket of Danish pastries. We eat while watching another "Then and Now" Rockamentuary on VH1, where Elton John, at the age of 28, has confirmed to himself and the world that he is a homosexual.

I tell Francesca that I am leaving San Francisco tonight on the Greyhound bus. "You had to get me to swallow first, huh," she jokes. She says that she knew I would leave today. Francesca is also leaving San Francisco tonight, heading down to LA to stay with her sister.

At the front desk of the hotel, I settle my bill and give the porter a half-full bottle of single malt scotch, for which he is very grateful. The total cost of my stay is only $30 dollars; for phone calls and for the breakfast Francesca took the liberty of ordering. However, that is the last of my Marriott reward points. No more big beds and cable TV. From now on, it's cheap hooker motels, guesthouses and hostels full of gap-year students, cheapskate holidaymakers, and Germans. Oh well, I've had a good run.

Marriott Courtyard
580 Beach Street
94105 San Francisco
(415) 947 0700
Great way to start the California experience and the building is earthquake proof.

Francesca and I say our goodbyes and she gives me her details in LA but insists that I don't contact her for two weeks while she gets settled.

I catch the 6:00 pm Greyhound bus from the downtown bus terminal. Every seat has been taken for the three-hour ride to Santa Cruz.

SANTA CRUZ,
7 SEPTEMBER 2003

When we arrive at the Santa Cruz bus depot it's 9:00pm and very dark with a crisp chill in the air. I grab my backpack and head downtown to try to find a bed for the night. The *Lonely Planet* tells me that there is just one hostel in town, but it has a curfew of 11:00 pm. Bollocks to that! No cunt is going to tell me what time to go to bed while I'm in California.

With not much luck of finding a place to stay, I hail down a cab. He tells me that there is a cheap motel just a few blocks from the centre. He takes me there for just $2. It is a motel called "Inn Cal," which might be part of a chain of motels in this part of California. A rake-looking Blonde receptionist puts me in room 213 on the first floor facing the car park and the soft drinks machine. The Marriott it is not, but for $30 a night, it's a bargain. I hang my up Arsenal top in front of a tacky, scenic painting to add a bit of colour to the four bland white walls.

First thing I have to do is call Amy and Maria, the college chicks from San Francisco. I ring the number that's on the Marxist flyer. There's no answer, Fuck! I look out of the window. The streets are deserted and I start to feel lonely. Now what the fuck am I going to do?

At the front desk, I ask the skinny, blonde receptionist if she knows of any reggae concerts in town.

"Yea for sure, honey," she screeches in a hick accent. "The only place that would be is the Catalyst Club on Pacific. That's the only place I know of in this town." She writes some directions for me and in doing so her little tits jiggle, as she isn't wearing a bra.

I am at one of the bars in the Catalyst and for a change I order a bottle of Bud, thinking of my budget. The Catalyst is Santa Cruz's biggest and only decent nightspot. Apparently, over the years some very well known bands have performed here including The Red Hot Chilli Peppers, No Doubt, Pearl Jam. Even Ladbroke Groves own, Big Audio Dynamite have graced the stage here. Tonight I have paid $20 to watch the Israel Vibrations, a reputable Reggae band that have Bob Marley's Wailers as backing vocalist. It's worth the $20 entry fee just to see them.

The crowd is a mixture of students; young causal surf types and aging hippies who have probably been here since the "Summer of Love." The majority of the students are on the upper tier playing pool.

I am half way through my second bottle of Bud when the Israel Vibrations take the stage. They kick off with a cover of Gregory Isaacs "Bobby Babylon." I like this kind of Studio One style old-school reggae. It's more pleasing to the ear than the new wave Dancehall, heavy-bass stuff that's come out of Jamaica in the last 10 years.

Still no sign of the girls. Time for a little browse. Best thing about being alone in a club, is that you feel almost obliged to talk to people, normally people of the opposite sex. Maybe I should forget about girls and just enjoy the reggae. Besides I have Francesca, don't I?

Do I fuck! She told me not to call her for two weeks while she "gets settled" in LA. What a load of bollocks. She is probably seeing what guy she can latch onto in that time. It is as if she is saying to take a break and see how we feel. When somebody in a relationship says to his or her partner, "Let's cool it for a while," it can only mean one thing. It's a bit like when Arsene Wenger told Adams to have a rest in the 97/98 season, when in reality he was having a nightmare and needed to be dropped.

Maybe I should not be so pessimistic. Maybe, it was just her way of telling me to have fun with some Californian girls and then see what happens in two weeks. Yea, that sounds about right. It is probably not a good thing to fall in love with the first girl you meet when you're travelling anyway.

I eventually catch sight of Amy and Maria; they are dancing with two young guys who look like students. I wait for the opportune moment when they go to the toilet, and like most girls, they go together. I track them all the way and when I'm within striking distance, I call out, "Hey girls!"

They welcome me in typical young, drunk girl fashion; both girls hug me with their young firm bodies. One of them grabs my arse.

"Hey, Mr Accent! We didn't think you would get here," says Maria.

"Yea, why didn't you call? If we knew for sure you were coming we wouldn't have come with our boyfriends," adds Amy. "Why didn't you call?"

"I did you didn't pick up. Boyfriends, eh?"

"Yea, that's Zach and Perry, right over there," states Amy, pointing to the guys they were dancing with.

The two girls start to chat with each other and then tell me to wait while they go to the bathroom. Maria returns, "Hey, come in here," she insists. I slip into the empty girls toilet unnoticed. She leads me to a cubicle where Amy is waiting.

"Hey Mr. Accent, want a line?" Amy has cut three lines of coke on the toilet seat. There was me thinking I was going to get more than a line. I take the rolled up dollar bill from Amy, squat down and snort my line. It's not bad either, a bit better than the stuff you get in London. Maria takes her line, rises, and kisses me. She breaks it then Amy has her turn, each time I grabbed their firm arses.

"Ok let's go," says Amy after we break the kiss.

"We just had to do that. We have never kissed an English man before."

"Oh right," I say disappointedly. Young girls eh! Oh well, it was half-decent gear, I suppose. They give me their number again and insist I call them tomorrow. They run back to dance with their preppy boyfriends. I stay in the cubicle and wait until my dick goes soft and the coast is clear.

Once out of the ladies, I stay for a few more numbers, then leave and get something to eat.

> **The Catalyst Club**
> 1011 pacific Ave
> Santa Cruz
> CA 95060
> www.catalstclub.com
> **Big Audio Dynamite has played there!**

I get myself a couple of burritos from Taco Bell and head back to my Hotel. Back in my room I hear "Huh, huh, Yeah baby, yeah," as I'm eating my Chicken Burrito Grande watching Entertainment news. Sounds like some hooker is being fucked in the room adjacent to mine. It does not last long enough to get me aroused. I am still eating my burrito when the hooker leaves.

There is nothing like waking up in a strange town when you have arrived in the midst of darkness the night before, especially when you can see the ocean. It is a beautiful, clear morning in Santa Cruz. The sight of the glistening ocean and the cool breeze that comes with it is almost enough to clear my head from the slight hangover and the come down from that impressive line of coke the college chicks gave me last night.

To clear my head further I hire a bike from the Family Cycle Centre, (which is the first bike hire shop I come across) and take a ride down along the bay. The women who owns the shop, is friendly as the day is long. She claims that I am the fourth

INN CAL Motel
370 Ocean St
Santa Cruz
CA 95060
(831) 458-9220
Cheap bills and very
quick cheap thrills!

English person this week who has hired a bike from her. She insists that I must lock the bike at all times when unattended. I agree and tell her that I know a guy in San Francisco who got his bike taken on a cycling expedition over Golden Gate Bridge.

I cycle up the scenic bay for the remainder of the morning. On the way back, I stop on the boardwalk and order some calamari and chips for lunch. While I'm taking my first bite of a calamari ring, which is cooked to perfection, giant seagulls surround me. They aggressively squawk at me and try to pinch my meal. Somewhat frightened, I jump up, grab my bike chain and begin to wave it in the gulls' direction to shoo them. These gulls are no wankers and are up for a fight.

The situation is attracting a bit of an audience; some Japanese tourists even have their cameras and camcorders out.

More and more gulls are coming; there must be at least ten of them now. I get a couple of my chips and throw them beyond the flying, scavenging beast. This distracts the majority of the birds who have taken the bait and allows me to make my escape.

The next morning I am on my way to LA. To my dismay I find out that, the Greyhound does not take the Number 1 highway along the Big Sur. The bus takes the 101 Freeway inland. That's no good, the Sur is part of my itinerary. I decide to cut my losses, and get off at the next stop, hire a car and drive along the Big Sur to LA.

Family Cycle Centre
914 41st Avenue
Santa Cruz
CA 95060
Hiring a bike and taking a ride along the scenic Pacific Coast is a must. Eating seafood on the pier is a miss.

MONTEREY,
9 SEPTEMBER 2003

I have been advised to go to Hertz car hire a block away from the bus station. Unfortunately, they tell me that they will not have any cars available until tomorrow and that I should come back then. One day in Monterey will not kill me, will it?

This is of course where Jimi Hendrix set his guitar on fire during a rendition of "Wild Thing" in 1967 at the Monterrey Pop festival. Being a massive Hendrix fan, I am honoured to spend a day here as a tribute to a piece of rock n' roll history.

I have list of motels I can try, but that can wait for now as I am a little peckish and I could sure do with a drink. There is a good-looking eatery/bar called The Blue Fin, which overlooks the historic Cannery Row on The Monterey Bay. I enter and I order a chilli burger with fries and salad.

"Would you like a drink with that?" asks the young, male bartender. I order a Corona and take it to a table on the balcony. In my thirst, I down the beer in two short minutes as I gaze at the Pacific.

The food arrives, and true to American form, it is massive. I lap up the chilli burger and order another Corona to wash it down. I am no alcoholic, but I just can't stop drinking at the moment, I have not stopped since I arrived in California. I am not sure how long my liver and kidneys will be able support this barrage of alcohol abuse they have had to contend with. I have to have some sought of dry night soon.

In the corner of the bar, I notice a jukebox. I feel that some music will supplement the beautiful Pacific Bay view.

The jukebox has an eclectic selection of 60s, 70s, and 80s classics, Seattle grunge, even some Britpop from the 90s blended with some Hip Hop classics spanning twenty years.

I choose five songs for a dollar;

"The wind cries Mary" by Jimi Hendrix,
"Ramble On" by Led Zeppelin,
"London Calling" by The Clash,
"What's Going On" by Marvin Gaye
And *"How Soon Is Now"* by The Smiths.

Now, these five songs are not necessarily on my desert island disk list, but they are the songs for the moment, the now. Now's the time and the time is now.

Before Jimi has finished sweeping up the dreary pieces of yesterday life, I notice that the bar has started to fill with locals lunching and tourist (mainly old retired, American ones).

I have Francesca on my mind while Robert Plant is *"Rambling On."* Yes I am *"going around the world"* as the song suggests, but I am not sure if *"I'm gonna find my girl"* or *"the Queen of my dreams."* I still have a lot to learn about Francesca, but I do like the fact that she is complicated and somewhat mysterious. Maybe Page and Plant were thinking about a mysterious girl like Francesca when they wrote the last verse, where *"in the dark steps of Mordor I met a girl so fair, but Gollum and the evil one crept up and slipped away with her."* Lord of the Rings maybe, but I'm sure by the time I've crossed the US/Mexican border it will all make perfect sense.

The sun continues to beam down on the bay on yet another perfect, cloudless Californian day. That could be the opening line of a song, but no song The Clash would sing! *"London Calling"* is a cry for help, not only from us Londoners, *"we ain't got not swing except for the rain or the truncheon thing,"* but for the entire world. They are forecasting nuclear disaster, global warming, famine and the impending Tory government. *"The Ice age is coming. The sun zooming in. Melt down expected. The wheat is growing thin."* Fucking unbelievable lyrics and all in the year of 1979. They were years ahead of the game and the album *London Calling*, set the standard for the 80s.

A change of pace in the music as marvellous Marvin Gaye tells us *"What's Going On"* in his world in 1971. Like Ghandi and Martin Luther King before him, Gaye's peaceful protest is even more poignant today than it was then. This song goes out to the Black Panthers and my Preston North End supporting mate, Larry, in Oakland, to Michael Franti, Spearhead and to all those who gathered at Golden Gate park for the Power to Peaceful concert.

The enigmatic Morrissey tells us he is "human and needs to be loved, just like anyone else does".

"Hey that's a great song. Did you put that on?" The voice belongs to a blonde woman in her early 40s, who is dressed smartly. She wears a knee length, navy skirt with a white, Ralph Lauren polo top. She looks like a cross between Linda Gray, Crystal Carrington in *Dynasty*, minus the shoulder pads, and Ellen Barking at the time of "*Sea of Love*." Her perfect hairdo is complemented with a lovely pair of green contact-tinted eyes and delicious lips that have possibly been pumped with collagen.

"Yea, It's The Smiths," I reply. "Are you a fan?"

"Are you kidding? They are one of my favourites. I spent four years at college in England and this was one of the anthems of my time there."

"Its *How Soon Is Now* is one of their signature tunes."

"Yea I know, it was on the album *Meat is Murder*, wasn't it?"

"Yes, you're right; it was on the US release." I am impressed. I love a woman, who knows her music. Maybe she doesn't know much about music and only knows the *Meat is Murder* album that she heard during her time at university in England.

"Hey are you alone? Can I sit with you?" she asks.

Fuck yea! "Yes, of course, be my guest," I respond with clear Cockney accent.

She continues, "Your accent, that's like a South London one, right?"

"Not quite, but I see what your getting at. I am actually North of the river, West London, Ladbroke Grove, Notting Hill.

"Notting Hill, cool." She wastes no time telling me about London and the rest of England. She studied Law at Cambridge. She stayed in old blighty and got a job at a Magic Circle law firm called Allen & Overy and later married an English music executive. Her name is Pam. She offers to buy me a drink. Who am I to refuse? However, I can't stay too long as I have find a place to stay.

She buys me another Corona and herself a glass of Californian Sauvignon Blanc. "So what brings you to little old Monterey?" she enquires.

I fill her in on the story so far and then ask her about the local hotels. Pamela says she can help find me somewhere without any problems. I show her the list of budget hotels that the young woman in the tourist office gave me. She doesn't look too impressed with my list of cheap hooker/ trucker motels.

"I tell you what" proposes Pam "let's finish these drinks and then let me take you to a few hotels that I know." Oh shit, I am well out of my league here cash wise. I can't justify nights at the Hilton or the Embassy on my budget. We leave the bar and walk to her car.

> **Blue Finn Café**
> **685 Cannery Row**
> **Monterey**
> **CA 93940**
> **831-371-7000**
> Great jukebox. The Queen Is Dead but God save The Smiths.

"What do you think of the *Queen is Dead* album?" I ask Pam, testing her music knowledge as we get into her Z4 BMW convertible.

"I think *The Queen is Dead* has taken too much of The Smiths accolades over the years. For me *Meat is Murder* is their best work," she answers.

Fuck me! this women knows her shit and I'm stupefied. "I prefer *The Queen is Dead*."

"It's a great album but it's a bit too depressing and suicidal," she counters.

"The Smiths can be dreary and suicidal sounding, but after hearing an album like *The Queen is Dead*, it takes you down the road of their anguish, despair and depression but then makes you want to live and better yourself," I philosophise. "It's not a depressing album at all; it's an album about facing your demons and dealing with the emotional uncertainties in your life."

"That's so true," she says, smiling, showing her gleaming whitened teeth.

We drive a few blocks along the stunning coastline and stop outside a classy looking hotel called The Beach Resort. Pam stays in the car while I go and check out prices and availability. Two minutes later, I return to tell her that they have no vacancies. Actually, that was a lie. The price was the problem, a $130 a night problem. Fuck that!

I would like to pull out the old Visa and pay for a deluxe room in order to impress Pam, but that would only be biting off my nose to spite my face, as I don't have that kind of cash at the moment.

So I insist that I stay at one of low budget hotels on my tourist information list. Pam suggests that I stay at her house. "It won't be a problem at all. It will be a pleasure having an out-of-towner like you stay over, I got plenty of room."

I pretend to be imposing on her, "Yea, but maybe we can try one of these motels on my list. Look this one isn't far," I say pointing to my tourist information list.

"Don't be ridiculous. It's not everyday I meet an interesting guy from London," she says, ignoring my list. "Besides, we still have a lot of music talk to cover. We have yet to mention The Smiths' first album for Christ sakes! Get in the car young man!"

Her house is a lovely four-bedroom beach condominium in Carmel about a ten-minute drive south of Monterrey. "But what about your husband?" I ask inquisitively as we pull into the driveway.

"Oh don't worry honey, he's dead," she says matter-of-factly. I hope that she didn't kill her husband like Sharon Stone did hers in *Basic Instinct*. In fact, wasn't that film shot in a small northern Californian coastal town?

"Oh, I'm terribly sorry to here that," I mutter, grabbing my backpack from the trunk of her car.

"It's been a long time. It's ok," she says as we go inside. "There are three spare bedrooms. Why don't you take the one on the first floor? You'll like the view of the ocean."

I check out my room and throw my backpack on the queen sized bed. "Make yourself comfortable, I'm gonna take a shower!" shouts Pam from the opposite side of the house.

I can't believe this is happening, my mind is in a state sedation, and I can't quite come to terms with it all. But hey! What the fuck, I'm going to take a shower too, in my en-suite bathroom. I grab my toiletry bag, only to realise that it is heavier than it was in San Francisco. Inside are two cellophane bags, each the size of miniature packets of sugar. I take them out and discover that they are filled with white powder. I Lick my finger, dab it into the substance and then taste it. Just as I thought, cocaine. Yes! and it must have been Francesca who put these packages in here, but why?

Maybe she wanted to leave something with me so that I would definitely have to contact her in LA. No, she isn't the insecure type.

Maybe she wanted me to have a good time in the two weeks that I won't be seeing her. No there's far two much blow here to consume on my own in a fortnight.

Maybe she knows that I am a poor, smelly, English backpacker and the proceeds from the selling of this shit will supplement my travels. No, I'm sure that she could do with the cash herself and for her poverty stricken family in Argentina.

On the other hand, maybe she's being pursued by her ex-boyfriend Creole, or by the police, and she doesn't want either of them to get their hands on the stash. Then in two weeks when the dust has settled in LA she can pick up her drugs. This seems the more likely outcome of the four theories.

I get out of the shower and put on my Arsenal top. This is the first top that features the new emblem, which I don't really like. Arsenal are supposed to be a club with history and rich traditions; the marble halls, the clock and the Art deco East and West stands have remained and been maintained during the decades of change, so why the hell didn't they keep the old style intricate cannon emblem? This new badge looks like it's out of a fucking cartoon.

Mind you, we are not the only club who have made changes to the emblem on their shirts. Man UTD, Liverpool, Chelsea and the Scum bags have all made changes. I have to admit that I have always liked the traditional Tottenham badge, with just the cockerel standing on the ball, but the less said about that the better.

"Hey that's an ASSenal jersey isn't it?" says Pam, who has showered and is wearing a knee-length strapless summer dress. Her forty-something, toned body would give most twenty year olds a run for their money. Her body is supplemented with fake tits, which are of DD proportions. It is also a body that has benefited immensely from years from paying top dollar for a personal trainer.

"ASSenal wasn't that good in the early eighties, Huh?"

"Please don't remind me." Yes, crap we were, but the eighties were when I first started supporting them.

Pamela continues, "When I lived over there Liverpool seemed to be the best team." Again, I am impressed, this time by her football knowledge. "My husband was a Chelsea fan."

Chelsea, fucking Chelsea. I don't care too much for those flash bastards from the Kings Road or for their mouthy supporters. Especially given the fact that I'm a Gooner born and bred in West London and being surrounded by the flash cunts all of my life. However, like most real Arsenal fans, I reserve the most hatred for those wankers at the wrong end of the Seven Sisters Road; Tottenham Hotspur.

The top of the table clashes games against Man Utd and Chelsea are now seen as our most important games of the season, but for us real Gooners the game we just can't lose is against the underachievers of N17.

Many if not all Arsenal fans hate Man Utd but it's only a rivalry in football terms and that's only been since the late eighties. North London enmity goes a lot deeper than that, You're talking seventy years of hatred. It started when we left Plumstead in South London of all places and moved to Highbury in 1913. Tottenham were at the time the only team in North London. So when we moved next door to them and then soon over took them in league status they couldn't bear it and the animosity has been there since.

I guess for Tottenham it was like being the only pretty girl in your class at school for the first two years, and then in the third year an absolute stunner joins, and you're no longer the only bird the guys are after.

I sometimes wish Tottenham could become a better side again in order to give the Derby more of an edge. Maybe bring back those glory, glory days. Well...not really, I love it when those wankers lose. But my point is to keep rivalry in football and keep the North London Derby alive, and for God sake stand up if you hate Tottenham! Because believe me they fucking hate us!

At the Shit hole of White Heart Lane you can almost taste the hatred. In fact, my first ever Arsenal game was a North London Derby at the Lane on Boxing Day 1983. Arsenal won the encounter 4-2, with Raphael Meade and my boyhood hero, "Champagne" Charlie Nicholas, each bagging a brace.

There is a warm breeze sifting through the slightly open windows and it slightly lifts Pam's dress, revealing her tanned, shapely, sexy thighs. She offers me a drink, and I get what I ask for, a single malt scotch with dry ginger ale. She has another white wine.

She insists that we go out for dinner tonight and has even reserved a table at Monterey's finest seafood restaurant. We have a few more drinks and share stories. We talk more about London and her experiences in the eighties. The mood is assisted by *"Shooting Rubber bands at the stars,"* a brilliant Eadie Brickell and the New Bohemians album that she inserted into her classy, Bang and Olsen stereo.

"This is one of my favourite albums. Do you know it?" she asks. I tell her that I got into Edie Brickell quite late, around 91'. I was a massive Hip Hop fan at the time. A group of New Yorkers called Brand Nubian used the break of Brickell's *"What I Am"* for one of their first releases called *"Slow Down"*.

We continue to talk, laugh, drink and impress each other with our musical tastes. First, she puts on a CD then I follow suit with one of mine, as if we are having a kind of "sound off." In my tipsy state, I put on *London Calling*, Patti Smiths

"Horse", *The Harder They Come* soundtrack and Public Enemy's *"Yo Bum Rush the Show,"* which belongs to her. Pam puts on Nirvana's *Nevermind*, and *Parallel Lines* by Blondie and *Raising Hell* by Run DMC which belongs to me. As the hours pass and the drinks continue to be poured, we forget about our table at the seafood restaurant. Instead, we order a Chinese take away.

Twenty minutes later the doorbell rings but it is not the food. It is one of Pam's friends; a preppy looking guy named Marty, a local real estate tycoon. He is taken aback by the fact she has me as a guest. She lies and says that I am a friend of a friend of hers from England. Well, she couldn't tell Marty that she picked me up in a café, just a few hours ago.

Marty comes in and takes a seat. He starts to do my head as soon as he opens his mouth. He babbles on about himself and meaningless local gossip. I cannot wait for this annoying wanker to leave. It is that classic situation where three's a crowd and the odd one out just doesn't get the picture. I can see that Pam feels the same way.

The doorbell rings again and this time, it is our food. Thank God! Marty does the right thing and fucks off with the take away guy. If he didn't, I might have chinned him.

"I'm sorry about that," Pam says apologetically while she prepares the food in her impressive, expensive looking crockery. "Marty can't leave me alone. He has the hots for me something bad, but you know, he's harmless. He thinks that because were both in local real estate, we should be an item, this dream, Carmel, real estate couple," she says, cracking open another chilled bottle of Californian white.

After dinner, Pam and I are sitting side by side on her sofa. The sun has long since gone down and we are enjoying the moment, listening to more music.

"So what are you going to do in LA?" she asks, sipping her wine.

"I'll probably be there for two months or so," I reply, feeling a buzz from the wine. "Maybe I'll check out some bands and try to join one of them and play some gigs. I need some cash to supplement this trip."

"You can play an instrument? Wow. What do you play?"

"Well, I have been known to mess about with the bass," I reply modestly.

"I'm impressed! I wish you all the best with that" She looks into my eyes and strokes my chest. "And how long will you be staying in Monterey?"

My body temperature rises and I get a little tingle in my pants.

"Well, up until today I wasn't going to set foot in Monterey, so every minute is a bonus. Had I known that I would be meeting a lovely woman like yourself, I would have made a trip to Monterey imperative."

"Oh, you're too cute." She leans over and kisses me. It's a moment of extreme passion that has been building all day. She is a very good kisser, with vast experience I can only imagine. She bites and probes my upper and lower lips and then works on my tongue. I implement a counter offensive with interest and attack her hefty chest. Each breast is more than a handful supplemented with eraser head erect nipples. I caress them gently but with authority. She groans with delight and wastes no time in grabbing my cock, which is erect as it gets.

She gets up and ushers me upstairs into her silk/satin kitted-out bedroom. At the bedside, she slips off her summer dress revealing a body of female perfection.

There is a growing trend at the moment, and that's the emergence of the sexy female forty something. Ok, women in their forties have always been a force to be reckoned with, but the recent wave of high profile females moving into the life-beginning decade; have done for the forty something's what Roman Abramovich has done for the beleaguered Chelsea Football Club which was staring in the eyes of bankruptcy at the end of last season. Elle McPherson, Andie McDowell, Liz Hurley, and of course Madonna are all prime examples of this.

Pam's pussy is soaking wet. I pull out the two fingers I had in there and give her taste of her own sexual medicine. I go in again, this time I squeeze three fingers in there. This has Pam cumming with a mighty groan. With her lower body quivering, the beast in me takes over and throws her on the bed. Each colossal breast gets a good sucking and licking. I take the opportunity and give them a Bombay Role (a tit fuck).

I suspect that her vagina has also been surgically enhanced, as it looks like one of an untouched nineteen year old, and I give it the licking it deserves. She cums a second time, this time squeezing my upper torso with her strong Amazonian legs nearly suffocating me in the process.

I use the condoms that are on offer and fuck her in every position in the book. I cum after a beastly, doggy-style pounding.

Après sex, I watch her every move as she walks to the bathroom for a piss. She has a body I can only describe as a curvy gymnast. She returns with a small wrap of cocaine.

"You don't mind if I do, do you?" she asks, gesturing to the coke. I am surprised, but somewhat happy, as it gives me an idea for a plan.

"I'm just so horny right now, and I love sex on coke." She offers me some, but coke has the opposite effect on my sex. For me the best sex drug is Ecstasy or MDMA, (Mandy as we call it in the Grove) the powdered form. But who needs Mandy when you have Pamela in front of you. After she snuffles a couple of lines, I fuck her three more times.

Although Pam has had a couple of lines she is fast asleep after having multiple, multiple orgasms. I am wide-awake as I have Francesca's package on my mind. What if the cops are eyeballing me, or maybe that wanker Creole has got his Latin hit squad tailing me?

My plan is to ask Pam if I can leave the stash here or at her work place or something. Since she is drug friendly, I don't think she will refuse.

"No! I've got a better idea!" says Pam while we are eating croissants for breakfast the following morning. "Why don't I drive you down to Santa Barbara? I have to go there in a couple of days anyway to tie up a few real estate deals and check up on a few of my properties. You can leave the packages at my house down there, that way the coke will be closer to you while you're in La La land honey. I'm sure you going need it at some stage for what ever you're going to do with it."

What a piece of thinking. I suppose I could stomach a couple more days living in a luxurious pacific beach condominium with an experienced, sex hungry, manufactured vixen.

"Ok, on two conditions; one, we drive along the Big Sur and two, I control the music." I affirm.

"The Sur is the only road I take baby, and I love your taste in music."

BIG SUR,
11 SEPTEMBER 2003

"And if you're in the Crown tonight have a drink on me. Go easy, step lightly, stay free," sings Mick Jones as Pam and I cruise down Highway One along the Big Sur. The coastal scenery is breathtaking.

It was well worth staying those extra nights with Pam. My dick may be sore from the amount of sex I had to give the insatiable, forty-something, but seeing these magical, wild coastline views makes it all worthwhile.

Pam's husband died about three years ago in a boating accident. I think she is a lonely person, not just as a result of her husband dying. I get the feeling that she wasn't really in love with him at the time of his untimely death. I can almost sense a tone relief when she talks of his passing.

We stop off at a tourist viewing point just short of the town of Big Sur Centre. I take pictures of elephant seal lions frolicking and fighting offshore. I then take pictures of Pam using the Sur coastline as a backdrop. We don't go on a nature trail like so many tourists do in this area. Pam tells that a friend of a friend died here while trying to negotiate the unstable cliffs, trying to gain an advantageous viewing point of the treacherous wave action and offshore rapids. I see that there is a true dangerous, wildness to the area and agree to knock it on the head. Apparently, it took 15 years for Chinese labourers and workers from state prisons to build the highway through this hostile terrain.

We pull into the small town of the Big Sur Centre. It is the kind of hub of the Sur (also known as the Village), with the only store, gas station and post office for miles. Pam suggests that we stay a night at a spa she knows and have a detox night, at her expense, of course.

The town itself is quaint and has a relaxed atmosphere, and is also the home of the Henry Miller Memorial Library. I wonder what Mr. Miller would make of my endeavours thus far. I'm sure the 'Prophet of Freedom' would not call it licentious behaviour and look at me with distain. I hope that he would have seen me as a visionary who has conquered his fears, broken away from society and is living with bravado and courage.

We check into the Ventana Inn & Spa, and are booked into one of the hotel's pricey cottage houses situated at the top of the hill above the hotel. The cottage is a secluded retreat. Its spacious airy interior has serene views of the Big Sur's wilderness forest.

Pam orders us some spa treatments; she will have the Grande Sur Hot Stone treatment and recommends that I have the Organic Sea Enzyme wrap and massage. Pam's treatments will take place outside in the Zen gardens. I head to the spa for mine.

A sturdy Philippine girl named Martha is my masseuse for the afternoon. According to the treatment menu, this body wrap uses sea enzymes to stimulate my body's metabolism, herbal green tea to balance Ying Yang energies and ginger root to invigorate the mind. What a load of bollocks!

Mary finishes me off with a relaxing Swedish massage. Unfortunately, I don't have any disposable cash on me to ask to be properly finished off, like I did in Thailand at that Sports bar last year.

Back at the cottage, Pam is naked in the outdoor hot tub sipping champagne, relaxing after her hot stone treatment. She says that this place would be ideal for honeymooners and jokes about us getting married. As I look at her zeppelin of a chest floating in the bubbles and the wonderful surroundings, I think that it wouldn't be such a bad idea. I jump into the hot tub and kiss her

Vetana Inn & Spa
Highway 1
Big Sur,
CA 93920
831-667-2331
www.vetanainnspa.com
Ideal for honeymooners.
Prices start at $300 at
night for modest rooms,
so rich in-laws are
required.

passionately. We then take our drinks into the cabin and make love on a rug in front of a wood fireplace, while the crickets outside serenade us.

SANTA BARBARA,
12 SEPTEMBER 2003

Having been spoilt by the splendour of miles and miles of rugged, wild coastal vistas of The Big Sur, my organic and naturist loins have been satisfied and I am ready for the big smoke once again. Los Angeles beckons, but first I have to store Francesca's packages in one of Pam's apartments here in Santa Barbara.

This town is dubbed the "American Rivera" in fact; it kind of reminds me of Marbella on the Costa del Sol in Spain. It has pleasant, relaxed white sand beaches, shops and galleries along historic streets with plenty of top-notch restaurants and cafes. However, unlike Marbella, there isn't a bar or café insight where one can have a "Full English" and watch Sky Sports.

It is 5:00 pm and I will be staying the night, as I don't want arrive at the bandit ridden, downtown bus station in LA when the sun has gone down; because in LA the freaks come out at night.

Pam tells me to put on something smart as we are going out for dinner tonight. She is getting the impression, like myself, that tonight will our last together, at least for the time being anyway.

This evening Pam wears a black, knee-length, Chanel dress with matching shoes and handbag. I go for a smart casual look; white Polo shirt with Aquascutum trimmings, Evisu Jeans and tan suede Paul Smith loafers. A walking clothing label I know, but that is just the way it is for a boy brought up on the North Bank in the eighties.

When we walk into the restaurant, like everywhere we have been together, we are the focus of attention. It could be for one of three reasons; one, Pam looks devastatingly gorgeous, two, I look devastatingly gorgeous, or three, they notice the age difference between us. Either way who gives a shit?

We sit facing each other in an intimate restaurant called "The Chase Bar & Grill." The décor is impressive enough; the interior is decorated with twinkling lights, which gives the place a kind of blissful ambiance.

> The Chase Bar $ Grill
> 1012 State street
> Santa Barbara,
> CA 93101
> 805-965-4351

I order the sea bass with roast vegetables and Pam the shrimp linguini. We wash are meals down with champagne to celebrate the time we have spent together.

With the drugs safely stowed away under the sink in the bathroom of one of Pam's plush apartments here in Mabella, I mean Santa Barbara, my mind is at rest. Pam is treating tonight as if it is going to be a while before she is fucked again and she makes the most of our last night together.

LOS ANGELES,
13 SEPTEMBER 2003

The Greyhound bus arrives at the downtown LA bus terminal. I cannot wait to get off this shit hole of a bus after the 92-mile journey from Santa Barbara. The highlight of the trip was a white, trashy crack whore asking me if I had a cell phone. She must have asked me at least six times. Maybe I should have asked Pamela to drop me here, but I think the six nights I spent with her were enough. Otherwise, our sex jamboree would have carried on here in LA. I would not say that she would be cramping my style, she's a top sort, but I just wanted to get to LA alone and with no extra baggage.

This grim, downtown bus terminal must be in the worst part of town, which is saying something. It's full to the brim with convict-looking bandits with their families and their masses of luggage. I have the option of getting a local bus to Central Station and then jumping on another local bus to Venice Beach, or just taking a cab.

My cab driver is from Russia, which is common in LA for a cab driver. In fact, he is Armenian, which is even more common for a cab driver in

LA. I tell him to take me to the Venice Beach Cotel. I have singled it out from the *Lonely Planet* as probably the pick of the hostels in the Venice Beach/Santa Monica district. The cab driver agrees with my choice and tells me that it is the most popular hostel with the travellers he picks up. It sounds half-decent and the *Lonely Planet* states that they give you a drink when you check in.

Do I get a drink at the hostel when I check in? Do I fuck!

The receptionist and manager is Katrina, a loud-mouthed Israeli, with an arse like two coconuts, who is a devout Manchester United fan. In addition, she has collected a fine array of English slang and idioms whilst managing this international hostel.

Her first question to me is: which team do I support? She then calls me a wanker when I tell her I am an Arsenal fan. She reminds me that we are playing Portsmouth tonight.

Her assistant, Jessica, is a Pretty, leggy blonde from Edmonton, not Edmonton that shit hole of a suburb in North London where many a scummy Tottenham fan comes from, but Edmonton in Alberta, Canada.

Tonight in order for me to adjust to the hostel way of life, I stay in a private room.

The hostel has a bar called the Aqua Lounge for the resident backpackers, but in reality, it should be called the Murky Dive, as the place looks dull as dishwater.

I get myself a beer from the subsidised bar and sit at a table with three guys who are all probably from the south coast, Gloustershire or maybe a posh part of the Midlands, as they all have non distinguishable English accents.

After sitting with these guys for twenty minutes, I am totally bored shitless. They have more or less taken the same route as I have. They tell tales of just travelling and going from place to place, but with nothing much happening when they got there. They then start talking of their future trips; from here, they are going to Fiji, then to New Zealand, Australia and finally south East Asia. Most of the backpackers I speak to are more or less doing the same trip.

A bit boring really, although for most of them, I'm sure it will be an experience and a half that maybe might just take them away from their white, middle class, conservative state of minds.

I don't meet many people who are going to Central or South America. Jessica is though. She and her sister, Jackie, are going to Costa Rica and Honduras. They are the two most interesting people I have spoken to so far in the hostel. Jessica is around 25, a bit shy but still has a lot to say for herself, once she warmed to me.

I go to the bar to get another drink even before my last one is half-empty, just to get away from those middle England bores.

There are two guys sitting at the bar. "Bunch of wankers, aren't they?" says one of them.

"Yeah I know what you mean," I reply.

"All they do every fucking night is talk about where they have gone or where they are going on their parent's money or trust fund," says the other guy.

They are Ian and Derek from Peckham, South London, Millwall fans! They pay for my drink. They have been here for three nights and tell me that all the action is in Santa Monica or on Washington Boulevard. They are going to end up at a bar/club called Gotham Hall tonight. They tell me I should tag along with them.

On Washington, the three of us hit a bar called The Venice Whaler, which is right on the pier. It's quiet for a Saturday night, but it doesn't seem to deter the South London lads, clad in Ben Sherman shirts hanging over their jeans, and white Reebok classics, South London style.

After a few pints, they shamelessly, confidently chat up a group of three girls. Ian, the louder of the two, is so loud and flash that the whole bar can hear him talking to girls, "Yea we had to get out of that hostel. It's full of wankers," he informs the girls at full volume.

"What's a wanker?" one of the girls asks. There is an immediate silent pause after the laughter has died down.

"Hey Richard, tell this bird what a wanker is, will you?"

The girl who asked the question is a big-boned girl named Nadine. I have to think about the answer for a while.

"Well Nadine, the word *wanker* has four meanings:

one, it's a slang term for somebody who masturbates. You Americans would say *jerking off*; we would say *having a wank*; two, it's a person, normally male, who is scared of something or somebody. I believe Americans call them *pussies or chicken shits*;

Three, a guy can be a *wanker*, if for example, he is a baseball player and in a game he misses an easy catch;

And four, *wanker* is a general term for an uncool person, like the other people in our hostel; *Wankers.*"

Ian hugs me. "Well put Richard, well put my son. Fucking bang on mate!" Ian and Derek are overwhelming the other two girls, who are both more pleasing on the eye and slimmer than what Nadine is, with their cockney charm. Even their foul language and piss taking isn't putting them off.

"Come on let's get the fuck out of here," says Ian.

We jump into two cabs to Santa Monica. Nadine and I get into one, Ian and Derek and two waifs into the other.

We enter the Gotham Hall nightclub on the Santa Monica strip and are greeted by *"California*

Love" by Tupac. The flash, cockney charmers head straight for the bar and order drinks for everyone. The club has a massive cinema-size screen hanging down from the high ceiling, showing music videos that correspond with the audio.

Again, Nadine and I are sectioned off from the rest of the group. She is actually really nice, she hasn't got "angry-fat-bird-syndrome" like many an over-weight girl I have met in my time.

She's from Wisconsin and came here to escape her family and her boring rural, Mid-Western nightmare. Her childhood sweetheart turned out to be gay, her dad blew his brains out after years of depression, and her mum is now dating a guy who tried to sexually assault her and her sister. Some story, yet she has no qualms in telling me it, given that she has only known me for a few hours. I feel sorry for her and at the same time start to think that she is cute with her shiny blue eyes and near perfect white teeth.

Girls who are large in proportions, big-boned, voluptuous or whatever term you like to use, are for me fine as long as they have big breasts to balance out their big frame. A cute face also helps. Nadine has tits in abundance and is very cute looking. I suppose a good-looking fat bird is just the same as an ugly fit bird. You know the old adage "Nice legs, shame about the face."

The Peckham Boys, now drunk out of their minds, head downstairs to the dance floor with the two size zero birds, leaving me at the bar with Nadine. She tells me that she works as a trainee criminal lawyer downtown. She seems to be really happy with her job, which makes me happy for her, as I have hated every job that I've ever had, no matter what. The very thought of being awoken by a screaming alarm clock on a dark Monday morning and then making my way to my soul-destroying, mundane job, makes me down my Jack Daniels and diet coke in one gulp.

We go on to talk about films and actors, her favourite actors are all British. She admires Dame Judi Dench, Kate Winselet and Rachel Wiesz. Her music taste is also very British. She loves all of the obscure bands from the 90s Brit-Pop era, like Kulashaka, The Bluetones, Dodgy and Cast.

"Radio Wisconsin would always play stuff like that at around two in the morning while I was studying," she says with a smile.

"But were not Oasis and Blur more popular here?"

"Oh yeah, but I have always gone for bands that are less popular at the time, you know. I am avid follower of bar bands; I hear England has a great scene." She asks who my favourite band of all time is.

"It has to be The Clash & Hendrix."

"That would be the Jimi Hendrix Experience"

"All right! Nadine don't show off"

"Sorry I just had to say that. Hey! We had a massive picture of the *London Calling* album cover on are wall in college, you know the one with the guy smashing his guitar on the floor."

"Yea I know it." That would be a bass guitar and the guy is Paul Simmonen", I say with an avenging smile.

I compliment her on her knowledge of British Rock music and on her smile. I tell her that it makes her very welcoming and easy to get along with. She blushes.

Downstairs in the club, the Peckham Boys are doing their best R&B steps on the dance floor. The waifsfs are with them dancing seductively. They look like Paris Hilton and Tara Reid. Nadine and I join them; she shakes her large, round arse very well.

The night ends with us giving each of our girls a good tonguing. Ian wants to take things further, but Derek and I are happy to meet them on a future date. We usher Ian into a cab and head back to the hostel.

> **Gotham Hall**
> 1431 3rd St. Promenade
> Santa Monica
> CA 90401
> 310-3948865
> **Big screen little, dance floor**

The next morning I have a splitting hangover and head to reception to get a towel so I can shower in the communal bathroom. Katrina, the loudmouth Israeli, laughs and tells me that Arsenal has only just about managed a draw at home to Portsmouth.

That's a great start to the day, and to make things even worse our old adversary Teddy Sheringham, Tottenham/Man UTD scum, has scored against us yet again, this time for lowly Pompy. It took a re-taken penalty from Henry to get us a point. That's two home-points dropped already. Just like fucking last season, when we dropped seemingly un-droppable points. How the fuck are we going to reclaim the title if we can't even beat newly promoted Portsmouth at home? Fucking Arsenal, bunch of wankers!

To rid myself of this hangover and the miserable feeling brought on by Arsenal struggling at home, I decide to take a walk along the beach. The great thing about the hostel is that it is only a stone throw away from the ocean.

I take a left on the Ocean Front, passing sideshow freak after sideshow freak after sideshow freak. The highlight of which are a Pacific Island looking guy juggling metallic balls while wearing a star spangled g-string, a midget with his feet facing away from him and a guy in a Zulu costume balancing snakes in a bucket on his head while riding a unicycle. To many, this is just another morning's viewing on Venice Beach.

I walk passed the guys who are game enough to work-out topless outdoors at the Muscle Beach Gym, and get as far as the Venice Beach pier. In front of me is the familiar sight of the Venice Whaler Café & Bar, where we pulled those birds last night. I decide that this will be an ideal place to have breakfast/lunch. It's already midday so let's call it lunch.

The place looks so different in the LA sunshine. It has transformed from a decent pick-up joint to a daytime sports café. I sit at the bar and order a white wine from the ginger goatee bearded barman, who looks like the lead singer of the Spin Doctors or Alexi Lallas who played centre half for the American "soccer" team in the 94 World Cup.

"You want some food with that, buddy?" he says in a soft laid back fashion.

"Yes please, I wouldn't mind."

"Take a look at the menu, right here, and just give me a hola when you're ready buddy."

It's a great menu. I order two appetisers: beer battered onion rings and calamari served with salad. By the time my food arrives, I have moved from the bar to a table on the upper deck with an ocean view. As I gaze at the Pacific, I wonder what Francesca is doing, then think about Pamela in Monterey and then of Nadine last night, but my final thoughts as always are back to the mysterious Francesca and those two packages of coke she left in my bag. I still have a week left before I call her.

The food is delicious and I order a Corona to wash it down. The barman clears the plates from the table with a smile "Enjoy the food buddy?"

"Yea it was great, thanks."

"Hey are you British, man?"

"Yea, English."

"Got that World Cup coming up soon, huh?"

"World Cup? No it's the European Championships next summer, mate."

"Isn't it the Rugby World Cup in November?"

"Ooohh, I seeeeee, sorry about that mate." I thought the Americans didn't have a clue, and didn't give a shit about Rugby.

"The guy who owns this place is a Kiwi. He's going crazy for it man," the barman continues.

"Yea the Kiwi's always have a strong team."

"He thinks they are gonna smoke every team in sight, man."

"Well, I've already got a bet going with a guy in San Francisco that England are going to win."

"I don't know much about rugby, but I'm sure my boss will take that bet," the barman says, leaving me to my view.

Before I know it, the Kiwi owner has come to my table. He is so cock-sure that the All Blacks are a far superior team than the English that he is willing to give me $1000 if we just get further than New Zealand. In return, I just have to give him just $200 if the Kiwis win. I take the bet and I give him my word that if the Kiwis do indeed win, I will return and give him $200.

> **Venice Whaler**
> **2-10 Washington Boulevard**
> **310-821-8737**
> **Meet the over confident gambling Kiwi owner.**

Back at the Venice Beach Cotel, I am told by the Peckham Boys that we are meeting the girls from last night at a bar on Main Street called the Circle Bar.

Jessica, the leggy, Canadian receptionist, asks what am I doing tonight, as she and her sister are having a rare night out. I don't tell her about the Circle Bar or Nadine. I don't want her know about my exploits, because I am getting the inkling that she might have a slight crush on me. Therefore, I leave the door to her and those long legs ajar. Especially now as I feel she has given me the green light.

At the Circle Bar, Derek, Ian and I are assembled in a tight corner. They are dressed unmistakably in classic "English lad" clobber; Derek has a burgundy Hackett polo shirt and Ian wears a white, short-sleeved Ted Baker shirt. Not to be outdone, I am wearing a white Paul Smith shirt that has tartan cuffs.

We catch sight of the girls, who are being chatted up by some local guys. The South Londoners are having none of it, and with their brashness and swagger make themselves known to the girls.

"Awight girls, how's it going? We've been waiting for you lot. Hey, you look lovely darling," says Ian.

"Those earrings are blinding, really suite ya. You look gorgeous babes," adds Derek. Then a kiss on each cheek and hug and like that the local guys have moved on.

"Hi Richard, how are you?" asks Nadine who looks twice as good as last night. All in black, her top is really tight around the waist like a corset and make her tits look invitingly bigger. I compliment her; first by saying she looks dynamite, then by asking if her tits are real.

Sunday night is a real busy night at the Circle Bar. You can barely move as a massive crowd have been squeezed into the tiny bar. One of the waif girls is a little claustrophobic and suggests we go outside for a while.

Outside Derek hugs her, "It's gonna be awight, darling. You're in the fresh air now."

"Oh your so lovely," utters the waif.

"Full of muppets in there anyway, place was doing my head in," adds Ian.

"Yea it was so hot," says the other waif, "and full of, what do you guys say? Total waaankers!"

We all laugh in appreciation of the waifs humour.

"Where do you girls live?" asks Ian.

"Just a few block from here from here," answers his waif.

"So let's go back there. What we are waiting for, for fuck sake? You don't wanna go back into that fucking sweatbox, do ya?" The girls have no answer in resistance to this barrage of blatancy.

> **The Circle Bar**
> **2926 Main Street**
> **Santa Monica,**
> **CA 90405**
> **This pick-up joint will have you going round and around until you bump into a prospective partner.**

The three girls share a three-bedroom apartment on Breeze Court, which is about five blocks from the bar. We are all seated in the lounge room when Derek pulls out a wrap of coke, which he, Ian and the two waifs consume gleefully. Thankfully, Nadine isn't a drug user, so I state that I'm going to remain on her level. She thanks me and puts her hand on my lap. I don't fancy waking up tomorrow with a hangover accompanied with that monged out feeling from the come down from Charlie.

Ian and Derek are getting louder and louder with every line they snort and the waifs are getting gigglier. Nadine isn't impressed with the all the cocaine-induced noise and suggests that we go to her room. The others barely notice us leave.

We're sitting on the edge of her soft bed, listening to the Millwall Boys taking the piss out of the waifs, who are laughing at everything. She has put on some music(The Cranberries Fist Album 'Everybody is doing it some why cant we') in order to drown out the noise and to assist the atmosphere.

"That was so nice of you out there; you know not doing any coke."

"That's no problem Nadine. I'm not a really a drug user, and as you can hear it doesn't do you any favours. Listen to those doughnuts out there."

She laughs as I look at her monstrous chest while she closes her eyes in the midst of hilarity. I can wait no longer to unleash them. First, I plant a soft kiss on her lips, biting and probing them in the same passionate way Pamela did to me. This works a treat as I feel her body temperature rising. I take the opportunity to give her tits a good fondling. They are firm and for me feel better than Pam's silicon pair. I can tell she's a bit inexperienced and somewhat nervous, so I make all the experience I gained with Pamela tell.

First I unclip her corset, which is also doubles as a bra. I remove it to reveal her chest. She has trademark melons, that must be at least a double E, but she doesn't have big nipples to go with them. I pause and gaze at them for a moment.

"I hate them, they're too big," says Nadine, embarrassed.

"Don't be ridiculous."

"If I had the money, I would get a reduction."

"No way! I think that should be outlawed, a criminal offence. Breasts are what make a woman a woman. Nothing can beat a woman with curves."

"Really?"

"Really." I kiss her again and make for her breasts. I use two hands and my mouth, as a mark of respect to each of the ample bosoms. I fuck her missionary and then with her on top. This makes me cum in an instant because my eyes are glued to her best assets while she straddles me.

"What's the best way for you to come?" I ask her as she hasn't climaxed yet and my ego wants a level playing field before we nod off.

"From behind," she blushes. I kiss her then get her on all fours. I am ready to go again because her cleavage is a wonder to behold. In the doggy position, I tell her to arch her back in order to give me easier access. She concurs and her big arse looks magnificent and round in the process. I go slowly at first, as experience tells me that this is the deepest position of entry. I soon up the tempo, when I see that she is giving her clit a good rubbing. I follow suit a give her arse a nice ribbing with my thumb. Nadine shortly shudders an almighty groan as she orgasms. That triggers me to shoot my load again.

I am awake the next morning and for the first time since I arrived in California it is raining. The pitter-patter of rain hitting the ground outside keeps Nadine in a deep sleep. I take a shower and get dressed. Before leaving, I kiss Nadine on the forehead.

"Hey Richard, thanks for a lovely night." She says half asleep. "For the record, nobody has ever asked what makes me orgasm. Thanks. Call me sometime."

On my way out, I check on the Millwall boys and peep into one of the waifs' bedrooms. The first room I look into is empty. In the other one, I find the Boys and the size zeros sprawled out naked on a double bed. I leave them to it and walk back to the hostel in the morning rain, which is instrumental in my recovery process from that heavy night.

At the hostel, Katrina again teases me about football, but my memories of Arsenal dropping two home points are all but gone. Jessica, who is also sitting at reception, asks me how my night was. I tell that it was average; and that we ended up at a party in Santa Monica. I still have aspirations and plans for the leggy Canadian and the door is still open.

I meet the South London Boys later in the afternoon at the Boardwalk Café right on the beach.

"Did you shag Fatty?" ask Ian, while he is tucking into his all-day breakfast.

"She's not fat at all, mate, it was just those massive tits that made her look big. Some girls are bigger than others," I say defensively.

"Yea all right mate." Says Derek

"So what about you guys? How did you get on?" I say, changing the subject.

"Had a right result with those Barbie dolls, mate," says Derek.

"Yea, we had a four-in-the-bed session. It was fucking blinding mate," adds Ian. "We all went into the same room. We told them that we didn't want to be separated because I made a promise to his mum! And they bought it! Then we were shagging them next to each other."

"Yea you were shagging her like a right poof! You can't shag to save your life, you cunt," teases Derek.

"Fuck off, you twat, she was loving it." Ian continues, "Well anyway, we both finished off and I asked them if they have ever, you know kissed each other, and all that. And right there and then they started on each other. It was quality mate. So we just looked at each other and swapped over, you know what I mean. I don't even think they noticed!" Ian said laughing.

"Yea it was fucking blinding," adds Derek, joining in with the laughter. "You should have fucked off Fatty and walked in, you would have definitely got some."

"No, I was just fine where I was thanks."

The South Londoners have pulled off an amazing feat and I'm happy for them. They may think that I had the booby prize, but I am more than satisfied with my night with Nadine.

They tell me that they are going to be having a few quiet dry nights in the hostel, as they will be going to Vegas on Thursday for a long weekend.

"Fancy coming with us, Rich?" asks Derek.

"I'm not sure, maybe."

"Come on, we'll have a right laugh, we'll be on it 24-7," adds Ian.

"Well you've got three days to decide. We're not going until Thursday."

I spend the night in the hostel with the Millwall Boys, Jessica, her sister and a few other young travellers. The South Londoners sit at one table playing poker, practicing their hands and bluffs for the Vegas trip. I'm at another table with Jessica, and the few young travellers. One of them is Diane, a flirtatious, twenty seven-year-old German, who has apparently been here longer than anyone else has. I almost fall asleep while hearing monotonous tales of her journeys through California and beyond. Diane is a typical German traveller, who likes the sound of her own voice.

Without going into to much detail, I tell a few stories of my own. During my chronicles, Diane and Jessica try to out flirt each other. Diane the Kraut, flirts by agreeing with and laughing at anything I say, even though it's not at all funny. Jessica gives me continued eye contact a plays with her long blonde hair, while I tell them of my gay night out with Malcolm in San Francisco. It all ends in a draw; Diane asks me to go rollerblading with her in the morning, and Jessica ask me to join her and he sister for a Chinese meal tomorrow night- Richard the Lionheart Lover is back and thats official!

I wake up in the morning and am told by Katrina that the German bird was waiting for me for around half an hour to go rollerblading. To be honest, I didn't fancy it anyway, Why would I. Besides I want to watch Arsenals opening Champions League game of the season against Inter Milan, which is on at 11:45am west coast time. Katrina tells me that all the games are shown at a British pub called the Cock n' Bull on Lincoln Boulevard. Jessica who is lurking at reception tells me that she isn't doing anything at present and would take me there to watch the game.

En-route Jessica tells me more about herself and her life back home in Edmonton; she worked as an accountant before coming to California and hated her job like 80% of the world. She's travelling to find out about herself and what she really wants to do- like 80% of backpackers around the world. She hasn't got a boyfriend back home, but to my surprise she is dating a guy who works at the hostel.

When we get to the Cock n' Bull Pub, we have to put a $10 entry fee into an old style beer glass that a small Scotsman is holding.

The bar has been purposely darkened, either to make it seem like we are back home on a dark autumn night, or because the whole setup is illegal and covering up the windows will not attract any unwanted visits from the authorities. If you ask me, the darkened windows just make the place seem even more suspicious. Nonetheless, I do feel as though I am in a pub in London on a dark autumn night.

Jessica and I take a seat at a table with the rest of the Santa Monica/Malibu branch of the Arsenal supporters club, which consists of a forty-year-old man, his two young daughters and a woman in her mid fifties, who looks like a cross between ZaZa Gabor and Barbara Cartland.

The latter is an ex-pat who has been living here since the seventies. She is an ardent Arsenal fan and comes here for every televised game. Her ageing, multi face-lifted mug with collagen lips and fresh, silicon breast implants just does not look right with the Arsenal hat and scarf she is wearing, but I am just happy that Arsenal has fans such as these in this eccentric part of the world.

The six of us are silenced as Inter take the lead after 20 minutes through Cruz.

I immediately head to the bar in need of a stiff drink when Van de Meyde sweetly volleys homes a second three minutes later. Even though they sell English draft beer here, I get a double Scotch as I watch Inter's front two of Cruz and Martins, run our defence ragged. If it wasn't for Kolo Toure it could be even more, but even he is powerless to stop the speedy Martins adding a third goal. His acrobatic somersaulting celebration adds insult to injury. Its 3-0 to Inter at halftime.

The young daughters of the forty-year-old man are in tears as their father is "effing" and blinding in his American twanged-cockney accent. The brunt of his abuse is being thrown in the direction of Pires, who is having a very poor game, but to be fair to the Frenchman, he's not the only one.

Jessica puts her hand on my knee and rubs it to console me, which is sweet of her but not enough to keep me from buying another scotch.

ZaZa Garbor is none too pleased either, "It's that fucking Wengers fault. He didn't do enough to bring in quality players in the summer. All we got was that fucking German keeper," she rants in a croaky American accent. She continues to rant on her way to the bar, "Fucking Arsenal. I'm going need another fucking facelift after this, what they are doing to me." The whole bar laughs in hysterics.

Arsenal re-group after halftime and give a better showing but the second half is scoreless and the game ends in a crushing 3-0 defeat for the home side, an awful start to our 2003/04 Champions League campaign.

Zaza offers to drive Jessica and I back to the hostel in her flash-looking, red BMW, but Jessica suggests that we go into Santa Monica and have some more drinks to get over the game.

"Why don't we go back to my place in Malibu for the afternoon?" Zaza offers, pulling rank.

"I don't mind," states Jessica. "I don't start work until 11:00 tonight."

"Yea why not, it will beat going back to the hostel and getting the piss taken out of me by that Man UTD supporting Isreali."

Back in London, I would have walked in the light drizzle of a dark Tuesday night back to my one bedroom flat and felt depressed with the Champions League embarrassment fresh on my mind, and with the prospect of going to work the next day

The Cock n' Bull
Lincoln Boulevard
310-399 9696
A British pub that looks like a dodgy British pub run by Glaswegians and Scousers.

getting stick from Spurs and Chelsea fans.

Here it is only two o'clock in the afternoon, the sun is shining and I'm sitting in a BMW convertible driven by a 47-year-old eccentric, ex-pat, sitting next to a young, sweet, innocent Canadian, heading for Malibu Beach.

While we drive down Lincoln Boulevard, ZaZa introduces herself as Eileen, and says that it's great to meet any one from her hometown, especially Arsenal fans. "Where's your girlfriend from, darling? She from London too?"

"No she's Canadian."

"No Shit, really? What part, baby?" she asks Jessica.

"Edmonton," I answer.

"Hey, let the girl talk for herself, man."

"Edmonton," Jessica squeaks.

"Shit Edmonton huh? I bet your glad to be out here, shit."

"Yea I was happy to get out of there for a while."

"For a while? I've been there once and I'm not going back. I've never seen so many backward country fucks. No offence honey."

"None taken." Answers the Jessica with wide eyes, looking at me softly laughing.

Eileen's as brash and loud as the Millwall boys, I wonder if they're related.

For the rest of the journey, Eileen tells us about herself and her history in LA; she started up as a back up singer for many of the acts out here in the seventies and is basically now another rich widower in Malibu.

We arrive at Eileen's house; it's an unbelievable mansion with beach views and two swimming pools. She has a Hispanic maid named Juanita, who fixes us a meal. Eileen suggests we eat our food in the garden. Jessica smiles at me in disbelief. You can tell that she has been backpacking for a good while, as she scoffs the gourmet meal as if it will be her last.

Eileen brings out a bucket of champagne with three glasses. "Help yourselves guys, I'm gonna take a shower and get out of my football clothes" she says as she walks back into the house "Fucking Arsenal, they'll be the death of me"

She reappears in a designer bikini and a sarong. "Hey you two I have some friends coming over for a kind of beach party."

"Beach party! It's a Tuesday afternoon," I reply.

"Hey this is Malibu not fucking erm… Marylebone baby." She gives Jessica one of her bikinis and gives me a pair of her boyfriend's board shorts. Jessica, although pale, has a breathtaking body. Her legs are long shapely like a synchronised swimmer, and are complimented with a sturdy, little arse and a toned sexy midriff. She appears shy at first to reveal her sporty, bikini body. She stretches her arms down in front of her with her hands linked to cover herself.

The first person who arrives is a guy about thirty-three years old. "Guys, this is José, my boyfriend," Eileen announces. José is a handsome Mexican who Eileen met while he worked in a bar in Marina del Rey. She now sponsors him while he goes to drama school. He has passed an English entry exam, and is now competent enough to start the course. They look an odd couple but hey, this is Malibu.

Eileen is throwing the pool party in honour of Jose's passing of the drama school's prerequisite.

I jump in the pool to cool off as the alcohol and the sun are beginning to make me feel drowsy. A few more guests arrive: A very camp looking gay guy carrying a very small dog that looks like an oversized rat and three very well-dressed women. Jessica joins me in the pool to avoid any uncomfortable introductions. The shy Canadian doesn't meet people very well.

I ask Jessica about her boyfriend at the hostel. She tells me that he is a young Swede who likes to surf and smoke, and that he has not taken her out once.

"So where is he now?" I ask.

"He's down in San Diego on a surfing trip with some of his friends."

"Why didn't you go?"

"It's not my thing."

"Surfing or smoking?"

"Err...both," she says laughing embarrassingly.

More guests arrive and a few join us in the pool. I ask José where in México he is from. He tells me that he is from a colonial town called Guanajuato, about three hours north of México City. I tell him that I will be heading down there soon and want to learn Spanish.

"Guanajuato is a cool place to learn Spanish man. Many students there," José tells me with his new found confidence in English.

"Ok Guanajuato it is then."

Eileen puts on some salsa music. This gets everyone out of the pool to show off their best salsa moves. There must be at least fifteen people here now. Jessica is impressed with my dancing, as I give her a few twirls. She doesn't seductively wrap her leg around mine like the Argie birds did, but her shy innocence is just as sexy.

"I am not suggesting anything here, but I think I need to lie down," utters Jessica. "The champagne and your salsa twirls have made me bit dizzy. You don't mind, do you?"

"No, not at all, don't be silly," I reply. The sun, the champagne, the dancing and Arsenals crushing home defeat has taken it toll on me too. I ask Eileen if we can use one of her many rooms for a rest.

"Hey you dog you! Vet that Arsenal frustration on that piece of Canadian country ass," Eileen says while dancing in her merry state.

"No we just want to rest."

"Yea whatever sweetie," she says, winking in my direction. "On the very top floor I have a guest suite. Go for your life baby." She waves us toward the house and goes back to her dancing.

The guest suite is fit for a rock star; it looks like a suite at the Savoy. I take a shower in the huge bathroom while Jessica lies on the bed for a rest.

I return to find her asleep, but my movements awake her. She gets up and decides to takes a shower too.

Ten minutes later Jessica steps out of the shower wrapped in a fluffy towel. "That's better. I feel really refreshed now."

I stand up and tell her that she looks cute when her hair's wet. She blushes a rosy red with embarrassment, but manages to thank me for the compliment.

I take the opportunity to kiss her intimately. She accepts my advances and caresses my head. Her body trembles as I stroke her back and her tight, firm buttocks. I lay her on the bed and slowly unravel the towel from around her. Her trembles turn into a shake as I run kisses down her neck and then along her shoulder. After licking and sucking her I ease her onto the bed, with legs spread and make for her pussy. Jessica puts her hands on my head and says, "Wait."

I look up at Jessica, who is looking at me with a wrinkled brow. "What's wrong?" I say.

"Look, I haven't even had sex with my boyfriend," she mumbles, wide-eyed. I'm surprised and sit on the bed by her feet. She sits up and covers herself up with the towel.

"I can't believe how easy it was to kiss you," she says. "I mean, it's not like you're not attractive to me, but I can't believe I let that happen. I can't believe I let myself do this. I feel so dirty," she rambles, looking from me to the bed to the door.

"Shh, shh," I whisper, trying to sooth her. "It was an impulse, there was nothing either of us could do about it. It was all meant to happen, everything; the football game, Eileen, the party and now this." Even Arsenal's Euro, Highbury humiliation, I suppose.

"But I've got a boyfriend."

"When I saw you come out of that shower, I felt that I had the right to kiss you," I reply, getting off the bed.

"I am so ashamed of myself, because I feel the same way too. I wasn't brought up like this Richard. What have I become?"

Okay, she's taking this a little too far. I feel like saying, "This is Malibu baby," but I think that would not go down very well.

"Please don't tell my sister or Katrina because they are both friends with my boyfriend." She sighs loudly and starts getting dressed. "I don't know what I'm going to do, but please don't tell anyone. This has to be our secret. Look, I have to go. I'll see you another time at the hostel maybe." And like that, she's dressed and gone.

After the bizarre and crazy times I have had thus far in California, I just can't comprehend and come to terms with Jessica's guilt. I get dressed and rejoin Eileen and the eccentrics of Malibu at the pool party. I have a dance with Eileen and tell her that I might be going to Vegas on Thursday for the weekend.

"Well honey," she says, "you'd better get your ass some rest these next two nights, cause your gonna need it."

"Yea, but my sleeping patterns aren't so hot at the moment," I tell her.

"Wait here honey, I'll be right back." She returns and hands me a pack of Xanax. "There you go honey. These suckers will put you to sleep."

As I leave, she gives me her card, which is like a business card but just has her name and number on it.

"Hey luv," she says losing her American accent, sounding more like Barbara Windsor, "don't forget the game on Sunday."

"What game."

"Hey baby," sounding like Goldie Hawn again. "It's the big one man, Man UTD!"

"Oh fuck, oh yeah."

"Get with the programme, baby! I'll be in the Cock n Bull if you don't go Vegas."

I laugh to myself, as I can't believe I'm being reminded about an Arsenal game, and a massive one at that, by a middle-aged, face-lifted widow in Malibu.

It's around midnight back at the hostel, I run into Derek, who is sitting alone in the Aqua Lounge drinking the last can of a six-pack of Budweiser.

"Hey Gooner, what you up to?" he asks.

"Ahh just had yet another bizarre day man," I sigh, sitting down next to him.

"Here, have a can and tell me about it. It's my last one but I think five is enough for one night, don't you?" I open the Budweiser and fill him in. He's impressed and entertained by my story though, I tell him not to tell anyone about the Jessica part. I ask him where Ian is.

"Ahh! He's in the room shagging some Aussie bird. She wasn't up for the spit roast so I left him to it."

"So you feel a bit left out tonight then."

"Don't worry mate, one way or another, I'll make up for it in Vegas. Are you coming or what?"

"Yea, I think I will."

I feel great having had two good nights sleep thanks to the Xanax Eileen gave me. My weekend bag is packed and I'm ready for Vegas. When I walk passed reception, Katrina who has been busting my balls all week about the Inter result and the impending clash between Arsenal and Man UTD all week, hands me an envelope.

"Jessica left it for you. She left yesterday without warning. Her and her fucking sister got these jobs in the Hills as nannies." Shocked, I look at the envelope.

Katrina continues, "Oh, it's probably her contact details, emails and shit. I wouldn't email that Canadian bitch, she's so fucking boring!"

I open the letter as I head downstairs. It reads:

Dear Richard,

After what happened the other day, I see this as the only way to deal with the situation. I thought I would be able to see you again, you know as just a friend or something, but I couldn't handle it right now. As I told you, I'm not the type of girl who sleeps with just anyone. Kissing you wasn't a fluke, I know, as I wanted things to go further without realizing it. I really like you, but I have high values and don't want to be in a position where I lose my inhibitions so easily again. As you may know I have taken a job in Hollywood Hills as a nanny. This job may be a way out of the situation, call me a wimp, but I can see no other way. I just can't.

Jessica

I feel rather relieved, as for once I should have thought with my head rather than my knob. Jessica is a lovely girl and after what happened on Tuesday I was thinking that maybe she would have dumped her boyfriend and wanted to start a steady relationship with me. This wouldn't have been an option any way, as I have Francesca constantly on my mind and not to mention I'm having the time of my life in California. Why spoil it by having a Canadian lumberjack's daughter as my girlfriend? I will have one final mad weekend in Vegas and call Francesca when I get back.

Ian and Derek have rented a red convertible Mustang. What else do expert from a couple of flash South London bastards?

"Oi, I heard you tried to give that Canadian bird at reception one the other day, you dirty bastard," rants Ian, who is driving the first leg of the trip.

"Yea, it wasn't meant to be," I reply as I look in Derek's direction with slight disdain.

"I bet she's got a really tight minge. I fucking love tight minges!" exclaims Ian.

"Yea, only cause your knob is so small!" teases Derek.

"Fuck off you cunt! I've got a big, fuck-off knob! Just ask your Missus when we get back to Peckham!"

We all laugh as we turn onto the Interstate 15 highway that will take us all the way to Vegas.

LAS VEGAS,
19 September 2003

We arrive on the strip at 2:00pm with Ian's funky house music blaring out of the convertible Mustang's speakers and with the wind hitting our faces feeling as if it's coming out of an electric fan heater. It must be over 100 degrees here. The boys are huge fight fans, so we are staying at Caesar's Palace, the scene of some of the most famous bouts in boxing history.

At the Caesar's Palace reception, we are told that they only have a room available for the first two nights. On Saturday, (which is fight night), we're going to have to find somewhere else to stay. The boys and I don't give a shit about all that, we are just happy to be here.

Ian tries to pay for the room with a wad of folded notes that he pulls from his pocket, but the receptionist politely smiles and says, that they are going to need a credit card of some sort. He fishes in his pocket and hands her a Visa.

The room they have booked must have at least set them back a grand for each night.

Ian looks at me and smiles "Don't worry Richard, you don't have to pay, you're sleeping on the couch. But you have to pay for your own brass though."

"Yea, you've had a right touch," adds Derek.

He's right, I have had a right touch, this suite is top draw. It is immaculately decked out in authentic, Italian furniture and has two Jacuzzis. While I'm looking around the place, I ask Derek, "What is it exactly that you two do in London to be able to afford a couple of nights here?"

"Building trade, night clubs and drugs," he replies.

"In Peckham in the winter and Ibiza in the summer," adds Ian, opening his bag.

"So why the hell are you two staying at a hostel?"

"We thought it would be a laugh," says Derek "You know what I mean. We were in a hotel in San Fran, It was all right and that, but me and funny fella over there were spending too much time together. And when we were out most of the people we met in bars and that were all staying at hostels. So we thought in LA we would give it a go, and stay at the Cotel."

"Yea, so it's great you coming along with us here to Vegas, you know, to split us up when we're bickering and fighting," adds Ian before throwing a pillow in Derek's direction.

We have a little nap before we go out. The first bar we strike is at the Venetian Hotel & Casino called the "V Bar". It's quite early and we get in without a fuss. At the bar, I get the three of us a double Jack and Cokes with three shots of Tequila each. We toast with a cheers.

Ian holds up his glass and announces, "Right this it, tonight is the night we have been waiting for the past year! Vegas is where we finally loose complete control of all senses and any fucking inhibitions that are still lurking about."

We down the tequilas and the Millwall boys down their main drinks in one. To keep up I finish my Jack and Coke soon after. Ian steps to the bar and orders another round.

While I wait for the drinks with Ian, Derek is already chatting up two slim blondes, who are sitting at the table next to ours. Before Ian has brought our drinks to the table, Derek is escorting one of them to the bathroom. That leaves the other girl sitting alone. I know Ian will try it on with her before he hands me my drinks, so I leave him to it.

First he whispers a sweet nothing into her ear. She returns the compliment and the next thing I know, she is escorting Ian to the bathroom. I sit there alone and dumbfounded.

The bar is filling up in their absence; nothing but gorgeous looking birds with massive tits, real and fake, and smartly dressed older guys.

The Millwall troopers emerge from the bathroom alone.

"Where are those two birds?" I ask.

"They're still in there fucking about with their hair and shit," replies Ian, taking a drink.

"So, what happened in there?" I ask, a tad envious of their blatant, no-nonsense style.

"Not much, all they wanted was a bit of coke from us and all we got was a bit of tit for our troubles."

The two girls who are wearing tightly fitted dresses return and join us at the table. Derek inconspicuously slips me a wrap of coke and whispers something into one of the blondes' ear. She comes over to me, "Hi I'm Trudy, what's yours?"

"My name is Richard."

"So Richard, do you wanna go to the bathroom?"

I look at Derek who nods his head at me.

"Yea let's go Trudy." I escort the thin blonde to the toilets while Ian and Derek look on and laugh.

We get into a cubicle in the elegant toilet.

"Well, are you going to pull it out?" she asks, looking at my pants.

I should pull out my cock, but I know what she wants. I give her the wrap of coke and she neatly creates a line about three inches in length along the top of the marble toilet. Like an anteater, Trudy disposes of the coke. Then with a pinch of her nose and a deep sniff, she looks at me in an inviting way. I can only smile back. She pulls down the straps of her dress and heaves out her silicon tits. She scoops up a small pile of coke and draws a line of it across the top of her rock hard massive bosoms.

"Well what are you waiting for?" Trudy asks. I didn't really fancy getting on it tonight, but I have never seen powder prepared on the anything like this before.

"Come on baby, hit it," she whispers, gently fondling her veined-silicon pair. I dive face first into the cleavage and run my nose side to side across the top of her breasts, vacuuming up the coke in the process.

My pecker is now rock hard so I pull it out and start masturbating, while Trudy continues to fondle her tits whilst dancing suggestively like a stripper. She spins around and seductively lifts her dress exposing and then sticking out her perfect little arse.

"Well, what are waiting for?" she again asks, looking over her shoulder.

I quickly put on an emergency condom and after a quick feel of her wet pussy, I slam my latex covered cock into the juicy, bald slit. I cum in less than a minute, as the erotic occasion has gotten to me. Coked up and all!

"That's great baby," smiles Trudy. She seems to be extremely happy that I have cum but pulls my hand away as I rub her clit trying to get her to orgasm so that we can have a level playing field. "That's ok baby, I'm fine," she declares. What a result! We get out of the cubicle when the coast is clear.

My first public toilet fuck. I didn't quite manage it is Santa Cruz with Amy and Maria, but this has more than made up for that disappointment. We return to find the other blond girl, alone.

"Where did my friends go?" I ask her.

"Oh them" She says with attitude "They were asked to leave by the doormen."

"What?"

"Yea they had some sort of argument with the bartender."

"Do you know where they went?"

"No, no idea. One second they were at the bar, the next they were being escorted out."

"Shit! I better go find them."

The girls say they want to stay here, as they have a few more hours to kill before they start work. They are strippers at a club called "The Palomino" and suggest we all meet there later. I am relieved, as I would rather be having a laugh with the South London geezers, rather than stay here in this pretentious bar these two simple, blonde Barbie dolls.

I bid them farewell, leave the bar and have a look around the casino area of the Venetian. There is no sign of Ian and Derek at the giant slot machines, the Roman column's or the gleaming marble walls. I leave and head for our suite at Caesar's.

> The V Bar
> The Venetian Hotel
> 3355 Las Vegas Blvd
> 702-414-1000
> Seeing is believing. Beautiful, jaw-dropping girls in a beautiful bar where strippers hang out before and after work.

I manage to weave my way through tourists strolling from casino to casino and the Mexicans handing out sexual service flyers on the packed streets of The Strip, and get to our suite at Caesar's. The boys are not there, but there is note stuck to the TV with Brylcream hair gel informing me they are at a strip club called Crazy Horse II.

After a ten minute cab ride, I'm standing in front of Crazy Horse II. It doesn't look like the kind of place that would contain stunning, sexual, provocative females. In fact, it looks like the goods entrance of a Bn'Q or an IKEA.

At the bar, I get myself a Jack and ginger. The bartender is equally as stunning as the strippers on show, whom are from all corners of the globe and Kansas. I browse the dark surroundings while a naked striper on stage, who looks like Alicia Silverstone, slides down the steel pole with her legs spread open in front of her. Maybe it is Alicia Silverstone, She probably needs a bob or two, I mean when was the last time she made a decent film.

"Oi Gooner!"

"Oi Gooner, you mug! Over here!"

The two Millwall boys are sitting side by side on a sofa, each with a striper gyrating and grinding on their laps.

"Thank fuck you made it! This is quality mate!" shouts Ian.

The strippers finish their tandem performance. The striper on Derek's lap, who is petite and Korean-looking, whispers something in his ear.

Derek's reply is, "Not now love, I gotta have a drink and talk to me mate."

The two strippers leave us to talk.

"What happened with you two at the V bar?" I ask, watching the both of the girl's perfect arses as they walk away.

"We were just having a laugh with that barmaid," replies Derek, taking a sip of his drink, his voice barley audible over the loud the top 40's Rn'B being played.

"All it was, was that she asked for a tip," says Ian, leaning forward putting his elbows on his Derek's knees.

"Yea, that's the norm over here. You normally leave a dollar per drink, don't you?" I say.

"Yea I know that you doughnut," says Ian, "But just for a laugh, when she asked for a tip I said to her, 'Yea I've got a tip for you love. Don't eat yellow snow.'" He slaps Derek's knee and we all laugh.

"Yeah there's nothing wrong with that is there! It's just a laugh innit?" Derek joins in.

"That's what it should have been, but after that she refused to serve us any more drinks, so I called her a fucking slag," says Ian, laughing again. "And the next thing we know, we're fucking being kicked out, buy these big, fuck off, bouncers."

"We waited outside for you, but you fucking took you time in the bogs with that blonde, didn't ya? What the fuck were you doing in there, you cunt?" Ian asks, looking at me.

"Nothing, just like you say, I just took my time in there." I finish my drink and change the subject. "So what are we up for now?"

"What we'll do," replies Derek, "is have a drink here then go back to Caesar's, 'ave a flutter on the poker, then go to one of the clubs, probably that Studio 54 at the MGM."

I help Derek get the drinks in. At the bar he tells me that he knows that I got a blowjob in the bathroom, as he got one too.

"How do you know?" I ask, faking innocence.

"I told her to."

"What! You have a way with words, don't you?"

"Yea maybe, its even more effective when you offer a bit of coke and $50." He laughs "don't worry it's my treat." Well there you have it; I knew it was too good to be true. Still, I got a bit more than a blow, so I shouldn't be too hard on myself.

"Whatever you do, don't tell Ian. He'll be gutted, as he only got a bit of tit and I won't hear the last of it."

Derek goes on to tell me that the Korean stripper that was on his lap said that it would cost him only $200 to shag her. He is contemplating it, as he is surprisingly infatuated with her. He continues to say that he loves Asian birds, especially those from Korea.

"Have you ever had a bird from North Korea?" he asks me.

"North Korea? Fuck! I've never even met anyone from North Korea," I reply.

In fact has anybody in the West met anyone from North Korea in the last forty years? The only thing I know about North Korea is that it's an extreme Communist, nuclear state, with a well-disciplined army and that they had a Striker called Pat Du Ip, in 1966, when they got to the World Cup quarter final in England. Furthermore, I certainly couldn't tell you if a North Korean bird was prettier than her counterpart in the south.

"I met this North Korean bird about four years ago," says Derek, watching the bartender pour our drinks. "I was selling pills at the Ministry of Sound and this bird wanted a couple. She was fucking gorgeous, I tell ya. It turns out that she was a diplomat's daughter. She was fucking unbelievable," he says now looking at me. "Even now when I think about her, words fail me, you know what I mean? We met each other a couple times after that, you know, while her old man was in London. We kept in touch for a while and then I took a trip out there."

"What! North Korea?"

"No! You Doughnut, It's a right drama getting a visa over there! Not any old cunt can get in. I met her in Shanghai and while I was over there I met a few of her mates from North Korea. I tell ya all of them were 10 out of 10 stunners. The people in the north of North Korea have this different kind of Asian look. I can't describe it. You're gonna have to go there and see for yourself," Derek pays and tips the bartender and grabs his and Ian's drinks.

I make a mental note to put a visit to the north of North Korea on my list of things to do before I die, while I grab my double Jack Daniels and ginger and make my way back to our table.

Back at Caesar's, the boys are playing $100 poker. I haven't got a clue about the game so I leave them to it and head for the $5 Black Jack tables.

The $5 and $10 Black Jack and Roulette areas are the busiest and you have to wait for a seat at a table at peak times in the popular hotels.

My first two rounds are unsuccessful. My first hand, I bust having

CRAZY HORSE II

Address: Not necessary. Every taxi driver will know the location of every strip joint in town.

Open 24 hours, but note: Like most strip joints around the world the best girls work between 9pm and 2 am. It's a good idea, especially on the weekend, to try off-peak times, as every out-of-towner will be there during peak times.

Some helpful tips for Vegas strip joints:

• Keep your wedding band on, strippers don't give shit whether you're married or not.

• Ask before you touch.

• If you can touch, stroke and not grope.

• Not all strippers are trashy bimbos from small town USA. Some are accountants, lawyers and nurses supplementing their incomes or paying for their kids to have a better life. Some have even been known to be high calibre graduates from Oxford, Cambridge, Princeton and Harvard paying off their student loans.

• Bring enough cash for a least one private dance. Strippers don't like credit cards. The joints have ATM machines but they charge a lot more than your average hole in the wall.

twisted on 16. My second hand of 19 was beaten by the croupier's hand of a King and a Jack. My third hand, was a four card 21, which beat the croupier's 20. This, along with the double scotch I ordered from the waitress in a toga, has given me a false sense of security and has me upping my stakes. After 20 minutes, I have lost $150.

Disillusioned with Black Jack, I head for the roulette tables. I fair a bit better here and have won back the $150. However after half an hour I am down another $100.

I grab another scotch from the waitress and take a seat in the lounge area of the casino. This is where many working girls hang out. I find out this information when I try to chat up a stunning brunette who lured me with her dark Mediterranean eyes. After a little flirtatious chit-chat, she asks me if I was staying here at Caesars.

"Yea I've got a suite," I boast in a tipsy manner.

"Well, maybe we should go to that suite," she purrs.

"Yes, maybe we should."

"OK, that will be $200 for half an hour whether you cum or not." Like the blonde in the bathroom at the V Bar, I knew that it had to be too good to be true.

The time is about 1:00am and the Millwall Boys have joined me after a fruitful spell on the poker table.

"Fucking two grand up we are!" brags Ian. "How's that for a night's work?"

"Yea, let's go to that club at the MGM Grand to celebrate," Derek suggests. "That Korean bird's gonna be there."

"Oh yea," I say excitedly.

"Oh yea! And I told her to bring two of her mates. I couldnt leave you two out, could I?"

At Studio 54, we have to wait for twenty minutes in the long queue. Once we're in passed the snooty, obnoxious bouncers and the fucking pointless red rope, I think to myself that it wasn't worth the wait at all. I was kind of expecting the Studio 54, to be like it was in New York in the mid 70's in its fabulous, flamboyant heyday and like it was in that film with Mike Myers and the gorgeous Salma Hayek. Now that might have been worth the wait and $20 cover charge, that I would rather have spent the on another couple rounds of Black Jack.

The only plus is the fact that the girls here outnumber the guys almost 2 to 1. The Millwall boys now completely high on coke and buzzing off the occasion are being their loud selves, insulting every girl they talk to, whether they are fat, thin, pretty or ugly. I have to hand it to them, because they still have that knack of impressing. I leave them to it and go for a stroll around the club.

I have a drink at the bar and spot a girl on the dance floor who is giving me a smiley eye while she dances in rhythm with the Hip Hop beat. I take note of her and wait until she makes a move.

Call it luck, but her next move is a walk to the bar, right next to me.

Confidence is a funny thing; it can come and go in a flash. Since mine is sky-high right now aided with that mound of coke I vacuumed off of that blondes cleavage in the bathroom at the V Bar, I waste no time in introducing myself to her. Betty is a teacher from Boulder, Colorado. I compliment her on her shapely, sporty legs. She says it's from living out in Colorado, where she hikes mountains and has competed in various outdoor pursuits for most of her life.

We are getting on well; we talk of the Denver Broncos, *Dynasty* and *The Colby's*. She is impressed that I know these eighties soaps and even more impressed that an Englishman can talk with confidence about her hero, Broncos legendary Quarter Back John Elway.

My flow with Betty is destroyed when we are joined by Ian, who interrupts our conversation by pulling me to one side, "Oi, get rid of fat legs. We got three strippers over there," he says with his usual brash bluntness. When I turn to Betty and tell that I will see her later, I can see the disappointment in her eyes.

At the table, I am introduced to the Korean and her two friends. They are also strippers at the Crazy Horse II. One of them has a boyfriend (a bouncer at the Mandalay Bay), who she is meeting after work. So that leaves one stripper for Ian and I to compete for. I love a bit of competition, but I wouldn't stand a chance against the mouthy

Millwall boy. I'm not saying that Ian has a better game than what I do, but there's no way he will just sit there and let me take this stripper away from him.

I find Betty from Boulder back on the dance floor and try to reacquaint myself with her. She tells me that she is leaving, alone. I try to persuade her to stay, but to no avail, her mind has been made up. Before she leaves, she says, "I'll see you at Club Ra tomorrow night. You can make it up to me then."

I sigh and hold my hands up in defeat. To make things worse Ian's barefaced, obnoxious charm is more than working on the single stripper. They are all over each other.

"This club is fucking shit! Let's go have a drink at Caesar's," announces Derek.

"Yea its two bob here, init?" adds Ian. He looks at me and laughs. "Didn't pull tonight then Richard?" I laugh at his gloating joke for a moment, but then remember my bathroom exploits at the V Bar and laugh some more.

> **Studio 54**
> **In the MGM Grand**
> **3799 Las Vegas Blvd**
> **Las Vegas, NV**
> **702-891-1111**
> **It's not New York and it's not 1977. Nice try though.**

The five of us are sitting in the lounge of the Caesar's Palace casino with The Millwall boys being their loud, obnoxious piss-taking selves and the girls are no more than giggling spectators. I am a mere gooseberry in the proceedings.

"Will you guys put a sock in it for a goddamn minute?" a voice shouts.

Alerted, the South London Boys stand up. "Who the fuck said that?" shouts Ian angrily, looking around the lounge.

A man in his mid to late forties sporting a cowboy hat surrounded by three younger girls rises to the challenge. "Hey guys, can you just keep quiet for a while? The sound of your voices is pissing me off."

Oh shit, I think to myself, this could be an explosive situation.

"Who the fuck are you, you cunt?" yells Ian.

"Hey, I've had a bad night all right, and now your British accents are pissing me off."

"Well get the fuck away from us before you get hurt, you plum!" shouts Derek.

"Hurt? Hurt by who?! You want some, pussy whipper? You want some, huh?" the cowboy taunts, as he steps towards us.

"Yea we want some Cowboy, let's 'ave it!" fronts Ian, moving away from our table.

"Yea, you'll get your mother-fucking head blown off, pussy whipper!" the Cowboy shouts, hooking his thumbs into the front belt loops on his jeans as he moves closer.

"Head blown off? What you got a shooter big man, 'ave ya?" bellows Ian, taunting the Cowboy. "Where we're from, we don't need guns. We fight toe-to-toe, man-to-man! We're English mate, football hooligans!" he rages, walking toward the cowboy with Derek in tow. "We fight each other for fun back home mate!"

I can see for the first time that the Cowboys' balls have begun to shrink. He backs up a bit; it must have been the "fighting for fun" part that did it.

One of the girls in his entourage pulls the Cowboy back by his arm. "No Lawrence, please baby no. Come and sit back down, baby."

"You heard the lady," Derek teases. "I think you should listen to your daughter."

The noise has alerted two security guards who step in and break up the Anglo-American friction and offer a peace treaty.

"Lawrence, I think it's time for you to go home. Please leave by the side entrance," says one of the security guards. As Lawrence the cowboy leaves, Ian teases him by imitating his young girlfriend's high pitched, Daisy Duke voice, "No Lawrence, please Lawrence." Lawrence gives us the finger and we all laugh.

"Who are ya! Who are ya!" the three of us sing in tandem jokingly.

It's a Millwall thing! Every Millwall supporter I have met in my life has the notion that they have the right to win every fight they participate in, no matter what the odds are. They are all under this illusion that they are invincible.

It's all to do with their notorious national reputation and the fact that most of them come from violent South East London dumps like

Deptford, Peckham and New Cross. These areas have the highest murder rate and one of the lowest standards of living in Britain and are inhospitable places at the best of times. Let alone every other Saturday, when hundreds of alcohol and cocaine induced Millwall thugs come out of the decrepit pubs and onto the streets of Southeast London; from the Elephant and Castle to the Old Kent Road.

With the exception of Dulwich and Blackheath, South East London is shit hole after shit hole of never ending concrete, urban sprawl. The products of this environment grow up and make their way to Cold Blow lane or the New Den as it's called today, the home of Millwall Football club.

The Caesar's Palace security guard now reads us our action points for the Anglo-American peace treaty. "You guys will have to leave by the front entrance."

"But we're staying here," I interject.

"You're guests of the hotel, sir?" he asks me in disbelief.

"Yea, here's our room key." I show him the plastic swipe card, room key with the Caesar's logo on it.

"Oh," he says somewhat disappointedly. "Well in that case I'm going to have to ask to return to your room."

We get to the sumptuous suite with the two strippers. I don't bother to try and make it a fivesome. I just shut the doors to the Millwall Boy's bedroom and crash out on my couch.

I am woken up the next morning by a slamming door. It must be the strippers leaving.

It ended a dream I was having of Francesca and Pamela in Monterey.

In my dream, Pamela was looking for a flatmate to rent the basement apartment of her house and Francesca is the successful applicant. One night, the bored and lonely Pamela seduces Francesca while she is doing her homework. Pamela strips the young Latina down to her bare skin and licks her body from head to toe, deliberately missing out her trim pussy. She then leads Francesca to the kitchen and rubs olive oil all over her. Pam then takes her clothes off and repeats the process on herself and then pours the remainder of the bottle of olive oil on the tiled floor. They start wrestling and kissing on the greasy, slippery floor.

The two perfect oiled bodies are a shining contrast in the Californian sun, when they slip into the 69 position, with Francesca's young, curvy, brown skin and Pamela's older, paler, siliconed, athletic body.

The kitchen door flies open. It's me. I walk in, slip on the greased floor and break my back. Next thing I know, I'm laying flat out on Pamela's kitchen floor looking at the ceiling while both she and Francesca lick my shaft and balls. But I can't see or feel a thing as I am paralysed from the neck down.

After breakfast the Millwall Boys and I are sitting by the pool with our legs in the water to keep us cool in the sweltering Nevada heat. Both of them have been boasting all morning about what happened last night. To keep a long story short, they each took a Viagra and apparently, they both fucked each stripper five times. I don't think they should boast since they took performance-enhancing drugs and ought to be disqualified!

Ian gets out his camcorder, "Here mate, just for you. I've got most of it on tape. Have a butchers at that mate."

I watch a scene where both strippers are on all fours facing each other giving each other a tonguing, meanwhile Ian and Derek are taking them from behind. Then they swap.

Its 10:00 pm. After losing another $200 on Black Jack and Roulette, I meet Ian and Derek at a restaurant at the Rio called "All American Bar and Grille". A croupier at Caesar's has been raving about it. Ian and Derek both order the biggest steaks in the house. I've eaten enough steak since arriving in California so I go for the fillet mignon and lobster tails served with a side soup and dough bread, grilled veggies and a jacket potato.

Our waitress for the evening is Cheryl, a local girl from downtown. She is overwhelmed by our accents and tells us she wants to go France, which she actually thinks is in London, as well as thinking that Europe and London are the same place. I give her brief Geography lesson covering the continent-country-city structure of Europe and then get the bill.

All American Bar Grille
In the Rio Suites
3700 W. Flamingo Rd
702-252-7767
All American by name...
Please note, that not all
Las Vegas waitresses
have missed essential
Geography lessons.

We jump into taxi and head for the Luxor. Fortunately, a night at Club RA was on the South London Boys list of things to do. Tonight, Brandon Block and Alex P, a couple of UK House DJs are headlining. Unfortunately, they are also both celebrity supporters of Tottenham Hotspur. Derek and Ian like the music they play but can't stand them because of their Tottenham connection.

Ian and Derek's have a similar level of hatred for Spurs as I do, but theirs is more for violent reasons. Tottenham's Yid Army have emerged as serious challengers to Millwall's Capital Hooligan crown in recent years.

We get into the club at around eleven and it's already a full house. The Millwall boys, who are on pills for the night, indulge themselves in water. I, on the other hand stick to my usual, Jack and ginger.

The progressive, euphoric House beats have Ian and Derek on the dance floor jumping with the masses. I'm not too keen on this brand of music, and certainly can't enjoy it without taking spaceman drugs, so I soak up the atmosphere by strolling around the place looking for Betty from Boulder.

After looking in all of the little nooks and crannies of the ancient Egyptian-themed club, I see no sign of her. Instead, I am pulled onto the dance floor by a trashy blonde, probably in her thirties. Embarrassingly, she is the worst dancer in the club. After a few more pounding House tunes she actually turns out to be the worst dancer in the world.

It is almost impossible not to stay in rhythm to a House or Techno beat, but this bird has managed the impossible. I reach my humiliation threshold when she starts hopping around me like a kangaroo. Before she has completed a full circle, I duck away to the toilets.

As I'm making my way through the crowded dance floor towards the toilet, feeling relieved to have escaped the clutches of white trash, I feel a fist punch my back. When I spin around, I'm delighted to see that it's neither the Millwall Boys nor the trashy Kangaroo dancer. Its Betty from Boulder.

"Hey, I saw that!" she says, laughing.

"Saw what?" I smile, checking out her muscular legs in the fitted jeans she's wearing.

"You! You on the dance floor with Cindy Lauper," she replies, flipping her long ginger hair over her shoulder.

"I know, it was bad, wasn't it? Did it look as embarrassing as I felt?" I ask, loving how her tight white shirt accentuates her midriff.

"Yea, it really did honey. I felt for you though."

"Did you see her impression of a kangaroo?"

"Yea that was the highlight!" she exclaims, laughing even harder.

We continue to laugh, while I lead her to the bar to get a drink. Even though she is sporty and muscular, she is all woman to me. I don't think the South London Boys would see things the same way I do, even in their state of euphoric ecstasy. They class any girl bigger than a size 10 as a "fat bird." Adding to that, the fact Betty has ginger hair, which will lead to the boys giving me shit-loads of stick tomorrow at debriefing. I can see it now, "How could you shag a fat ginger bird? She looked like Charlie Dimmock gone wrong!" I'll have to duck out of here with Betty without them seeing me. I shouldn't really care what they think, but I do.

Its 1:00 am, and Tottenham Hotspurs own Brandon Block and Stevie P have entered the fray. The crowd go wild as they are introduced as UK House superstars. The two London DJs lap up the adulation, as you would expect any flash Cockney DJ in Las Vegas to.

Betty tells me that tonight is her last in Vegas. The last night of any holiday is traditionally shag night, or as Americans would say, put out night.

Fishing for a green light, I ask her where she is staying.

"At Circus Circus," she says, while putting her hand on my knee. That's a green light if ever I saw one and it's time to go. I wait out side while she tells her friends she is leaving.

Club Ra
At the Luxor
3900 Las Vegas Blvd
702-262-4000
Occasional flashy
Cockney DJs spurred on
by the occasional trashy
local.

Circus Circus is on the opposite the end of the strip from The Luxor, so we jump in a cab. The gulf in class between here and our suite at Caesar's is huge. I could have impressed her by taking her to our suite, but that would almost certainly have meant some sort of interruption from Ian and Derek. Instead, I'm here in the moderate surroundings of a twin room at Circus Circus.

"I really hate that Techno shit," says Betty as she pours two drinks. She only has vodka, mixed with regular Coke, which will have to do.

"Yea it's not really my cup of tea either," I reply.

"You drink Vodka, don't you?" she asks, still pouring drinks. "It's all we got here."

"That will have to do," I say, sitting on the only chair in the room. "Who's we, by the way?"

"We, is my friend Mary, who is still dancing at the club," Betty says, handing me my drink. "She won't be back for at least another two hours."

We cheers and Betty downs her drink and goes to bathroom. I can hear her taking a shower. Maybe she was feeling hot and sweaty from dancing at Ra. A few minutes later, she comes out wearing a robe.

"Hey Richard, I'll level with ya. I'm no slut, I'm not saying I'm a saint either but I choose who I sleep with very carefully."

This outburst surprises me, I mean I knew we were going to have a shag, but I thought it would one of those long-winded efforts, where you have to maybe psychologically talk a bird into it and convince her she is doing the right thing. I mean she is a schoolteacher. However, I like surprises.

She continues, "Now I don't beat around the bush in situations like this, so let's cut the crap, all right?"

I take a sip of my drink, still shocked and now slightly unsure of what is going to happen here.

"So Richard, we have about two hours so let's not waste time huh." She throws off her robe revealing her muscular physic of femininity. "I'm a woman who knows what she wants."

I play along with her, feeling the mood pick up a bit.

"Well Betty, what does a girl like you want?"

"I want you to eat out this pussy, and eat it good, That's what I want."

I do just that. Her clit is the biggest I've ever seen. It must be the mountains and the high altitude of Boulder perhaps. I don't need to pull or part her lips or probe my tongue in there in search of the sensuous trigger. She orgasms with ease.

"Ok that was pretty good Richard, but that's just an appetiser for me," she says, while sucking her index finger. "I like nothing better than fucking, and I especially like to drive. You don't mind if I drive Richard, do you?" she asks in a pouty little-girl voice.

I'm not a sexist, I am all for equal opportunities. Betty straddles me; first, while facing me, then she spins around and squats on my cock. The sight of her expanded arse working my shaft and her sound of her screaming American accent brings me to an unwanted orgasm. Unwanted, because we still have about an hour and a half before her roommate arrives back from Club Ra.

As I expected she hits me with it, "I want more baby, we still have soooo much time."

I am a man, and I'm with a girl I don't know in a post-orgasmic state of mind. My energy levels have died and I'm no longer aroused. Now Betty is nothing but a ginger bird from Colorado who looks like Ray Parlour. Right now, I just want to be alone on the sofa in the suite watching a 'Then and Now' Rockumentuary on VH1.

"You not getting away that easy, baby." Betty grabs my limp cock and wanks it while she flicks her gigantic clit with two fingers on her other hand. This gets me hard again. I attempt to mount her, but to no avail. She holds firm and flips me back onto the bed. "I told you baby, I like to drive," she grunts.

I meet the South London Boys by the pool the following morning for a debriefing. "I saw you chatting to that ginger bird with the fat legs again. Did you shag her?" asks Ian.

"Nah just had a couple of drinks with her, that's all," I reply quickly. "How was your night? And how were those pills?"

"The pills were fucking toilet, mate," answers Ian. "They gave us a rush in the beginning but after ten minutes it was gone."

"Yeah those fucking bumble bees were pony, they just made us drink water and fucking piss all night," adds Derek. "We got them from this dodgy Hawaiian at the Cotel"

Today is Saturday and it is also fight night, which also sadly means we have to check out of the suite.

> **Caesars Palace Hotel & Casino**
> 3570 Las Vegas Blvd
> 702-731-7110
> **The suites are just made for flash bastards like Ian and Derek.**

We phone some of other cheaper hotels in order to find a room; Stardust, The Flamingo, Riviera, Bally's, Treasure Island but there're all full. I recommend we try Circus Circus; maybe we can have Betty's now vacated room. We have no luck with any of the above and are now stranded in the Stardust car park.

"You know there's a hostel here in Vegas," I suggest. "I know it's a step down from the suite, but we're running out of time and choices."

"Yea alright, we may as well have a look," Derek replies.

"Leave it out. How the fuck can we stay there, after staying at Caesar's?" says Ian disapprovingly.

"Yea I know, but let's just have a look. It won't do us any 'arm, will it?" Derek prods. "It's either that or we go back to LA and miss out on a Saturday night in Vegas."

"Fucking hostel in fucking Vegas, you're having a laugh," whinges Ian "I'd rather go back to LA."

I tell him that there will be shit loads of birds in Vegas tonight and we shouldn't miss out on fight night, as anyone who is anyone comes to Vegas on fight night. Fortuitously, as I speak, three glorious looking girls walk into the Stardust reception.

"Ok, we'll have a quick look," says Ian, eyeing the girls.

We get into the rental and drive to the far end of Las Vegas Boulevard, which takes us into downtown. The streets here are notably narrower than those around the strip. The place also has a sense of realness compared to the strip, which by day, looks like a giant toy town in the middle of the desert.

Downtown is where Las Vegas started. I have visions of Al Capone and Lucky Luciano as we make a sharp right onto Stewart Street, where the hostel is located.

"This is a fucking dump!" Ian exclaims while he scans the area. "We can't stay here."

I agree with Ian, "Yea, I think you could be right." The surrounding area looks like a bad scene from a gangster rap video. We are only three blocks away from Freemont Street, the tourist part of downtown, but we may as well be a million miles away.

Nevertheless we park the car and approach the grim looking hostel with caution. At the entrance, we walk passed a good-looking, young unshaven guy with a backpack and an acoustic guitar.

"Alright lads, how's it going?" He says with a cockney accent.

"You from London?" Ian asks, with more of a cockney accent than usual.

"Yea," says the stranger, holding out his hand.

Ian shakes it and asks, " Oh yea, whereabouts?"

"Stevenage."

" Stevenage! That's not London, you cunt!" Ian says, releasing his hand.

"Yea, but its London, when I'm out here, you know what I mean," says the young handsome guy defensively.

His name is Will, a Plastic Cockney as we call them, also known as a Mockneys. On my travels if I had a pound for the amount of people who say they are from London but are in fact from places like Reading, Brighton, Chelmsford or indeed Stevenage, I would be able to afford a suite at

Caesar's tonight. I can understand why they say this to Americans or anyone not from Blighty. But to say it to three guys who are actually from London is asking for abuse.

Will looks like a cross between Colin Farrell and JK the lead singer from Jamiroquai. He tells us that he was going to stay here until he saw the rooms. "I get into this room and there's this geezer in there with fucking turn tables. Then another one comes out of the bathroom high as a kite on heroin, I said fuck that."

"So what are you doing now?" I ask.

"Well, I actually prepaid the room, so I'm waiting to get me money back."

"Then what are you going to do?"

"I ain't got a clue, might get a cheap hotel or somemink."

"D'ya wanna ride with us? We're in the same boat, it should be all right." Derek and Ian both agree with me to take on the pretty, loud-mouthed, plastic Cockney on as a passenger. I can see that Ian was more reluctant to have him ride with us, as he sees Will as a fast-talking, rival.

> **The Las Vegas Hostel**
> Address: Down and out in downtown Las Vegas.
> According to Pretty Boy, you may have wannabe DJs and smack heads as your roommates.

Will gets reimbursed by the receptionist and then puts his backpack and guitar in the mustang.

Having a good-looking white boy with us will be an advantage no matter what the situation is.

"Lets go back to we were last night," says Derek.

"What, Club Ra?" asks Ian.

"No you doughnut, the hotel where the club is."

"The Luxor," I confirm.

"Yea that's it," Derek says. "I just remembered I was talking to this bird last night, she's like the front desk manager, she was all over me. I reckon she can sort us out. It's better than staying out here, innit?"

The four of us head for the Luxor. Pretty Boy Will is sitting next to me in the back. He tells me that he was travelling in America with his best friend, who got lovesick after three weeks in New York and returned to England, and like me, he's now on his own. His favourite place so far was Miami. He is heading to LA to pursue a music career and wants to join a band. Maybe he and I can do that together.

At the Luxor, Derek and I get out of the car while Pretty Boy and Ian remain in the Mustang.

"So what's this bird's name," I ask Derek as we walk into the lobby.

"That's the thing, I'm not too sure but if I see her I will definitely know her."

"Fair enough," I say shrugging.

"I didn't tell Ian this. He wouldn't have shut up about it and he was already doing my head in as it was."

We scan the reception area of the Luxor, looking for, as Derek puts it, "a fit blonde." Unfortunately, it must be the "fit blonde's" day off, which makes sense; I couldn't imagine facing a day of work after a night dancing to euphoric techno music. We return to the car and tell the others that they have no vacancies.

"Why don't we try over there?" suggests Pretty Boy, pointing across the street. We all look across the road at a hooker motel called the 'The White Sands. It's one of the very few motels on the strip and looks out of place adjacent to the imperious Luxor. Desperate, we cross the road and ask if they have room for four. The young receptionist, who looks like she could be Greek, says that she can offer us two rooms at the price of $50 apiece. Having spent more than half a day looking for a room, we cannot refuse this.

Ian doesn't want to share with Derek, with whom he is constantly bickering, and he certainly doesn't want to crash with Pretty Boy. "I'll jump in with you Rich," insists Ian, nudging me with his elbow.

"Yea no probs, but you can't bring any blokes in the room after twelve," I say, teasing him.

"You cheeky bastard, you don't have to worry about all that. I'll 'ave a bird back here by eleven," he boasts.

"How the fuck can you bring a bird here? We're not in the suite anymore mate!"

"I'll take her to the Luxor," he says winking with a cheeky grin, "have a few drinks there, get her drunk and just walk across the road to here. She won't know the difference after a few cheeky tequilas."

"She will in the morning," I say laughing.

"I won't give a fuck in the morning," he replies, joining in my laughter. "I'll just fuck her off into the car park if she starts doing me head in."

The strip is gridlocked with flash cars and limos, full of fight fans in town for the showdown between Oscar De La Hoya, aka Golden Boy, and "Sugar" Shane Mosely. It's a rematch, Mosley having defeated the Golden Boy by a unanimous points decision in the first fight.

The four of us congregate in our room to plot out our last night in Vegas. Pretty Boy insists that we go to a strip joint called "The Crazy Horse." Ian looks at Derek and I and shakes his head.

Pretty Boy continues, "Yea I hear they got some right sorts in there."

"We were there on Thursday night and pulled a couple of cracking strippers," boasts Ian.

"Bullshit!" shouts Pretty Boy.

"Bullshit?" Ian challenges, "We swapped over and everything, had them tonguing each other, the lot."

"Nahh."

"Yea we got it on camera, have a look," Ian says, going to his bag to get his camcorder.

While Ian gives Pretty Boy a private viewing with a running commentary, Derek and I take a walk up the strip to a burger joint called Fat

Burger. We return with fat bellies after eating gigantic burgers, and find Ian and Pretty Boy getting on like a house on fire. Pretty Boy has finished watching Ian and Derek's orgy and now has arse-licking respect for them.

Pretty Boy seems to have done his homework on Las Vegas. He talks non-stop about all the places he has read about. According to him, our first stop tonight should be the lounge bar at the Bellagio.

We get there at around 8:30 and it's very crowded. Ian and his new sidekick Pretty Boy spring into action, immediately hitting on a group of four classy-looking girls. With Pretty boys film star looks, attracting the birds then with Ian's brash charm keeping their attention, their going to be a force to be reckoned with on fight night in Vegas. The four girls turn out to be hookers, but it was an impressive start to the evening all the same.

We have a flutter before we leave; astonishingly I win $200 on roulette, choosing a Red-Red-Black-Red-Black-Black sequence. This puts me in a great mood; it's funny what a bit of cash can do.

The next bar on Pretty Boy's list is in the Viva Las Vegas lounge at the Hard Rock Hotel. No matter what the girls looks like here all of them have obscenely huge fake tits. It's like being in a Russ Myers movie.

Derek says he is getting a migraine and heads back to the motel for a lie down. I have a mind to go back too; my night with the dominant Betty from Boulder is beginning to take its toll.

Pretty Boy has attracted the attention of two attractive girls, who look and dress like they are from Europe. They turn out to be Russian and since there are two of them and three of us, I play the odd man out and leave them to it. It's not because I'm lacking confidence. A pretty Boy he may be as his nickname suggests and Ian might have the gift of the gab, but I reckon I can give them both a run for their money. It's because I recently had bad experience with a Russian bird in London. I enticed her back to my flat just off Ladbroke after meeting her at the Propaganda Club in Soho. She gave me the best sex I'd ever had, the highlight being when she put her legs behind her ears and fingered her minge and arse simultaneously, begging me to fuck her in both.

Anyway, the next morning while I was half-asleep, she kissed me goodbye and left her number, saying that we should do it again. When I got out of bed an hour later, I discovered that she had stolen my wallet, my laptop and my Venus Fly Trap. I fucking loved that plant! So much so, I used to kill flies and feed them to it just to watch it shut its trap.

I not saying that all Russian birds are dodgy, but on this occasion, I leave Ian and Pretty Boy with the two Russians and I Fuckovski.

I take a cab back to the motel. I fall asleep with Francesca on my mind, something I find myself doing a lot lately when I am alone.

"Oi Richard." I hear a voice whisper in my ear as I'm being shook. I manage to partly open my eyes. It's four in the morning and Ian's back with Pretty Boy.

"You don't mind sleeping in with Derek while me and Pretty Boy here take care of those two Russian birds, do you?"

"Yea sure," I say getting dressed and grabbing my valuables. I'm not one to cock block and I would expect them to do the same for me. I give them both a celebration hug then head into the other room.

"Oi Svetlana, Tania in here," shouts Ian softly.

To cure his migraine, Derek has to smoke a couple of potent skunk weeds to send him to sleep. It's not what the doctor ordered, but with Derek in a deep sleep, I see that it has done the trick.

Derek has only smoked two of the three he rolled earlier. I am sure he will not mind if I smoke his remaining spliff. I take it outside and smoke it.

While I drag the potent smoke through my lungs and puff it into the night sky, I again think of Francesca and our impending confrontation in LA.

Once I've finished the joint I head back to bed, but I can't help but listen in on what's going on in the other room.

I try to picture the scene as I hear one of the Russian birds say "fuck me harder" and then in turn here Ian say, "Yea go on handsome, give it some violence!"

I laugh and shake my head as I walk into the other room. Give it some violence he says! There are many terms for having sex; shagging, fucking, banging, etc... etc..., but giving it some violence, that's a new one, but I suppose we are talking about a Millwall boy here.

That skunk was heavy shit. It's 9:00am, I feel like shit, and that Nevada sun piercing through the cheap curtains of this hooker Motel with no air con isn't helping.

I take an invigorating, cold shower and then convince Derek, (who is now wide awake) to join me for breakfast.

Yesterday Pretty Boy suggested, that we should have a buffet breakfast at the Bellagio.

At the Bellagio breakfast hall, we are seated after waiting in a long queue for about twenty minutes. There is a magnificent array of food to choose from, food that we normally wouldn't dream of having for breakfast; fried rice, pasta, and even sushi. We both pass on the sushi as I don't think it would go down too well with a hangover and the mongey feeling from the skunk. However, we can't resist the French toast, waffles, pancakes and the personalised omelettes.

We lap up the feast, in a total oblivion to anyone else in the breakfast hall. We are both so hungry that our attention is only focused on the Big Breakfast.

We wash it all down with champagne decorated with a strawberry and then toddle out of the Bellagio ten pounds heavier.

On the long walk back to the motel, Derek tells me about the migraines that he gets every so often, because he's slightly short sighted. He has glasses but hates wearing them - he says they make him look like Jarvis Cocker or something out of University Challenge, and he can't be arsed to put on his contacts every morning. When he gets back to London, he's going to get expensive laser eye treatment. He goes on to tell me that he is not looking forward to getting back to Peckham.

Buffet Breakfast at the Bellagio
3600 Las Vegas Blvd
Las Vegas, NV
888-987-6667
Obesity in America has reached near epidemic proportions. It's easy to see why, when you see what on offer here. However in the Bellagio's defence, they were serving low carbohydrate and fat free, egg white omelettes.

"I have an eighteen-month-old daughter with one bird," he says, "and the day I left, another girl who works at one of the clubs I serve at, told me that she's three months pregnant with my child. Fucking drama mate."

My hangover has gone so Derek's story gets my full attention.

"Yea, I should be happy," he continues sadly, "with a baby on the way and that. But I failed the first time and I'm sort of scared I'll fail again. I didn't want this, just yet."

"How or why do you think you failed?" I ask with concern.

"Arhh, you know, I was always out and away for days on end without so much of a phone call. Always chasing skirt, getting drunk and high," he says, looking down at his shuffling feet.

"A bit like you are now then?" I comment, and we both chuckle. "But maybe now you're getting a second chance at fatherhood," I suggest, trying to put a positive spin on things.

"Yea I thought that, but the girl who's pregnant is a not the kind of girl I want for a missus, if you know what I mean."

"What, is she a girl who's always out and in the clubs?"

"Yea, 24-7. She's a fucking stunner though," Derek says, with a smile in his eyes.

"But you know, Derek, women change when they get pregnant," I tell him, trying to reassure him. "They get that mothering instinct, and if a change is needed to be made, it will come naturally."

"Yea maybe," he replies, not buying the philosophy. "But thanks, eh?"

We get back to the Motel and find Ian and Pretty Boy hysterical.

"Those fucking Russians slags have had it away with our money!" shouts Pretty Boy, looking distraught.

"Yea and my fucking video camera!" adds Ian, who is throwing clothes around the room covering and uncovering the furniture.

I leave and walk into my room and return with Pretty Boy's wallet and Ian's wad of cash.

"What the fuck?" Ian says with a stunned look on his face as he takes his cash.

"How the fuck did you get them?" asks Pretty Boy, opening his wallet to make sure it's his.

"Last night when you brought back the Russian birds, I gave you guys a hug, remember?" I say, sitting down in the chair. The two of them nod and I smile. "In doing so, I picked both your pockets" Then I tell them about my Russian experience in London.

"You haven't got my camera have ya?" asks Ian, still stunned.

"No, I've got that," interjects Derek.

"Thank fuck for that!" Ian says relieved. "But why the fuck did you take it?"

"When I came back early last night, I felt like having a wank, and there's nothing better than watching yourself shagging in order to knock one out, you know what I mean" he replies.

So, I got those Russian girls wrong. I have never been one to follow stereotypes anyway. But Ian and Pretty Boy did get the shags of their lives, so the tag Russian women have of being the best in bed still stands.

When the excitement dies down, we decide to stay one more night in Las Vegas to celebrate. We can't be bothered to check out so we stay another night at the White Sands Motel.

"Yea, tonight we can go to a club, maybe the Rum Jungle at the Mandalay Bay, and then watch the Man U Arsenal game." Pretty Boy pipes up.

"Tell me you're not a Man UTD fan." I say to him, shaking my head.

"Fraid so mate. I take it you're a Gooner then."

I knew there had to be something I hated about Pretty Boy. He's the worst kind of Man UTD supporter, "A Cockney Red", but in his case a Mockney Red!

I know too many of these annoying London-based Man Utd Muppets to mention. It just doesn't make sense to me. I have always thought football, in a supporter's sense, to be a tribal thing. Support your home team! In addition to that, there's nothing better than going up north as a flash cockney bastard, (as we are known to them), all clobbered up in the latest gear standing out like peacocks in the bars of Manchester, Liverpool and Newcastle. Then letting their birds know where we are from and why we are here.

The four of us have an afternoon nap then have a feed at that Fat Burger joint. We get back to the hotel and get ourselves a few drinks to charge us up for the night ahead. Ian and Derek have two lines of coke each, Pretty Boy has one, and since tonight is our last night in Vegas and its Arsenal biggest away game of the season, I have a cheeky one.

The Rum Jungle on a Sunday is, of course, on par with Pretty Boy's Las Vegas Guide. I have to give it to him; he has been spot on so far and he is right again. This is the most popular club on the strip on a Sunday. We get there at 11:00 pm, just in time to avoid the queues, the cover charge and most importantly the door bitch, who is just about to start her shift.

In the magnificent two-story bar, we each order a different kind of rum, as they have thousands here each illuminated with a laser beam. We must have each drank at least seven different rums from all corners of the globe, the best being Ray Nephew from Jamaica and the Bozcov Tuzemsky from the Czech Republic being the worst.

It's now midnight and the four of us are dancing to commercial R&B and Hip Hop. Ian and Derek then find a couple of girls to sell coke to, they then take them to the bathroom. Pretty Boy and I ignore the mass of stunning girls and start a drunken, heated discussion about football. Who is the better player Pires or Giggs, Viera or Keane?

The club closes at 4:00 am, only two hours until kick-off. We can't find the Millwall Boys anywhere, so Pretty Boy and I head off to the MGM Grand, where they will be showing the game on one of their many sports screens. In fact, they have over a hundred screens showing different sports from around the world. We even have the option to watch the game in our own booth with a 17" screen, and we do just that.

In order for us to sit there, we need to have at least one sports bet. Pretty Boy puts $50 on Man UTD to win 1-0 with Van Nistlerooy scoring the first goal. I'm not so adventurous, I just put $20 on an Arsenal win.

The game is the usual tense affair that occurs at Old Trafford when these two great teams meet, with Man UTD having the better of the opening exchanges. They go in at the interval level at 0-0. Pretty Boy and I are both nervous wrecks in the midst of the tension. To calm my nerves, I go into the casino and blow $150 on Roulette.

Arsenal get more into the game after the interval and create a few chances. Edu comes the closest to breaking the deadlock, striking a free kick just over the bar. We are matching them in a physical sense too, which is a change from the norm here, where the Neville brothers especially Phil, (who always has the game of his life against Arsenal), kicks Viera and the rest of our midfield off the park.

As Pretty Boy tries his luck with the waitress, the game is heading for a draw. Then suddenly Pretty boy and Man UTD get a massive boost as we are reduced to ten men. Rudd Van Nistlerooy has got Viera sent off, by playacting his way to getting our captain his second yellow.

With only 45 seconds left Man UTD are awarded a very dubious penalty. Pretty Boy and the best of 67,000 Mancunian Muppets at old Trafford go wild. Moments later the 4,000 travelling Gooners and I go wild as the cross bar rattles, the cheating Van Nistlerooy has hit the bar. The final whistle is blown seconds later. Parlour, Cole, Lauren and Keown in particular let the cheating Van Nistlerooy know how they feel about his cheating ways.

So the spoils are shared, Pretty Boy and I shake hands and head back to the motel. I am the happier of the two of us with the result; Pretty Boy is not only pissed off with that last minute penalty miss, but had Van Nistlerooy scored, he would have won over $300.

It is 9:00 am, Derek and Ian are wide awake in one of the motel rooms, sitting on the bed talking cocaine-induced shit with the two girls and their stylish gay friend they served up in the Rum Jungle. It looks like they have been at it since leaving the club. Pretty Boy and I ignore them in our exhausted state, and go into the other room for some much-needed sleep.

The two Millwall boys wake us up at around two in the afternoon. "We've gotta leave you lazy bastards. The bird at reception has given us a late check-out, but we gotta leave now," Ian announces.

The White Sands Motel
3889 Las Vegas Blvd
Las Vegas, NV 89109
The very cheap annexe of the Luxor

Pretty Boy and I get dressed swiftly, pay for

our room then jump into the back of the Mustang. Ian starts the engine and we head back to LA.

In the car, Derek turns around and gives Pretty Boy a piece of paper. "One of those birds fancied you rotten, didn't she Ian?" he says winking away from Pretty Boy.

"Yea, she was going on about you looking like Colin Farrell and all that all night," Ian says smiling, looking at Pretty Boy in the rear view mirror.

"Really?" asks Pretty Boy excitedly.

"Yea really, give her a call," Derek says, handing Pretty Boy his mobile phone. "Just say it's Russ, she'll go wild mate!"

Pretty Boy dials and puts the phone to his ear, "What's her name?"

"Mate, I was on gear all night!" Derek says, facing the front again. "I can't remember a bird's name! What's up with ya? Just give her a call, you muppet!"

"It's ringing," says Pretty Boy with excitement. "Hello, it's Russ, Derek's mate from last night," he says in a cool voice.

"Yea I'm all right, and you? Is your friend with you?" he asks with a smile. "Tell her it's the guy who looks likes Colin Farrell?" He looks at me and winks.

Then his expression turns to a frown. "What?!" he shouts, looking confused. "Nah mate! Who told you that? No!"

Ian and Derek start laughing.

"No I am not in the fucking closet! What makes you think that?" continues Petty Boy on the phone. He looks up at Ian and Derek, who are laughing and realises he's been stitched up. They let me in on the joke and we all laugh as we turn off Tropicana Avenue onto the Number 15 freeway to Los Angeles.

Five minutes onto the freeway, we see a sign for a discount outlet mall, which was of course, in Pretty Boy's Las Vegas guide. The South London Boys are happy to go there, so that they can add to their designer wardrobes.

As expected, the first store they hit is Burberry. I trail behind, as the three of them lengthen their strides in the excitement and anticipation.

Burberry has become the symbol of the CHAV Movement in Britain. But what is a CHAV? I ask myself. Am I a CHAV? If a CHAV is somebody who is from a working class background, who likes to wear designer clothes, then maybe I am. Were the casual, football hooligans of the eighties CHAVS? Didn't they wear Burberry and Aquascutum of the like when going into battle on the streets and terraces? And what about the Mods (who were mostly from working class backgrounds) with their slick designer suits, and what about the Teddy boys who wore expensive drape suits a decade before.

Its all about the underprivileged, and working class sticking two fingers up at their peers, who look down at them. It has been this way in Britain since the 19th century. But I guess the Burberry

CHAV moment has probably taken the whole thing a bit too far.

Derek has bought two Polo shits with the Burberry tartan on the collar. Ian has purchased a pair of jeans and a Burberry cap. Pretty Boy has bought himself a shirt covered in the Burberry tartan and a T-shirt with the word Burberry printed all over it. Yuk!!! Oh well, we have to give him allowances, after all he is from the urban sprawl town of Stevenage.

"I'm gonna wear this for the West Ham game," insists Ian, while admiring his new cap.

Millwall will be playing West Ham in a league fixture for the first time in nearly ten years, as a result of the Hammers relegation last season.

After browsing Ralph Lauren, Tommy Hillfiger, and Timberland we sit down for a coffee and a muffin at Starbucks. While we are sitting, the Millwall Boys talk about the long awaited confrontation with West Hams ICF.

"I tell you what, they're not gonna come down the Old Kent Road and take liberties this time, I'll tell ya," states Ian passionately.

"The ICF (Inter City Firm) are a bunch of has-beens, we're gonna piss all over them," adds Derek.

While they continue to blabber on about East and South-East London hooligan pride, I see a familiar face trying on a pair of sunglasses in the Quicksilver store. It's that cowboy Lawrence, the guy we had the spat with at Caesar's Palace the other night. I make the guys aware of this.

"Right, drink up lads, there's something I have to take care of," says Ian, chugging down the last of his coffee. He throws Pretty Boy the car keys.

"Handsome, get in the motor and sit in the driver's seat. keep an eye out for us. And as soon as you see us come out of the main entrance start the engine," he instructs Pretty Boy.

"What? I don't understand," Pretty Boy says shaking his head, walking back to the parking lot.

"Just do it, Pretty boy, I'll explain later," says Derek as he pulls out a wrap of coke from his pocket. He opens it and offers it to Ian, who takes a quick pinch up each nostril. Derek copies his mate's actions and returns the wrap to his pocket. They offer me some but I decline. "You sure Gooner? You might need it."

"No I am quite sure, I'll be ok.

"Suit yourself, anyway let's go. Just follow us."

We keep our eyes on Lawrence's every move; he seems to be alone. Ian and Derek have a score to settle from the other night. It must be a Millwall thing. I thought the Anglo-American dispute had been resolved when Lawrence was kicked out of Caesar's, but I suppose I'm going to find out what Ian meant by "fighting for fun."

We tail him for ten minutes, until he goes to the bathroom.

"Right this is it," commands Ian. "If the toilets are empty we'll take him out. Richard, you watch the door." Ian gives me his old cap and puts on his new Burberry cap. Now our faces are hidden from the cameras.

We enter the bathroom. It is empty apart from Lawrence who is taking a shit in one of the cubicles. I guard the door, as per Ian's instructions, making sure nobody enters, trying to think of something to say if someone tries.

Derek boots in the cubicle door where Lawrence is taking a dump. Ian drags the cowboy out with his pants around his ankles.

"Who's a British bastard now, Lawrence?" Ian shouts in the cowboy's face, prior to landing a ferocious head butt on the bridge of his nose. It splatters like a tomato being bashed by a mallet and sends the cowboy to the tiles. Ian and Derek give him a beating like the one Billy Bats got in the film *Goodfellas* from Robert Di Nero and Joe Pesci.

After a series of punches and kicks, Lawrence is knocked unconscious with the Millwall Boys leaving him star-shaped, on the bathroom floor with a bloody, broken nose, his pants around his ankles and shit still leaking out of his arse.

171

The three of us coolly and calmly walk out of the bathroom and out of the mall. Pretty Boy starts the car and we jump in and get back on the freeway 15 to Los Angeles.

After five minutes of driving Pretty boy breaks the silence, "What was all that about?"

"We just had to teach a cowboy a lesson. He will think twice the next time he comes across a bunch of British bastards," mumbles Derek.

"Yea we just kicked the shit out of him," adds Ian jokingly.

I briefly laugh at Ian's gag then ask worryingly, "Do you think he will survive that beating?"

"Who gives a fuck?" Ian replies curtly. Derek remains silent.

"I fucking do! He knows where we were staying. All he has to do is go back to Caesar's and get your details."

Those local Nevada cowboys are all related in one way or another, it's all one big family out here and everyone else is just a temporary lodger paying rent. I'm sure it will just take one phone call and there will be half a dozen guys wearing Stetsons packing Colt 45s waiting for us when we enter the Cotel.

"Don't worry about all that, you mug!" Ian says chuckling. "Those Nigerians and Eastern European cunts in London aren't the only ones who can get away with credit card fraud. You don't think that was my real name on the card, do ya?"

LOS ANGELES,
23 September 2003

We arrive at the Venice Beach Cotel at 6:00 pm and are greeted, as usual, by the loudmouth Israeli, Katrina.

"Hey guys, I expected you last night, but it's your lucky day. I have room the four of you. Who's your mate by the way?"

I introduce her to Pretty Boy. "What team do you support?" she asks him.

"U-N-I-T-E-D!" sings Pretty Boy, knowing she a Man UTD fan.

"Yea those Arsenal bastards were lucky last night," she starts.

"Fuck off, we deserved the draw," I say cutting in.

She and Pretty Boy start the sort of mouthing off that you normally would expect from Man UTD fans when they get together anywhere in the world. I pick up my backpack and head for the dorm before they start bragging about their treble triumph of 1999 and that FA cup semi-final at Villa Park.

That semi-final was for me, one of lowest point for me as an Arsenal fan and believe me there has been many, and it still hurts just thinking about it. With the game locked at one apiece, we were cruising, Man UTD were down to ten men (Keane the man dismissed). We also had a goal from "Le Miserable" (Nicholas Anelka) disallowed, and then had a Bergkamp penalty saved. Despite these set backs I sill thought the game was ours to be won.

As the epic "Thriller at the Villa" moved into extra time, we still looked the more likely of the two teams. But we just could not break them down. The game was heading for penalties, when a wayward pass from Vieira(of all people), found its way to Giggs and the rest is a Man UTD song.

Other low points that deserve a mention are; The Littlewoods Cup final against Luton in 1988 and another FA cup semi final, this time a 3-1 defeat against The scum at Wembley in 1991; Gascoigne, Lineker et el. I cannot talk any more about the later as many Arsenal fans are still waking up screaming in a cold sweat, at that nightmare moment when Gazza smashed in that free kick past Seaman. We have beaten the Scumbags in two semis since, but I for one, still feel that that defeat, on that Sunday morning at Wembley is a defeat that will never be totally rinsed out of Gooner blood, unless Tottenham are going for the League and Cup Double and we beat them to prevent them achieving that fate. And that, I pray will never happen.

The four of us are in a four-bed dorm, with two bunk beds. From experience, I go for the top bunk above Pretty Boy. Last year, when I was in Koh Phangan, a Swiss guy told me a story about a bunk bed collapsing and squashing the backpacker occupying the lower bunk to death. Could be an urban legend but I'm not taking risk, in this un-maintained, shabby hostel.

Once in the room, we all crash on our bunks and fall asleep instantly. The extended weekend in Las Vegas has taken its toll on all of us. Even the coked up Millwall boys are out for the count.

It's now seven in the morning, and I'm the first to rise. The other three are still out cold. Incredibly, I have slept through the night for an impressive eleven hours. We are lucky enough to be in a room that overlooks the freaks of Venice Beach and the ocean; the ball-juggling Islander in a g-string is still here, and yep so too is the Zulu on the unicycle.

Later that day, the Millwall Boys announce to Pretty Boy and I that they will be heading to San Francisco tonight and then flying home two days later. I am saddened by this announcement and it leaves a lump in my throat.

I like most people who have been brought up north of the Thames, hate South London. I also hate Millwall and their supporters. But these guys have made me change my mind. Isn't it amazing what travelling does to you?

175

The last two weeks have been like the essence of a dream, it was something outside the norm. I had the wildest time first here in LA and then in Vegas with two people I have never met before and in all probability will never see again. Spending time with them sometimes made me homesick, and sometimes even lonely, but the whole time I felt more alive than I have felt for a long time, including that first night spent with the gorgeous Francesca.

With the Millwall Boys gone, that leaves Pretty Boy and I. He has already become friendly with a couple of young Scouse girls. I leave him to it and give Francesca a call.

As expected, I hear the relief in her voice. She is happy to hear from me and can't wait to meet with me. Francesca has an ulterior motive, of course, but she will be a sight for my tired, sore eyes. She is staying nearby in Marina Del Rey. Walking distance. She tells me to meet her at a coffee shop called the Cow's End on Washington Boulevard.

I arrive early, dressed casually in a white, short sleeve Ted Baker shirt with the *La Times* in hand so I can read something while I wait for Francesca to arrive. I don't think I could stand sitting in the strange looking café alone, looking around aimlessly, sipping my latte to make time pass.

With the *LA times,* I could catch up on what's been happening in this fucked up world for the passed month or so.

However I don't get to find out how many Iraqis have been killed in the latest spate of Islamic sectarian violence, or how Israel will retaliate after yet another bus bombing in Jerusalem, because when I get there Francesca is sitting on a stool at the window waiting for me. She looks even more stunning than the last time I saw her. We hug tightly and kiss. We both order lattes, and then fill each other in on we have been up to.

"So, have you got a new girlfriend?" she jokes.

"Yea, about four or five," I answer and she laughs.

She tells me that she has found a job in Hollywood as a massage therapist, and then nervously asks me about the packages she left in my toiletry bag. I then tell her, equally as nervous that I don't have them.

"What! what do you mean you haven't got them, no Richard?"

"I mean, I haven't got them with me."

"So, where are they?" she asks through clenched teeth.

"They are in Santa Barbara," I reply, trying to keep it cool.

"Santa Barbara! What the fuck are they doing there man?" she asks with a furrowed brow.

"I left them with a friend," I tell her, looking into her beautiful hazel eyes.

"What friend? You haven't got any friends in the whole of fucking California!" she yells, taking a sip of her latte looking around the café.

I tell her enough of what she needs to know about Pamela.

"So you meet some chick and gave her my drugs?"

"I didn't give them to her; I just stored them at her house like I told you," I say, trying to calm her.

"Well your just gonna have to go and get them," she says angrily.

She has done well in making me feel like the person who has done wrong. "Why the fuck did you put the drugs in my bag in the first place?" I ask her, putting the pressure back on her.

"I had too much heat on me in San Fran," she says, calming down. After a deep breath she continues, "I stole the drugs from Creole's apartment. Naturally he accused me of stealing them, but he couldn't prove a thing without the evidence. He was even down here for a while checking up on me," she says, looking at me with big, hazel, innocent eyes. "This is why I didn't want you to contact me for two weeks."

"So now he's gone?"

"Yea he's gone, but I can't do shit, he's got contacts down here."

"So what are you going to do?" I ask with concern in my voice.

"Well first thing first, you have to go to Santa Barbara," she says coolly.

I call Pamela's mobile number. She answers and tells me that she is in Santa Barbara and will be for at least another ten days.

"Hey Pamela I need that thing."

"Sure no problem honey, just tell me when you want it."

I tell Francesca that her drugs are safe. "Ok I don't need them today, so I guess I can wait for a few days," she says, her mood becoming lighter now that she knows her drugs are safe and nearby. "Come back to my apartment and I'll cook you something. Are you hungry?" she asks, wrapping her arm around mine as we walk to her abode.

> **The Cow's End**
> **34 Washington Blvd**
> **310-574-1080**
> **Not normally a place where drug running arguments are settled over a gourmet organic coffee.**

At Francesca's trendy apartment, she tells me to take a seat in the dining room while she cooks lunch. "I'll cook you a traditional Argentinean meal," she says, giving me a quick kiss on the lips.

"Oh yea, what will that be?" I ask, watching her walk into the open-plan kitchen.

"I got some beef steaks from back home," she says, taking out a brown paper package from the fridge. "Argentinean beef is a lot better than the meat you get here, you know."

Francesca maybe a drug-dealing liar, but overall, she is a decent girl with all the usual insecurities that come with girls, but like no other, I have met.

179

"How do you like it done?" she says while the steak sizzles on the stove.

She presents me with a massive plate of the medium rear steak (just as I ordered) and roast vegetables then pours us each a glass of red wine. I agree with Francesca, the steak is better than any I have had here. In fact, it probably the best I have ever tasted, anywhere.

"So tell me Richard, did you fuck her?" she asks casually while we're eating.

"Fuck who?" I ask, slowly chewing the meat.

"That woman in Santa Barbara, or where ever she is from," she says, taking a sip of wine.

"Oh no," I lie, shrugging a shoulder. "She was just a woman I hitched with from Monterey."

"Liar!" Francesca yells smiling mischievously at me, "I have spent two nights with you, and I know that's bullshit," she says, pointing her fork at me.

"Anyway is doesn't matter to me, its not as if we're going steady or anything," she says shrugging and continuing to eat. She goes on to tell me about her job as a masseuse in Hollywood. She provides treatment for the rich and almost famous and is paid really well.

"So why are you so desperate to get the coke back?" I ask, helping her clear the table after we finish eating.

"The money from the sale of that shit will go back to my family in Buenos Aries," she tells me, as we pile the plates in the dishwasher. Her family back home, like many in Argentina, are living on the bread line after the collapse of the economy. "It will also pay for my flight back to Argentina, I want to go home and continue my studies at university."

She cannot believe I am staying at the hostel. In truth, I am short of cash and need to find a job. "Without a green card, that's going to be difficult. What other skills do you have apart from accountancy?"

"Well, I can play bass guitar and write songs," I tell her.

"That's fantastic!" Francesca advises me to look in the local entertainment classifieds, and being her usual nice self, she runs down to the local shop to buy me the two most popular entertainment industry classifieds.

While she's gone, I scan the trendy apartment; it is unbelievably stunning. I wonder how Francesca can afford to live here being a masseuse. She must have some top-notch clients and they must pay her really well, or maybe she does extras. At this stage I wouldn't rule out anything.

While I continue to sip my glass of wine, the phone rings and startles me. After three rings, the answer machine picks up.

"Hey baby, how are you," says a man's voice with either an eastern European or Arabic accent after the beep. "I'll be back tomorrow, see you then. I've missed you these past few days, honey."

Who the fuck was that and what the fuck was that all about? What kind of shit this girl into? Who is she with now? Some eastern European gangster? Oh well I think I'll just play dumb. I erase the message and wait for Francesca's return.

On her return, we browse through the classifieds together. There are plenty of jobs on offer for singer-song writers, but unfortunately, I cannot sing.

There are ads for bands looking for musicians, including bass players. Francesca takes down all the phone numbers.

"Hey, what about this?" says Francesca excitedly. The advertisement reads:

"*Singer looking for band members to play three gigs a week at a University bar. Call Nigel for more information.*"

"Well what are you waiting for?" Francesca urges, pushing the phone in my direction. I give Nigel a call and setup and audition for tomorrow.

I spend the night with Francesca; it's not a problem as her "flatmate," a Turkish graphic designer, is in New York.

Since my last night with Francesca I have been with three or four different girls. However, being in bed with Francesca is really the only time it feels right, and all of the other girls are insignificant, distant memories. After having sex with her, I have no feelings of doubt, guilt, thoughts of back home or of Arsenal.

In the morning, I walk back to the Venice Beach Cotel and find Pretty Boy in bed with one of the Scouse girls. A big guy from Manchester is in the bottom bunk opposite. I wake Pretty Boy and tell him about the audition, convincing him to come along as he is desperate to show California how good a lead guitarist he is."

I introduce myself to the stranger from Manchester; his name is Dan, but insists we call him Manchester.

"You don't mind if I tag along with you guys to that audition, do ya?" he asks. His accent is a very strong Mancunian one, he sounds a bit like Liam Gallagher or Bez from The Happy Mondays.

"Can you play?" I ask cautiously.

"A bit of drums me. I once had an audition for Oasis and the Roses" he casually tells us.

Oh well, I suppose it will not be any trouble to bring a drummer. This would complete the band I suppose. We get dressed and jump in a cab to Westwood, where the student bar is.

"So what happened with those auditions, Manchester?" I ask during the ride.

"Well, I was just a bit too crazy for those guys."

"Err...define crazy," I say, thinking I may have made a mistake in letting him come along.

"My dad listened to 'The Who,' man, and he idolised Keith Moon. When I was thirteen he bought me a drum set and showed me a video of

The Who's Keith Moon playing the drums, and that's where I got my crazy style from."

Ok, that doesn't sound so bad; I'm an admirer of Moon and 'The Who' myself.

We get to the bar and are greeted by Nigel, a young conservative, Goth type wearing a black 'Pixies' t-shirt and tight black wrangler jeans. He is delighted to have three guys auditioning from England.

"All my favourite bands are from the Britain," he states, telling us that his influences are 'The Cure' and 'Led Zeppelin.'

"All the best bands are from the Britain," replies Manchester with patriotic passion.

"Hey I don't dispute that, man," says Nigel, holding his hands up.

Nigel comes from a rich family and currently has aspirations of starting up a rock n' roll band. Before this, he tried to get his pilot licence and spent six months learning to fly. When he got fed up with that, he started rally driving. Then after realising he wasn't as brave as he thought, he jacked it in and is now setting up this rock band.

He has already bought all of the instruments and has them in place; a set of Yamaha drums, two Rickenbacker electric guitars and a Fenders Precision bass, which I am satisfied with, although I would have preferred a Fender Jazz bass for more variation. He has aspirations of cutting a CD, being signed and touring the world. Delusions of grandeur, maybe, but he is paying top dollar to achieve his dream. Nigel is forking out $1000 a gig. Split between the three of us, that's over $300 each, so why not try and help Nigel realise his dream.

"I haven't got the talent to write any of my own songs," states Nigel. "So Richard, what songs have you brought with you?"

I have written two songs: *"The Cybil Shepherd"* and *"Hooligan Supporter."*

"Ahh! Yeah cool. Pretty edgy stuff, man," Nigel murmurs as I show him the lyrics. I tuck them back in my pocket after he's finished looking at them since we will not be auditioning either of the songs.

"Why don't we do *'My Generation'* by The Who, man?" Manchester suggests.

"Yea I know that. Are we all okay with that?" asks Nigel looking at Pretty Boy and I.

"I know it," boasts Pretty Boy. "Piece of piss! Those Townsend chords are nothing special."

"Don't worry about me, I know The Who," I tell Nigel, while I tune the bass.

"Right, let's get this audition started then!" shouts Nigel, grabbing the microphone.

Pretty Boy and I plug our guitars into the Marshall amps.

"A one, two! A one, two, three, four!"

Pretty Boy kicks off with opening twanging cords. After three bars I join him with the bass riff. Manchester catches the rhythm and adds a pulsating, up-tempo, battering rhythm on the drums, which is slightly off the tempo Pretty Boy and I have set, but we soon match his pace. Nigel catches the beat after the fourth bar and starts nodding his head.

"Ok repeat that intro again." This time Nigel joins with Daltryesque soulful shouting,

"PEOPLE TRY TO PUT US DOWN!"

I am impressed. He sounds like a cross between Robert Plant and Sting.

We finish the song with all four of us sweating profusely looking at one another, nodding in appreciation.

"Ok that's great fellas. Let's have a drink because you're hired!" Nigel is absolutely ecstatic. Maybe he feels this particular dream of his might be realised.

Our first gig will be on Friday night and rehearsals will be on Thursday and Friday morning. Yesterday, none of us would have thought we would be in a band. Nevertheless, that is what travelling and life is about, adapting to change.

"Ok I'll do it," says Pretty Boy, after we get back to the hostel. "It will be a laugh, but I've only got another six weeks here before I leave for Australia."

"I've given myself six weeks here as well," says Manchester, "but the money is too good to turn down. I've got an open ticket, so I can always change my flight,"

"Hey Pretty Boy, you're not thinking straight," I point out with a smile on my face. "Just think of all the college birds you can get while playing in a band."

Pretty Boy nods his head and smiles, "If it goes well, I'll stay."

I call Francesca and tell her the good news.

"That's really great Richard," she says distractedly, "but I'm gonna need that thing by the weekend."

"Can't it wait until next week?" I ask, disappointed that she's not happier about my newly found rock n' roll status. "I have rehearsals on Thursday and Friday."

"Sorry baby, I need the cash, and I have friends who will be in town from New York this weekend. I just have to have it by Friday."

"Ok Francesca, you win. You'll have it by Friday," I mutter then hang up and start cursing the Argy bitch. Today is Wednesday, so I have two days, one really, as I have a rehearsal tomorrow morning.

I immediately get on the phone to Pamela. We will be meeting tonight in Santa Barbara as she's still there on business.

SANTA BARBARA, 24 SEPTEMBER 2003

Everything was coming together; my feelings for Francesca were flourishing again and I have just landed a well-paying gig, playing music to a college crowd in Westwood. Now I am on the fucking road again, going back on myself, all in the name of drugs.

I get to Pamela's and get the welcome I was expecting but not wanting. She smothers me in kisses and caresses my body.

"Oh I missed you baby," she says, trying to unbutton my shirt. I gently push her hands away, as it just doesn't seem right. It's great to see her again but Francesca and her packages are on my mind. "Are you ok baby?" asks Pamela with concern. "Are you in some sort of trouble?"

"I'm fine, could do with a drink though."

While she's pouring me a glass of white, I go up to the bathroom to get the packages, but only one is there.

"PAMELA!!!" I yell, running down the stairs with the one package.

"I'm so sorry, baby," she whimpers, looking like a deer caught in the headlights, "but I have done something really stupid."

I can feel rage bubbling in my stomach. "What the hell have you done with the other package?"

"I had a party last week here with some friends and clients. They wanted some coke and I didn't know where to get any. I would have asked you if I knew your number. I'll give you the money for it, you know that," she says walking toward me, holding out my drink.

I take a sip and think for a moment. I suppose it will not be that bad if I get the money, after all that's what Francesca wants in the long run. But my problem is, I don't know how much each bag would cost. I take another sip then ask Pam for a kitchen scales to weigh the remaining bag. It's two kilos.

Next I ask Pamela if I can make an international call in order speak to one of my best mates in London. He is delighted to hear from me and talk briefly about what's going on in London and of Arsenal's unbeaten start to the season. Then in Cockney code I ask, "What's the damage on Bob Marley?"

"How much?" he replies.

"Two."

"Two big ones?"

"Yea."

"£2000."

"Cheers mate."

"No problem. But wait, one more thing."

"What's that?"

"I'm coming to LA next week, I've got to get away from London for a while."

"Really?"

"Yea really."

"Fucking sweet, mate! That's great!" I say enthusiastically. "Email me your flight details and I'll pick you up at LAX."

Patrick is half Scottish and half Jamaican. We have known each other since we were five years old.

We travelled the country together following Arsenal since we were in school but stopped going together for a few years, when he became an active member of The Herd, Arsenal's young hooligan gang, at the age of sixteen. However his hooligan activity came to an abrupt end in 1993 when he was beaten to a pulp and left unconscious by Stokes City's Naughty Forty firm after a midweek league cup tie.

Patrick hasn't held down a regular job or girlfriend since he left school. This has also coincided with him being on the drug scene; I think that started after we witnessed Arsenal winning the title for the first time in our lifetime at Anfield in 1989.

After Michael Thomas' last gasp winner in the championship decider, the two of us headed for the Cream Fields rave in Liverpool. There we met some scally, Scouse drug dealers who welcomed us with open arms as they were Evertonians and were delighted that we piped their cross-city neighbours to the title. In a night of mass celebration, the scallies gave us a cocktail of LSD and Ecstasy. The LSD in particular made the title win at Anfield seem like we were celebrating our 18 year wait for the title on Mars with a thousand party guests from Venus.

Patrick was never the same after that experience. Now he is a kind of a drug connoisseur. He knows any new drug that's on the street before it gets into the hands of any dealer, the benefits of taking it and of course the side effects.

I'm not sure how I'm going to take to having a very familiar face around me out here, especially Patrick and his drug obsessions. Up until now I have been an unknown commodity to everyone, a new face in new towns. Fucking great. Now I am going to be faced with someone who knows me inside and out. I don't feel too good about it; still all that will be out weighed by the laughs we are going to have I'm sure.

Pamela is annoyed that I don't spend the night with her, but is very understanding when I tell her that I have to get the money and the package back to LA ASAP, as I have immense heat on me at the moment.

I catch the 11:00pm Greyhound bus back to LA.

LOS ANGELES,
25 OCTOBER 2003

I get to Francesca's at 1:00 am.

"She did what?!" yells Francesca. She is more upset about the missing package than I thought she would be.

"You've got the cash, so what difference does it make?" I say trying to appease to her.

"What difference does it make? I'll tell you what fucking difference it makes," she fumes. "It means that the drugs have been sold on the streets, and if so much of a grain finds its way to my ex, it will only be a matter of time before Creole traces all the leads back to YOUR stupid British ass," she yells, pushing her index finger into my chest for emphasis.

"Look, you're fucking over reacting, nothing got sold" I retort, getting pissed off with this unnecessary attitude. "She only gave it to a few yuppies at one of her pretentious real estate house parties in Santa Barbara," I tell her, taking her hand in mine. "None of the stuff would have gone back to San Francisco," I say matter-of-factly.

"Well for all of our sake's, we just better hope that's the case," she says, storming off to her bedroom.

These drug dealers must be bio-scientists if they can identify whether a few grains of cocaine belong to them or not.

Francesca comes back into the kitchen and makes me a drink, "I'm sorry about my outburst," she says, handing me the glass.

"I think I understand so no problem, eh," I say, raising my glass and taking a drink.

"Thanks for going through all this trouble to get the package back from Santa Barbara," she says with a sigh, running her hands through her hair. " I guess I'm just worried about you." Standing in front of me, she holds my face in her hand and kisses me softly.

"Worried about me, was ya?" I ask with a smile.

"Maybe, but hey, you want go and see a hockey game tomorrow night at the Staples Centre?" she asks, letting go of my face and walking to the kitchen.

"Who's playing?" I ask, taking another sip of my drink.

"LA Kings and the Vancouver Canucks," she says, pouring herself a glass of white wine.

"I have rehearsal in the morning, but I'm free after that," I agree. It will be a good way to relax.

Pretty Boy, Manchester and I arrive at rehearsals half an hour late due to the fact that we are all clueless about the LA public transport system. Nigel is relieved that we have turned up at all.

I hand the guys the music sheets for the songs I think we should perform for the set. I have taken it upon myself to be the music manager. Pretty Boy just wants to perform and get his hands on the college groupies, Manchester can't wait to unleash his frustrations of growing up in dull, rainy Manchester out on that Yamaha drum set, and Nigel, despite his great singing voice and enthusiasm, just hasn't got the musical know-how.

Some of the songs we will be covering are as follows;

Should I Stay or Should I Go – The Clash (this is a well-known track that the student crowd should be familiar with),

Don't You Forget about Me (Ska version) - Simple Minds (this track is featured in many an American teen flick, so it should go down well),

Some UK Ska/punk classics to show them what were about and where we are coming from, like *"Too Much Too Young"* – The Specials, *Three Minute Hero* – The Selecter,

In the City – The Jam, *Teenage Kicks* – The Undertones.

And to make them feel at home again, some US commercial plastic punk anthems like: *Basket Case* - Green Day, *Self Esteem* – The Offspring, *The Anthem* – The Good Charlotte.

We rehearse the songs and as expected they all work well with our natural but raw talents. We have one more session tomorrow then it's our opening night on Friday. Nigel is happier than ever and gives us the money for the first gig in advance.

"What about a name for the band?" he asks.

"Oh leave that to me," I reply, unplugging the bass from the Marshall. "I'll have one by tomorrow."

"One last thing," he says, coming over to me, "What about those songs you have written? Maybe I can familiarize myself with the lyrics for a later gig."

Up until now I have been very possessive with my lyrics, but I have to give them to someone at some point, so I reluctantly hand Nigel my two songs.

"oh yes Cool. *'Hooligan Supporter'* and *'The Cybil Shepherd'*. I really like those titles man." Nigel reads the lyrics on his way out.

Hooligan Supporter

Hooligan supporter, what you gonna do?
Hooligan supporter, what you gonna do?
Hooligan supporter
Kill each other?
Hooligan supporter
Or kill the boys in blue?
Fire in your eye
and a knife in your pocket.
You want to fight
with anyone who wants it.
All kitted out
in the labels of your crew
You want to fight
with the boys in blue
Saturday's here
What will it bring?
A punch? a kick?
or the truncheon swing?
The nation's against you
What has life brought ya?
NOTHING! So you're a Hooligan supporter.

Chorus

The terraces
are your territory
Stand your ground
for death or glory
Your life has something

but nothing to do
You don't need a job
join the dole queue
Social, economic,
political torture
But you don't care
So you're a Hooligan supporter

Chorus

Enemy of the state
but to others you're the big face
An English embarrassment
The English disease,
And don't care you're a Disgrace
But Billy is a lawyer
Johnny is a banker
Billy doesn't run
And Johnny's not a wanker
A criminal record
will come back and haunt ya
So watch out
If your a Hooligan Supporter

The Cybil Shepherd

She had style she had grace,
That curvaceous body and a beautiful face.
Hook on drugs
Addicted to her
No direction from school
Ask the taxi driver.
Wasn't high, didn't fight
Moonlighting on, it's Thursday night

Cybil oh Cybil
You outshone the Moonlight
And thought for civil rights
Cybil oh Cybil
You outshone the Moonlight
And thought for civil rights

Got in trouble, fighting, abuse
Cybil was the star
We couldn't care about Bruce
Had a feeling,
When I was stealing
Could I find a girl?
Who was just appealing as
Cybil oh Cybil
You outshone the Moonlight
And thought for civil rights
Cybil oh Cybil
You outshone the Moonlight
And thought for civil rights

She had style she had grace,
That curvaceous body and a beautiful face.
Hook on drugs
Addicted to her
No direction from school
Ask the taxi driver.
Wasn't high, didn't fight
Moonlighting on it's Thursday night
Cybil oh Cybil
You outshone the Moonlight
And thought for civil rights
Cybil oh Cybil
You outshone the Moonlight
And thought for civil rights..(Repeat twice)

CYBIL!!!!!!!!!!!!!

Having just been paid for the future gig, I was willing to splash the cash and pay for a taxi to the Staple Centre. Francesca and I take our seats for the game between the Kings and Canucks. Neither Francesca nor I are interested in ice hockey, but the game was an exciting, bruising encounter, with The Kings winning 3-2.

Outside, the Kings fans celebrate their team's victory and taunt their Canadian counterparts, who have probably made the long journey south to cheer for their side. A few Canadian fans give the middle finger in retaliation. We hear a policewomen's voice requesting for backup, for possible riot situation. Both Francesca and I laugh.

"A riot!" she says calming down. "That's funny! You should see it when Boca Junior plays River Plate back home in the derby of Buenos Aires."

"Yea I bet, it must be fucking mental," I say, picturing a derby game at White Heart Lane against the scum.

"Fucking mental?! There have been times when the police don't even turn up! They just let them fight!" she says, laughing again. Yea, I have to admit these hockey fans are pretty lame compared to a full-scale riot at a football match in England or in Argentina as it would seem.

Now, I am no thug, but I have always been fascinated with football hooligans. I see it as a kind of a *'Fight Club'*. In normal circumstances a football hooligan (in Britain at least) would normally only look to fight another hooligan who wants to fight them. So I don't really see much wrong with that. The Thing I do not condone is bully boy thugs picking fights with normal fans who wear club colours that are clearly going to the game to innocently cheer their team on. If thugs want to fight each other, what's the problem with that?

While Francesca continues to boast about the viciousness of derby in Buenos Aires, I think back to one Saturday morning in March 1985.

LONDON
MARCH 1985

I went to a Catholic Comprehensive school in West London. Incredibly, the Arsenal fans out numbered the Chelsea and QPR fans. This was because most of the Arsenal team of the late seventies and early eighties were Irish and half of the boys at the school were of Irish decent. So naturally, they all admired Brady, Stapleton, O'Leary, Jennings, and Rice.

Arsenal were playing West Ham on the coming Saturday. Word had got round that the Gooners would be ambushing West Hams ICF at Kings Cross. Kieran McShay, an Arsenal freak in my Form class, had convinced Patrick and I to be part of the Herd of Gooners who would be waiting for West Ham.

In those days The ICF would normally travel from the East End and start their assault on Highbury from King Cross smashing every pub, and kicking the shit out of any Arsenal fan along the way and then take over the North bank. This year however was going to be a different story.

I shit myself as soon as Kieran told me about the plan. Patrick and I thought that he must be mad. This is the fucking ICF we were talking about! - Arguably the finest hooligan firm of the casual generation. But Kieran had an almost mesmerising, persuasive way about him, so we pensively agreed to go along.

That Saturday, we got to the Metropolitan Line as it was from Ladbroke Grove and got off at Kings Cross at 11:00am. As expected, there must have been at least 400 stylish Gooners scattered across the grounds of Kings Cross station, turned out in their best Aquascutum, Pringle and Lyle & Scott gear. They looked more like a bunch of golfers teeing off at St Andrews, than a crew of thugs looking for a tear up.

For the occasion I wore an Aquascutum scarf that I could only wear at weekends because I had nicked it from Mr Young, our trendy Geography teacher. Both Patrick and Kieran had previously super-glued eagles onto their acrylic, Marks & Spencer v-necks in order to turn them into Lyle & Scott jumpers.

Kings Cross is a massive station so we were split into two groups. The hardcore Gooners, lead by a legend called Denzil, were waiting to ambush the ICF when they get off the westbound tube. The younger crew known as the Herd, lead by Milton, would bring up the rear from the Main Line part of the station.

At 11:30 exactly, the ICF arrived in North London, flash and brash as usual. Earlier, back in Mile End, the police had spotted them gathering and escorted them to King Cross. On this cold Saturday morning in March 1985, they got the surprise of their lives. The first batch of Gooners roared and charged at West Ham's finest as they came off the west bound train and onto the concourse. The ICF retreated to the platform in shock; they then regrouped for a counteroffensive.

The police managed to get early control of the minor skirmish, which then resulted in a stand off in the concourse of Kings Cross, where the Hammersmith and City Line is now.

The Gooners backed off up the stairs and onto the streets outside the Main Line station to join us and the other 200 or so young Arsenal. The ICF were confident on taking this Arsenal firm, whom they had pissed on year after year. As expected, the ICF broke free from their flimsy police escort and charged out of the station and onto the streets of Kings Cross to confront their North London adversaries.

To their surprise, the Gooners had doubled in size.

I heard the infamous West Ham war cry of, "I-C-F! I-C-F!" and my heart and my bollocks jumped out of my mouth. Back home, I should have been watching the object of my schoolboy fantasies, Sarah Green on *'Going Live'*, but instead I was with a bunch of football thugs looking to kick the shit out of each other. I could see the fear on Patrick and Kieran's faces too. This is where we actually realised we were just a bunch of thirteen-year-old schoolboys.

The Gooners roared and ran at the ICF. All of the rear guard Gooners rallied around us then shouted, "Come on lets go! Let's have them!" Fuelled by adrenalin, our young legs took us with the rest of the Herd. The Gooners must have had the famous ICF on the run because we ended up back in the station.

I have bungee jumped in New Zealand, white water rafted on the Zambezi River and ran with the bulls of Pamplona, but that Saturday morning in March 1985 was the biggest adrenalin rush of all.

LOS ANGELES,
26 September 2003

Tonight is our first gig. Things should go smoothly so long as Manchester can keep his composure on the drums. He's a great drummer, but he tends to get a bit carried away half way through some of the songs and goes into Keith Moon mode.

Our last song of the night will be The Foo Fighters "*Monkey Wrench*," where I have given Manchester licence to have a solo. "Yea," he says nodding. "It will sound like a John Bonham's solo, like on Moby Dick on Led Zeppelin II."

"Ha, yea sure it will," says Pretty Boy sarcastically.

Pretty Boy is a class act. He can play every Hendrix riff including all his live stuff. I can hold my own on the bass, and Nigel just has to sing.

We arrive at the college bar in Westwood at around 7:00 pm. A small crowd has assembled for happy hour but we won't be on for another two hours.

"I hope more birds turn up than this," says Pretty Boy, looking around.

"Who gives a shite? I just want to plays those fucking Yamahas, man," Manchester says, eyeing up the drum set.

Nigel arrives with his 10 out of 10 stunning girlfriend; she looks like a cross between Tara Reid and Jessica Simpson. We all marvel at her beauty.

Pretty Boy taps me on my shoulder. "What's she doing with that mug?" he whispers in my ear. "I can't fucking believe it!"

"This is LA, mate. If you got the cash anything's possible; bands, birds, the lot," I reply.

The bar starts to fill and by the time happy hour finishes at 8:30, the bar is two thirds full, with enough birds for Pretty Boy to showcase to. But no sign of Francesca though, who said she was going to come and show support.

We are introduced on stage by Nigel's dad, who owns the bar. "Ladies and gentleman! Tonight I have a special treat for you! We have a band making their debut tonight. So without further ado, give it up for "The Metamorphosis!"

Yes, that's the name I came up with after a deep thinking process:

Metamorphosis, change of form (by magic, natural development, etc.); change of character, conditions, etc.

I thought that description is significant for the status quo and our music.

A one, two, a one, two, three, four! We kick off the gig with a cover of *"Basket Case"* by Green Day just to get the student crowd going. They lap it up and soon some of the crowd are dancing wildly in the small space in front of the stage.

We have a half hour intermission after performing an explosive Ska set.

Still no sign of Francesca. I call her from a pay phone, but there is no answer. Oh well, who gives a shit. It's not just Pretty Boy who is getting admiring looks from the young female students in the crowd. While we're sipping beers at the bar, two girls stand beside us at the bar.

"Great music, we really like Ska," says one of the girls.

"Thanks," I reply. "Glad you liked it."

The girls, both short, blonde, college chicks are not studying at UCLA like most of the students here; they are majoring in English and Drama at USC. I turn my attention to Caroline, who isn't wearing make-up. I like the natural look; it gives girls a look of honesty.

"One of the drama teachers at our college used to be in a famous Ska band back in England," she tells me.

"Oh yea, what's her name?" I ask, curious about her music knowledge.

"Sarah Jayne. She always tells us that she was a guitarist in an all-girl band called the 'Body Snatchers'"

"The Body Snatchers" I exclaim, almost choking on my beer. "No fucking way! That's bull shit!"

"No honestly!" she says giggling. "Hey do you know them?" Caroline asks.

"Yea of course I do! I was a fan of all the Ska bands at that time."

The Specials, The Beat, Madness, Bad Manners, and not forgetting the Body Snatchers, of course. It was 1979 to 1980, the two-tone era; I was only seven or eight years old, but I would say that those bands have had the biggest influence of my short, fledgling musical career.

"Hey Mindy, these guys have heard of the Body Snatchers," says Caroline excitedly.

Mindy who has already got her tongue down Pretty Boy's throat, breaks when she feels Caroline shaking her arm.

"Hey Mindy! These guys have heard of the Body Snatchers!"

"Who the hell are the Body Snatchers, man?" Mindy asks, irritated that she's been interrupted.

"You know, our drama teacher's Ska band from the eighties."

"Oh shit, no way!"

Its time to go back on stage for the second set. Pretty Boy tells the college chicks that we'll have a drink with them after the set.

We get a rapturous applause when we finish our set with *"The Anthem,"* even with Manchester's monstrous, uncoordinated solo. The appreciative crowd request an encore and we give them *"Too much too Young"* by The Specials- A classic.

Manchester, who has performed wonders on the drums tonight, heads back to the Cotel, alone to smoke a few joints to wind down.

Nigel gets a hug from his girlfriend and leaves with her. Pretty Boy and I head over to the two USC chicks and after a few drinks, they suggest we go across the road to another bar called Maloney's.

There is a massive queue outside the popular student bar.

"Ahh fuck, look at the line," says Caroline with her squeaky accent.

"I've been here before. There's a back entrance we can use," Pretty Boy lies, winking at me. I don't know what he's got up his sleeve, but I'm curious to find out all the same.

Around the back of the bar is a small alley full of bins, empty boxes and bottle crates that are piled against the wall. There is a back door, two in fact, but Pretty Boy had no idea where he was going or what he was doing. Before I know it he has Mindy pinned against the wall, kissing her aggressively. He lifts up her top and savagely fondles her cleavage. This sort of thing isn't really my style.

Caroline almost feels obliged to kiss me so she pushes herself against me. I catch myself from falling over as she gives me slobbery drunken kisses. I softly push her away and start kissing her neck. She moans, and pinches my arse, but she isn't Francesca, and I'm not really that aroused.

As I pull my mouth away from her neck, my eyes focus across the street at the bar where we were playing. They must be playing tricks on me, because a woman looking exactly like Francesca is walking past the bar, holding hands with a tall dark-haired guy. I push Caroline away from me and walk to the sidewalk as the woman leaves the guy she's with and goes into Nigel's dad bar.

He lights up a cigarette while waiting for her, meanwhile I duck behind the queue in front Maloney's, still watching the entrance. My eyes weren't playing tricks on me! It is Francesca who comes out of the bar, looking in my direction, slightly worried. She says something to the guy, kisses his cheek and they continue on their way.

"Are you okay?" Caroline asks, drunkenly stumbling over.

I grab her as she trips on the curb of the sidewalk, and take her back to the mouth of the alley. Pretty Boy has Mindy bent over a couple of empty beer crates, shagging her doggy style. I turn Caroline away from the scene and sit her down on the curb, as I know what is soon to follow. Just as Pretty Boy is shooting

> Maloneys
> 1060 Gayley Avenue
> Westwood Village
> CA 900244
> 310-208-1942
> Long queues on the weekend. No back alley entrance.

his load up Mindy, Caroline starts vomiting up the alcohol she has been drinking since happy hour. I reckon it was the combination of the cheep beer they were selling and the sight of Pretty Boy's skinny, pale, arse flexing and contracting that made her puke.

I am woken up the next day by the sound of Pretty Boy getting dressed.

"Where the hell are you going so early?" I mumble, pulling the blankets over my head.

"I got to meet that Mindy bird from last night," he says excitedly.

"You what?" I ask, flipping the blankets down. "It's 9:00 in the morning!"

"I know, but I gotta meet her at a café in Westwood; she wants to buy me breakfast."

"Fair enough." I mumble and roll over, pulling the blankets over my shoulders.

"Do you wanna to come? Maybe I can get her to bring her mate along," he says shaking me.

"Ahh no thanks mate. I need to get some sleep," I reply, looking over my shoulder. I don't think Pretty Boy has quite got the concept and functions of a groupie.

"Why didn't you shag her anyway Rich?" Pretty boy asks me before he leaves.

"She wasn't up for it," I lie. "Besides the site of your skinny white arse going at it was enough to put anyone off."

"Fuck off you cunt. See you later."

I spend the rest of the morning lying on my bunk wondering who that was with Francesca last night. It must have been that guy who left that message on her phone. It definitely didn't look like Creole.

When I finally get out of bed, I walk past the reception at the hotel. Katrina asks me if I am watching the Arsenal game.

"What game? It's Friday," I say, half ignoring her, pushing the button on the elevator.

"Yea I know its Friday but Arsenal are playing Newcastle in a minute."

"What, stop pissing about?"

"Yea no shit! It's a 7:45pm kick off, 12:45am LA time. You can watch it in my room if you want," she says matter-of-factly, tossing me her keys.

Her room is like an oasis in the midst of this backpacker squalor. It is almost a lavish one-bedroom apartment featuring all the mod cons including a good size TV. Katrina, being the football freak she is, already has the TV on the Fox Sports football channel.

Newcastle haven't got the best of records in London in recent years, so it's no surprise that we win a tense affair, 3-2. A Gilberto header sandwiched between two King Henry strikes and two Newcastle equalisers is just enough to get us the three points on a rare Friday night of Premiership football.

"Lucky bastards," says Katrina, who has entered her room. The Israeli is not shy and gets undressed in front of me.

"What do you think of my body?" she asks fishing for compliments, now naked apart from her black, cotton g-string.

"Not bad," I reply. Her body is firm with C-cup breasts and big brown nipples. I gaze admirably at the body that she has probably kept up since she served in the Israeli army.

"Don't even think about it, Ritchie boy. I would have shagged you by now, if I really wanted to," she teases, with one hand on her hip.

"I wouldn't be so sure about that?" I reply, leaning back on her bed.

She chuckles waving a hand in my direction. "I know you Richard. Besides, I don't like sloppy seconds."

"I don't know what you're talking about," I say coolly, wondering what she's heard.

Katrina laughs again while stepping into her ensuite bathroom. I know she was talking about Jessica, but what could she have heard. Fuck-all happened.

After our successful first gig last night, Nigel has given us the afternoon off. He thinks there is no need to rehearse. Manchester is hungry and wants to get a late breakfast so I take him to the Venice Whaler. The friendly, gambling Kiwi owner remembers me and our bet from a couple of weeks earlier.

"Don't worry," I reassure him, after he reminds me, "I haven't forgotten the bet."

We order the same thing; cheeseburgers and fries. He's in hysterics when I fill him in about Pretty Boy's back alley shag.

"I was supposed to go to back to the room smoke a joint then fall asleep," says Manchester, "but when I got back to the hotel, I got chatting to these guys outside. It was weird, like, we had this spiritual connection." He takes a bite of his burger and continues, "I ended up getting a ride with them down to the canals for a smoke."

"A ride?" I ask, "What were they driving?"

"They weren't, they had push bikes. I hitched a ride on one of their handle bars."

"So what were you smoking?" I ask, interested.

"I almost ashamed to admit it," he mumbles, slowly chewing some fries.

"Come on, it can't be that bad, can it?"

"Yes it can, man. We smoked crack."

We have been warned by the hostel staff to keep away from the unpredictable vagrants of Venice Beach, who come out when the sun goes down. Talking to them is one thing, but getting a ride on a push-bike and smoking rocks with them, I don't know…

Manchester and I finish our burgers in silence. Well, I suppose like most bands, the drummer is always the crazy one. I hope he doesn't overdose, combust or choked on his own vomit like his heroes Keith Moon and John Bonham.

We finish our brunch and I ask Manchester if he wants to accompany me to Francesca's place, a short walk from the Venice Whaler.

I have yet to see Manchester chat up a girl. I don't think he's an Iron, so I ask him what kind of girls he likes. Having spent a bit of time in San Francisco, I think I can spot a gay guy if I saw one.

"Strictly Asian," he says seriously. "I haven't got time for anything else. I can't wait to get to Thailand and beyond man." Manchester went Asian after he found out a girlfriend of his wasn't carrying his child, but his best mate's. He sadly turned to heavy drugs at the same time he started dating girls from India, Pakistan, Vietnam and China. Not that turning to drugs makes you turn to Asian girls, I must clarify.

At Francesca's, the dark-haired guy who was walking with her the other night answers the door, "No, she is not here, she is at work," he says with a Turkish accent. "Who are you, anyway? How do you know Francesca?" he says with slight aggression.

"I am a good friend of hers from San Francisco," I reply with a camp inflection in my voice, putting one hand on my hip. "We used to dance together in San Fran."

Manchester picks up on the situation. "Yes and I'm his boyfriend, Sebastian."

"Oh, I see," says the Turk, with a slight scowl. "She's working in Hollywood," he says curtly, stepping back to close the door.

"Thanks baby. I'll give her a call on her mobile. See you now," I say twiddling my fingers at him as he closes the door.

So that was Francesca's flat mate, more like her Turkish boyfriend. My feelings for her have gone up and down like a roller coaster since I have known her. After last night's no show, then seeing her holding hands with the Turk and now this, my emotions are at the bottom of the track. I think that's the reason that I am still interested in her. It's not just her beautiful face and perfect figure, as those two physical aspects are dime a dozen around these parts. It's the fact she sends me to the bottom of the grave with every disappointment, and when I see her again, I'm reborn into a state of ecstasy and forget all that has gone before.

We have been given orders from Nigel to go to Maloney's the rival bar of his dad's and discreetly spread the word about the Metamorphosis. Our first gig last night may have been a musical success, but the bar was still only half full, or half empty as he put it. Pretty Boy does most of the work, as he is a favourite with the young ladies. Manchester and I talk to the guys and the older ladies. We manage to pinch at least thirty punters from Maloney's, most of them young girls.

I see that Francesca isn't part of the crowd again; however we have pulled off yet another crowd-satisfying gig.

The next morning Katrina hands me a message; Francesca has called. I call her immediately and she says that she needs to see me today. She wants me to go to the Kodak Theatre on Hollywood Boulevard then call her when I get there.

Before I go, I check my hotmail. Patrick has sent me a message containing his flight details. He asks if there is anything I want bought over. I reply with a short list; a jar of Bransten pickle, a Lyle & Scott t-shirt, a couple of newspapers (one tabloid, one broadsheet) and a lad's magazine, either *Loaded* or *Maxim*. I write down his flight details and then head out to meet Francesca in Hollywood.

It is around midday and I am sitting in a bar in the Kodak Theatre on Hollywood Boulevard. On the way here, I was a bit of a tourist and stopped to look at the stars on the Walk of Fame that are such a familiar site. It was like seeing the Golden Gate Bridge for the first time. I never seen it before but I knew it so well.

I took pictures of Robert Di Nero's, Eddie Murphy's and of course Cybil Shepherds' stars.

After having a drink at a bar in the Kodak theatre, I give Francesca a call. She says she can't make it to the bar but I should meet her at one of her client's houses in the Hills. "For fuck's sake!"

I mumble to myself, walking back to the bar. "What the fuck am I doing with this Argy bird?" I down the scotch I ordered and leave.

The house must be worth over four million. I ring the doorbell and Francesca answers with a smile.

"What's all this about Francesca?" I demand angrily, before she can say hello. "For once, I need to know the truth."

"Ok," she says, ushering me inside. "This house belongs to client of mine, like I said."

I look at her. "And who's this client?" I ask curtly.

"Her name is Karen Welsh. She's a lawyer uptown," Francesca replies, turning away, bored with my attitude.

"Ok, so where is she now?" I demand, stepping toward her, continuing the interrogation.

"This is the honest truth," she says whirling around, holding her hands palms toward me like she's been caught out. "She left on a flight to Hong Kong this morning and wanted a massage to relax her, because she hates flying."

"So what are you still doing here?"

"Well, in the past three weeks we have become real close friends," she says, as we move into the front hallway of the house. "She asked me to stay while she's away, as I was having trouble with my current housing situation."

"Oh yeah, problems," I retort with a huff, "with your Turkish boyfriend roommate?"

"Ok, so I was kind of seeing him," she says with her hands on her hips. "Look Richard, I needed a place to stay," she continues, folding her arms defensively.

"So you were paying for the rent on you back," I shout accusingly.

"Fuck you, Richard! Fuck you!" she yells pushing past me and then running up the spiral stairs of the luxurious mansion in tears. I feel like Clark Gabel chasing Janet Leigh as I run after her. I find her in the master bedroom lying face down on the bed, crying her eyes out.

"I'm so sorry Richard, I didn't know what to do," she apologizes, when I sit on the bed next to her, her voice muffled by the blankets. She looks at me with her beautiful sad wet eyes. I know that she's a lying toe-rag, but these tears are real.

"I need the money for my Mamma and Papa in Argentina. We have nothing," she sobs, bringing on a fresh bout of tears.

Despite the lies and all the other shit, I take pity on her. I pull her to my chest. I hate seeing her like this, but it always seems to be one drama or another with her.

We slowly rock back and forth while she cries on my shoulder. I wipe her eyes and hold her face in my hands.

"So what now?" I ask with a sigh.

"Can I trust you?" she sobs, wiping her eyes.

"I'm on your side," I whisper, brushing her cheek with my hand. I brace myself for more "truth."

Francesca sits up and pulls her legs underneath her. "As it stands, I have two guys after me; Creole in San Fran and now Mehmit in Marina del Rey."

"Ok, well that Mehmit seems like a nice guy, right?" I say cautiously.

"Yes and no. He's an extremely nice guy, but his family won't take too lightly to their son being robbed."

Here we go. "So you robbed him too?"

"Yea," she mumbles, looking at her hands.

"How much?"

"Ten grand." She looks up at me with a frown. I look at the ceiling and take a deep breath.

"How the hell did you get ten grand out of him in just over two weeks?" I ask in disbelief.

"I didn't. He borrowed me five the rest was stuff I kept stealing from his house."

"Ok," I say pausing to comprehend the trouble she's got herself into. "And Creole? What's the latest in San Fran?"

"Not good I'm afraid. And not good for you either," she says with a serious look.

"What d'you mean?" I ask slowly, starting to panic.

"I mean those drugs that your fancy woman in Santa Barbara gave out," she smirks, "some of it made its way back to San Fran and to Creole."

"Oh for fuck's sake, how the fuck could that have happend!" I shout, bashing my forehead with the palm of my hand.

"Don't panic, I haven't heard anything about him finding the source," she says, putting her hand on my shoulder. "Saying that, it's only a matter of time. If I were you I would give Miss Santa Barbara a call to make sure she's safe."

I use the phone in the bedroom, while Franesca goes downstairs to cook something for dinner. There's no answer, it goes directly to Pam's voicemail. Worried, I hang up without leaving a message and join Francesca downstairs.

We don't talk anymore about her situation, but keep things light. She calmly switches the subject and asks me more about my life back home. I elaborate a bit more about my daily routine; waking up on a grey London morning going to my uninteresting, soul-destroying job in the city, then at seven o'clock after standing on a crowded Tube on the dirty Central Line, I make my way to my local boozer to get pissed with my unemployed friends in order to forget about my shit day at work.

After dinner, we retire for an early night. I have a dream about diving off the Golden Gate Bridge in to a pool of Crystal champagne full of celebrity mermaids.

The next morning, Francesca is in the kitchen cooking breakfast.

"You don't have to say a thing about yesterday. I'm just sorry I got you into this mess." She says stirring pancake batter "Look Richard, I don't want you to go anywhere near my apartment, things are too hot up there right now whether Mehmit thinks you're my gay dancing queen friend from San Fran or not." She laughs lightly and shakes her head, puts down the bowl and spoon and turns to me. "I'm leaving LA tomorrow and I think you should too."

"What? Why do I have to leave?" I contest.

"It's only a matter of time before Creole gets to LA and Mehmit lives and works in Santa Monica. It's just a bit too hot for you," she says with concern in her voice.

"But I have commitments here now in LA with the band, not to mention I have a friend coming over from London in two days."

"Okay," she says throwing up her hands and raising her voice. "It's up to you but I think you should at least move out of the Venice Beach/ Santa Monica area."

"Maybe you're right," I mumble, setting the table. "Where are you going anyway?"

"First I have to sort out a few things in Palm Springs, and then I will be in San Diego for about two weeks," she says as she pours some batter into a hot frying pan. "From there, I will cross the border into México then fly back to Buenos Aeries." The pancakes cook fast, and Francesca expertly flips them.

"Why don't you just fly home from LAX?" I ask, pouring orange juice into some glasses.

"Too risky," she says briskly, licking some batter off her finger, pouring more into the pan. "My visa has a few inconsistencies. If they run a check on me, I might be detained and I just can't risk that." She smiles at me as I hand her a glass of juice.

Later I convince Pretty Boy and Manchester to check out of the hostel and move to the Orbit on Melrose in Hollywood. I tell them we will be nearer to work and all the nightlife on Sunset. We say our goodbyes to Katrina and wish her the best of luck, but I don't wish her the best of with the rest of the current football season.

> **The Venice Beach Cotel**
> 25 Winward Avenue
> Venice Beach,
> CA 90291
> 31039976
> A loud-mouth Israeli will greet you, but without the promised *Lonely Planet* drink.

The Orbit Hostel on Melrose is noticeably cleaner than its Venice Beach counterpart. We get a room for four, with the imminent arrival of Patrick in mind.

Patrick arrives on a delayed American Airlines flight the day Arsenal play out a drab away 0-0 draw with locomotive Moscow in the Champions League. As usual, we are struggling in Europe. However on the scale of things a point away in Moscow is a good result, especially after what happened against Inter at Highbury, and the fact that we were without Vieira, Campbell, Ljungberg, Gilberto and the non-Flying Dutchman.

Patrick is as pleased to see me, as I am him, and the Bransten pickle. On the way to the hostel, I fill Patrick in on most of what has gone.

"Please, please," begs Patrick. "Please let me be your band please!"

"I don't know mate. It's not my band," I tell him as we arrive at the Orbit.

"Come on Richard! How can you have a Ska band without horns?" He has a point. Patrick is an adept saxophone and trombone player. But he hasn't played since he left school about ten years ago, and has had no desire to play in that time either; however he just can't resist the excitement of being part of a band in California.

The next morning at rehearsals, I introduce Patrick to Nigel and the rest of the band.

Manchester and Pretty Boy welcome him, but Nigel is adamant to adding horns in the band. If Nigel knew anything about Ska, he would have been looking for a sax or trombone player months ago. Eventually, he agrees to bring Patrick on board after Patrick softens him up with talk of The Cure and the Pixies on the strength of my tip off.

Manchester and Pretty Boy have devised a plan for us all to go on a Hollywood bender and get wrecked for the rest of the day. This will entail seeing the sights and getting pissed in the process. Patrick, like Pretty Boy and Manchester, has never been to Hollywood before, so he persuades me to take part in the splurge.

After rehearsals we get a cab to the very start of Hollywood Boulevard. Pretty Boy, who has become more of an alcoholic than I have, is craving a beer. We walk all the way to the Kodak Theatre and have a drink at one of the bars there. Our heavily tattooed bartender is another resident of LA who is either a budding actor or a wannabe rock star. On this occasion, the spiky haired freak is a guitar player without a band. When we tell him about our band, our friendly, welcoming bartender becomes a jealous, obnoxious one.

Normally I would order in a nice slow, clear English accent. But today, as this obnoxious prick is being difficult to get along with, I leave Manchester with his strong Salford accent, along with Pretty Boy and Patrick with their uncompromising Cockney accents to tear into him.

The problem starts when the bartender says that he can't understand a word any of them are saying. Both Pretty Boy and Manchester take offence to this, and hurl a barrel of abuse at him. The fracas has caught the attention of a Kodak Theatre security guard, who enters the bar and escorts us out for being guilty of a public disorder.

All of us now pretty tipsy have ended up in the Graumans Chinese Theatre comparing our shoe sizes with Shirley Temple's, Jayne Russell's and the like. Just outside the theatre, an attractive girl is looking for audience members for the Jimmy

Kimble show. We all reckon that it will be a laugh and decide to be part of the show.

We queue and get our tickets for the show. Unfortunately, it has now been four hours since we agreed to attend the show, and are now all drunk out of minds and high as kites. Once again, I have succumbed to the temptation of cocaine and on this occasion it accompanied by a few dabs of MDMA that Patrick got his hands on from some lowlifes back in Venice.

At the lobby of the theatre, we explore the surroundings and notice a sectioned VIP area complete with champagne and hors'deuvres, which have obviously been laid out for Kimble and his guest. There is a female security officer, guarding the feast.

"Eh Pretty Boy," Patrick says hoarsely, "charm that bird, will ya, so we can nip in and swipe some of those VIP goodies." The plan works and we are two bottles of Veuve Cliquot richer. Drunk and high we take our seats in the studio theatre.

Jimmy Kimble enters the stage with the verve of a seasoned performer, as Patrick pops open one of the bottles of champagne. The cork rockets into the studio lighting hanging from the ceiling and ricochets down into a bag of nachos on a fat girl's lap. We burst into fits of laughter and catch a security officer's attention. He doesn't have time to confront us as Kimble has started his opening comic routine.

The four of us are now in stitches and Kimble's jokes that now seem twice as funny as usual are adding to the hilarity. Manchester and Patrick start to heckle Kimble, who to his credit, comes back with some witty retorts. Pretty Boy adds to the heckling, shouting sarcastically "Oi Kimble you wanker! You're funny, aren't ya?"

"Right that's it! No more!" Kimble yells to the security. "Get them outta here!" he orders, "I can't work like this."

Ten security guards swarm on us and escort us out. Kimble has the last laugh as he calls us extras from Mary Poppins and takes the piss out of our London accents. He does a better impression of a Cockney accent than Dick Van Dyke, that's for sure. As we exit the female security at the entrance reclaims the bottles of Veuve Cliquot from pretty boy's clutches with a firm side swipe, saying "I'll take those honey, and don't bother calling"

Disappointed with our early exit we head for a few bars on the Sunset Strip. The first bar we hit is the Saddle Ranch. The coke has wore off but the MDMA is still lingering and we are still drunk. The bar has a mechanical bull that proves too much of a temptation.

Pretty Boy is first on; the male waif only lasts a pathetic five seconds. Patrick fairs a bit better, as he gets up to 20. Manchester is the pick of the bunch with an impressive score of 40 seconds. I am reluctant to jump on the bull because even in my drunk state I was able to read some of the disclaimer we all had to sign, which reads something like the *"Saddle Ranch will not take responsibilities for death or any serious injury."* With that in mind, I last a very cautious 10 seconds. Manchester wins the pot of cash that we all put $20 into, for the rider who stays on the longest.

After another round of drinks the guys spot an assorted set girls at a booth in the corner that will be their fist target for the night.

I'm not really in a pulling state of mind, even in my drunken state. I still manage to have Francesca on my mind, wondering if I'll ever see the Palm Springs-bound Argentinean again.

The boys waste no time going over and introducing themselves. I am introduced to them, but I show little interest to the girl who I have been paired with. Her name is Shanice, a very good-looking Haitian.

"You don't talk much, do you?" she says softly.

"Oh yes I do, you should hear me," I jokingly reply.

"I should hear you what?" Shanice is a lovely, witty girl from the valley. But it doesn't seem like anything will materialise from this, as we are left dumbfounded when they

> The Saddle Ranch
> 8371 West Sunset Blvd
> West Hollywood, CA
> 323-656-2007
> Read the small print
> on the mechanical bull
> death warrant.

get up and leave. They tell us they are going to the Sky Bar, a bar that has a notoriously strict door policy.

The four of us approach the smartly dressed doorman guarding the roped entrance of the Sky bar. I tell him that we're a British rock band opening for Radiohead on their US tour.

"Yea we've just arrived and we're staying at the Renaissance in Hollywood," I say confidently.

"Our tour manager told us that this bar would be the place to come to," adds Patrick causally.

"Ok boys, you have a nice evening." says the doorman as he unlocks the carabineer with his thumb and drops down the rope to let us pass.

I don't know why they have those ropes there. It not like they can stop a bum rush once you have got past a monster of a doorman.

I am very impressed with this place; looking at it, I think it's the best bar I've been too so far in California There's an intimate sheltered bar that leads to an outdoor swimming pool surrounded by king-sized beds. The bar has probably the best view LA has to offer, as you can see the whole of the sprawling metropolis from here.

Patrick taps me on the arm, "Look! It's fucking Mick Hucknall from Simply Red! Can you believe it?" he yells, pointing at the ginger singer.

Fucking Mick Hucknall, my sentiments exactly! He, along with Eamon Holmes, is the most hated Man UTD fan at Highbury and probably in the Britain. Actually, to be fair to Hucknall, Eamon Holmes is more annoying than the ginger, soul-singing womaniser.

We notice the girls from the Saddle Ranch sitting on a bed by the pool. I take a seat next to Shanice and offer to buy her a drink.

"No, let me buy you one," says the dark and lovely Haitian. She escorts me to the bar and buys herself a glass of champagne and a Scotch and ginger for me.

Shanice is a dancer who has shaken her big round booty in many a Rap video. Her ambition, like many is to be an actress, and she is determined to achieve that goal, like many a bartender, construction worker, massage therapist or pool attendant in LA.

She has the looks, but I fear that her arse is too big for the big screen, let alone television. Maybe shaking her jacksy beside Snoop Dogg in a rap video is as far as she will get. Speak of the devil, no not Snoop Dogg, but another well-known rapper is sitting at a table in front of us. He has sent one of his entourage to the bar to speak with Shanice.

"Hello baby, how are you tonight?" says the flamboyantly dressed sidekick, as he sidles up to the bar.

"I'm fine," answers Shanice.

"Yes you are, yes you are," he says, stepping back to look her over. "My man over there would like you to join him for some champagne," he oozes, gesturing to the well-known rapper at the table.

"I'm sorry, but I already have one," she says, taking a sip from her glass.

"But baby, we got the whole nine over there," he brags, trying to persuade her.

"Sorry, I'm just fine here," she turns her back to him and looks at me.

The messenger returns to the well-known rap star without the booty.

I wont reveal this well-known rapper's name, for security reasons, as I don't want a cap in my ass when the traffic lights turn red on me at an intersection.

It's great that the fame-hungry Shanice has opted to stay with me at the bar, even though the multi-platinum selling artist is doing his best to woo her.

The conversation between us is just starting kick into gear when the well-known rapper approaches us himself. Oh no, I think to myself, now I have no chance of keeping her at the bar.

"Hey baby, what's up?" he asks with gangster suaveness stepping in between Shanice and I.

"Hey you know, we're just having a drink," Shanice says casually, gesturing to me.

I boldly introduce myself to the Rap star. I see this as a counter offensive. "I like your style," I tell him, offering my hand. "Your rap technique is true old school, real New York B-Boy style."

"Hey thanks man," says the Rapper, looking at my hand, and then shaking it. This takes his attention momentarily away from Shanice, but not for to long as he gets his gangster lean back on.

"Hey baby, I think you could be looking just fine in my next video," he offers subtly. Thankfully Shanice isn't that shallow and continues with her cool uninterested attitude.

"I keep telling my boys back home that you're better than Jay-Z and NAS," I persist.

"Yea I know you London boys know how to rock," he replies, turning my way again. "I love touring the UK man."

"As long as you keep it street, you will have a massive following in London," I continue, taking a sip of my drink.

"Hey man, London and the UK know how to show love, you know what I'm saying." Now he is fully facing me and Shanice is a mere spectator.

"You're flying the flag for Queen's Bridge man, MC Shan, Craig G, Tragedy, NAS and now you."

"Hey man you're getting deep now. You know your mother fucking shit," the Rapper says, impressed. "You know what? I'm gonna buy you a drink." Who am I to deny him?

"Mr. Bartender! Get my man here from England a bottle of that champagne." A bottle of Crystal arrives with just one glass; the well-known rapper has totally forgotten about Shanice.

"Hey man, I'm going to head back to my boys over there. You have yourself a nice evening" We do a ghetto-style handshake and he struts back to his table.

Shanice is speechless as I sip my glass of very expensive champagne.

"I have never seen anything like that before," she gasps, amazed that I could tame the ultimate Alpha Male. "That was just amazing!"

I ask for another glass, pour Shanice a drink and escort her out to the pool area to join the others. Patrick and Pretty Boy are chatting away with their respective girls. Manchester, however, is in a world of his own. He is totally ignoring the girl he has been paired with. This is because the Pilipino girl he wanted is all over Pretty Boy.

Patrick and Pretty Boy decide to stay with their new partners, while Manchester, Shanice, the left out girl, (who is actually quite cute) and I get into a cab. We do the gentleman thing and get the cab driver to drop the girls off in the Valley prior to heading back to the Orbit.

> **The Sky Bar**
> **8440 Sunset Blvd**
> **West Hollywood, CA**
> **383-650-8999**
> **Rub shoulders with stars from the music world and Mick Hucknall.**

After another successful Saturday night gig in Westwood, where Patrick made his début on sax on some up tempo, Trojan Ska numbers, Manchester and Pretty Boy head off with a couple of pretty, Japanese students with chunky legs, who are majoring medicine at UCLA. Patrick and I head to the Cock n Bull in Santa Monica to watch the Arsenal/Liverpool game at Anfield.

We put our $10 into old fashioned beer glass that the fat Glaswegian at the door in holding and take our seats with the rest of the Santa Monica/

Malibu Arsenal supporters club, who seem to have grown in members since the Inter game. There are now ten of us; a few tourists and an old Cockney pensioner have joined the fold. Eileen is here with her Arsenal hat and scarf on with her outrageous fake breasts on full view.

"Hey Richie baby! How's it hanging?" she says in her croaky Goldie Hawn accent. "Where's the lumberjack's daughter?"

"Who?" I ask.

"Come on! That sweet Canadian thing you showed around my house," she says chuckling.

"Oh, you mean Jessica," I say, shaking my head.

"Yea you know who, you dawg you. Hey who's you friend?"

"This is Patrick, my mate from London," I tell her, gesturing to Patrick.

"Hi Love, 'ow are you?" Eileen switches to Barbara Windsor. "Richie baby, why don't you get us some drinks while me and Patrick here 'ave a little chat." She hands me a $100 dollar bill and I do just that.

While I'm waiting to be served by the Scouse bartender, I watch as Eileen and Patrick get on like a house on fire. Patrick has landed on his feet here with Eileen; she is right up his street. He has a thing for older ladies, much older ladies.

This started when we were teenagers. We once stole some dirty magazines at WH Smiths in Paddington Station after arriving back in London after an Arsenal away win at Swindon in 1992.

I remember us running excitedly all the way up Platform 12 to the Hammersmith and City Line to catch our tube to Ladbroke Grove, only to be disappointed on the westbound platform when I realised the magazines were titled *50+*, *Wrinkle City* and *Grannies Exposed*. Patrick rolled them up and tucked them into his jacket and said he would dispose of them later.

The teams emerge from the Anfield dressing rooms. There is a bigger cheer in the pub when the Liverpool side is announced. Dodgy Scousers run this pub, so it has to be expected.

The cheers get louder as Liverpool are running us ragged in the first half. I go to the bar and order a much-needed double scotch. Before I get back to my seat Kewell has given Liverpool the lead with a great finish. I down my drink and head straight back to the bar for another.

It's almost like being an away fan in the corner of the Anfield Road end as the bar erupts into a frenzy with us Gooners left sitting at our tables.

Liverpool should have been at least three up before half time, but incredibly, we get an equaliser. Edu has scrambled in a corner. Patrick and I jump onto the table to celebrate and are greeted by hugs and kisses from Eileen on our decent.

Patrick has never been a fan of Robert Pires, and has been dishing out abuse the Frenchman's way. I am partial to handing out abuse to our own players myself; with Wiltord, Luzhny and

Grimandi baring the brunt of it in recent seasons. But as far as Pires is concerned, I can see no justification to the level of abuse thrown at him despite his shocking start to the season.

The second half is a much better showing from Arsenal, who have at last come to terms with Liverpool's three-pronged attack of Kewell, Owen and Diouf.

With the game locked at 1-1 Patrick and I are nervous wrecks. I am on about my sixth scotch and Patrick has convinced Eileen to join him in some MDMA dabbing. I am not sure that's a good idea at the moment but Ill leave them to it as there are more important things to worry about right now, the Scousers being on the attack being one of them. Yet again, we manage to chase them down and break up another wave of Red pressure.

Pires receives a short pass from Edu. The Frenchman cuts inside and sends a powerful curling shot from 28 yards into the top corner, giving Dudek no chance. A magnificent goal that sends Patrick and I onto the table again, this time Eileen joins us in the celebrations. We chant at the mass of Liverpool fans "2-1 to The Arsenal! 2-1 to The Arsenal!" in the tune of The Pet Shop Boys *"Go West."*

The now fuming Scouse owner kicks us out without a warning to spite us.

Typical Liverpool fan. Wanker! Can't take losing. They have been this way since 1990, when they last won the championship. They dominated the nation for nearly three decades from the era of Mr Shankly to Dalglish. They were so used to winning, but now they are just, quite frankly perennial underachievers as far as the league is concerned.

We leave without a struggle, as there is now just 10 minutes remaining and Arsenal are cruising to a victory that looked very unlikely after the first thirty minutes of play.

The three of us wait outside the Cock n' Bull until we hear the remaining members of the Santa Monica/Malibu branch of the Arsenal supporters club greet the final whistle with a cheer. Arsenal have dug out 2-1 away victory at fortress Anfield.

Eileen invites us back to her beach house for a drink to toast the victory.

I can see myself coming out of the Anfield Road end with the rest of the Gooners, singing our hearts out after this memorable triumph, and then spending the rest of the night in College Square or on Mathew Street taking the piss out Scousers and probably shagging one of their birds.

Eileen's boyfriend has gone back to México for the week, so the house is empty when we walk in. She cracks open a bottle of champagne.

I must have passed out as I am awoken a little while later by the sound of Patrick fucking Eileen. She's screaming the house down. Patrick is one of those lucky bastards who have been blessed with a whopper of a cock. Even the PE teachers at school made envious jokes about it. And if Eileen's screams are anything to go by he knows what to do with it.

In the morning, we jump in a cab back to Melrose. Patrick thanks me profusely for introducing him to Eileen.

Later I call Francesca, who is now in Palm Springs. She again tells me to leave LA, as it is too hot at the moment with her two ex lovers looking for her and anyone associated with her. "Look Richard, they both know your face," she says with concern.

"Ok, ok give me a week or so and I'll be in San Diego."

"Ok, I'll be there in ten days or so," she informs me. "Promise me you'll keep a low profile, and for God's sake keep away from Santa Monica. You haven't been there, have you?"

"No, not at all." Well not exactly. But I couldn't imagine Creole or Mehmit in the Cock n' Bull watching a Premiership game at two in the morning.

"In San Diego, I promise there will be no more bullshit," she says sweetly. "I swear baby, I've done what I had to do, and I plan to start a fresh in San Diego."

I don't believe a word of it; she's probably just left some millionaire playboy's hotel room at the Palm Springs, Four Seasons. But still, Francesca is Francesca and I can't stop my feelings for her, no matter what.

We don't have a gig tonight, so everybody decides to go on a date; Patrick is meeting with Eileen again, Pretty Boy has a secret date, Manchester will hang with one of the chunky-legged Japanese students and in my lonely, insecure state, I head to the valley to meet with Shanice.

She's has offered to cook for me; all I have to do is turn up, with a bottle. When I ring the doorbell, she answers wearing in a tight sexy black dress that accentuates her curvy, hourglass figure. Shanice has cooked me a Mexican meal and we start with nachos and dip. I open the bottle of sparkling Californian white that I have bought with me.

Shanice, as well as wanting to be an actress, is studying naturopathy. She tells me that she is a great believer natural remedies. Her mother was diagnosed with stomach cancer and after two course of chemotherapy, the cancer still lingered. The doctors gave her six months. Then in a last desperate attempt to save her mother, Shanice sent her to a Chinese doctor. After three months of seeing him, the cancer was completely gone. Now, she always recommends Chi-therapy rather than chemotherapy. I think it's a load of bollocks myself but if it makes her happy.

The bubbles from the sparkling wine have gone straight to Shanice's head and she has become giggly. I have been with girls with big arses before and learnt the best way to their heart or in this case to their panties, is by complimenting them on their rear-ends. The combination of the bubbles and my compliment has Shanice forcefully, kissing me. She is the aggressor in this moment of passion and doesn't want me to take control. I try to push her onto the sofa. But with her solid legs she manages to stand firm. So I judo flip the Haitian and start undressing her while she lies on the sofa. I notice that she isn't wearing any knickers as I slip her dress off.

Shanice has very little to offer in the tit department but I'm really only interested in her magnificent, round, arse. I kiss her lips for a bit then have a lick and taste of her pussy. She spins around and sticks out her arse so I can kiss and lick each cheek. I lick her pussy from the rear. With emergency condom on, I enter her dripping vagina from the rear slowly, as requested. While I'm fucking her, I pull and yank her weave as if she were a pony. She can feel it when I cum which leads to her a groaning to a climax.

In the après sex moment, Shanice looks at me almost in shock. " I thought you English were conservative and unadventurous in bed," she says smiling.

"Don't believe the hype," I reply, pulling my pants back on.

"Well I won't because you know how to get down baby." She gets up and puts some music on, to add to the ambience.

"What the fuck's this?" I ask, as REM blasts out of the speakers.

"REM."

"Yea I know what it is, but why are you listening to it?"

"I like it," she says defensively.

"I was expecting you to throw on some Rn'B or Hip Hop or maybe some cool soul, you know maybe some Marvin or Stevie."

"Don't believe the hype, baby," she says, flicking her index finger off the end of my nose as I grimace.

"Ok, I'm impressed that your music taste is eclectic," I tell her, sitting up on the couch. "But if you like REM, I recommend you start listening to The Smiths."

"The Smiths? I don't know them." Initially, I am shocked, then I remember Shanice is only 22 and there can't be too many African-American birds or Haitians for that matter at that age who listen to the Smiths.

"I'm gonna write that down and get me a Smith's album tomorrow." I'm very impressed by her urgency and willingness to try something new. "Is there a particular CD, I should look for?" she says getting a pen and paper.

"Check out '*The Singles*,' it has their best stuff on it and will show you what they are all about."

I leave the Valley for rehearsals in the morning with a packed-lunch of the food that Shanice cooked last night, which we didn't touch. She has intricately rolled me enough fajitas to feed the band during our lunch break.

Nigel is in an upbeat mood, as he has learnt the words to my songs. We will be performing them for the first time at our next gig on Friday. That will be the penultimate gig, as I plan to leave the band after Saturday's performance.

After speaking with Francesca, I phone Pamela again from a pay phone to make sure she's okay. I start to worry as I get her voice mail again. To be on the safe side, I don't leave my contact details in the message. My thoughts are of Pamela being bludgeoned to death by Creole and his crew.

At the Friday gig, my songs are well received by the student crowd with a rapturous applause, especially *'The Cybil Shepherd'*. Nigel should be on cloud nine, as he performed the songs to perfection in his own idiosyncratic style. After the gig, he pulls me into a back room.

"Shut the door behind you please, Richard," Nigel says, agitated. "I bought you in here to tell you that I'm leaving the band, which basically means Metamorphosis is finished."

I should be really pissed off with this news, but as I was going to announce my departure the following night, I am relieved.

"Why? What's wrong?" I ask, pretending to be upset.

"It's nothing to do with you, Manchester or Patrick," he tells me, pacing. "It's Pretty Boy; I can no longer work with him."

"Why? What's he done?"

"Pretty Boy and my fiancé are having an affair. The pretty bastard is fucking my fiancé, man!" he says through clenched teeth, running his hands through his hair.

So that was who Pretty Boy's secret date was with. "Well Nigel, I don't know what to say"

"You don't have to say anything. I can only say sorry to you, Patrick and Manchester," he says with a lump in his throat.   "For the inconvenience I will compensate you, of course."

"Ok, do you want me to tell them now or later?" I ask.

"Please Richard, please. I would like it done quietly. I have put the money I owe you all in this package here," he says handing me a brown envelope. "It's cash for ten gigs. That should make up for the inconvenience." That's a right touch, and it has saved me a hell of a lot of hassle! Fortuitously for me Nigel's stunner has led to the break up the band, a la Yoko Ono and Nancy Sprungen.

Later at the Orbit Hostel, I break the news to the rest of the guys. Pretty Boy shows little remorse for his selfish actions. I obviously don't give a shit, but Manchester and Patrick are gutted, until I tell them about the severance package Nigel has given us. It works out to be over $2000 each.

"I don't know about you guys, but this spells the end of my stay in LA," I announce. "I'm moving on to San Diego on Sunday."

"Eh man, that will be perfect for me, man," says Manchester.

"Whatever, I'm with you, Rich," says Patrick.

We all look at Pretty Boy. "Sounds good, but I have met the girl of my dreams. It all depends on what happens with her. I guess I will knock around here for a week or so in the meantime."

On our last night, we talk our way into a club on La Brea called the Garden of Eden. I dance night away with a petite, school teacher from Palm Springs called Missy, Pretty Boy and Patrick have teamed up and pulled two naive wannabe actress/models, and Manchester is grinding on the dance floor with a Malaysian bird. In all, it's the perfect way to spend our last night in Los Angeles.

> **Garden of Eden**
> **7080 Hollywood Blvd,**
> **Entrance on La Brea**
> **Los Angeles,**
> **CA 90028**
> **Great end to a great stay in a great city.**

We all leave the club empty-handed apart from Manchester, who is trying to coax the Malaysian back to the hostel. While the rest of us wait to see if the big Manc can use his Salford charm to persuade the young Malaysian, the two wannabe actresses that Pretty Boy and Patrick were talking to come out of the club.

"Hey girls, where are you going?" asks Patrick.

"We've got a party at the Hyatt to go to. Some model from Paris is throwing it," replies one of the wannabes.

"Can we come with ya?" asks Pretty Boy.

"I don't see why not," one says, looking at the other. "But if your not allowed in, it's not our fault, all right?"

"All right!" we all say in unison. All roads lead to the Hyatt on Sunset. We get in without any problems. The only problem is the Malay bird that Manchester bought along; she was doing our heads in, continuously whining about being bought to a hotel room.

The party is in two deluxe rooms next-door to each other and full of the most beautiful models you will ever see; both male and female. The four of us look like pieces of coal in a bag of platinum. We stick out like sore thumbs, not only in the way we look, but in the way we're acting, as we are all pissed out of our heads and high as kites.

I don't take any more of the cocaine Patrick has bought out with him, but I have visions of The V-Bar in Vegas, as he and Pretty Boy escort the two try-hard, wannabes into the bathroom for a few lines and whatever else comes with it.

I get talking to a striking model from Bratislava with chiselled high cheek bones named Christina. Her English is pretty bad so our conversation is limited to a simple introduction. In fact most, if not all of the models here are from Europe.

I glance over at Manchester, who is trying to get his tongue down the Malaysians throat, but she isn't having it.

Making conversation with these models is proving difficult, as their goods looks are not supplemented with matching personalities.

Manchester, with the Malaysian on his arm, announces to me that he and his new girl are leaving. I guess the shy Malay didn't want an audience, and would rather accept the Mancunians advances behind closed doors.

Finally the bathroom four return with smiles. It's amazing what a bit of coke can get you these days. With Manchester gone and the other two occupied with their coke hungry models, I start feel a bit out of sorts and out of place. I can't be arsed to get a taxi home so I find a nice spot on one of the beds and crash.

I am awoken by Patrick pouring water over my head at 7:00 am. Normally I would have knocked him out for this stunt, but he only did it because the Arsenal/Chelsea game is about to kick off on the TV. What a touch, I can't believe it. We had agreed earlier that we would just catch the result in the morning, as we had no intention of ending up at this EuroTrash Party.

I notice that the room is empty apart from us, the wannabes, and the gorgeous, Parisian model who threw the party. I make myself known to her in my semi-conscious state.

"Hi, my name's Ester," she says with a soft French accent. "You come from London also?"

"Er yea, er.. great party." I say wiping water of my face "Did you have a good night?"

"No it was shit," she says, sounding like she's sneezing. "Those are not my friends, I hate those bitches."

"Oh," I say, taken aback.

"Yes I kicked them out two hours before." Hold on a minute, if this spoilt French bird had a tantrum and fucked everyone off, how the hell did we survive her Gaelic wrath? Easy, Patrick sorted her out with a couple of lines.

"Your friend tells to me that you are supporters of Arsenal, no?"

"Err… Yes of course, for sure." I reply trying to remain composed from the shock of the hearing the word 'Arsenal' coming from the stunning model's mouth.

"Yes in France, everybody is liking Arsenal because of the French players," she beams.

"Yea and she kicked those other mugs out so that we could watch the game in peace," adds Patrick, returning from the bathroom.

"Yes, I would prefer it if I watch football," she says, taking a seat on the bed beside us.

It's funny, wherever you are in the world; you watch English football in the strangest of places with the strangest people, but I reckon this situation will take some beating. The wannabes and Pretty Boy are honorary Gooners for the afternoon, well for the morning if you like here in LA. Pretty Boy of course hates Arsenal, but he hates Chelsea even more. Like me he has many friends, back home who are Chelsea fans.

Growing up in West London, I was naturally surrounded by mouthy Chelsea fans. I even stood on the shed with them a few times. Although the atmosphere at the White Wall of the shed was fantastic in those days, I couldn't bear standing shoulder to shoulder with those Arsenal-hating, flash cunts. In addition to that some Chelsea fans in the early eighties were known to have had links to the very far right. Of course they were not the only club targeted by the National Front, who saw the terraces as the ideal place to get their ignorant, fascist views aired, but Chelsea were on my doorstep so I saw becoming an Arsenal fan as an ideal form of rebellion.

Pretty Boy decides not to watch the game. Instead he takes the two waifs, who have no interest in this mouth-watering London Derby to the other room.

With five minutes gone, Arsenal get a free kick just outside the box. Henry and Edu stand over the ball. Edu shoots at goal; the ball deflects off Parlour's leg en-route into the bottom corner of the net. Parlour wheels away in celebration as if he meant it. Only the likes of Pele (not the Romford form) in his prime would have had the speed of thought or the audacity to score a goal of that calibre but anyway its 1-0 Arsenal.

Patrick and I jump up and down in a celebratory huddle. Even the young Parisian model joins in the celebrations. She sings *Allez Arsenal, Allez*

Arsenal. It doesn't sound quite right coming out of her cute French mouth, but I am just as happy to see her supporting Arsenal, as I was Eileen and the Malibu crew.

Three minutes later Chelsea are level. Crespo's equaliser, an unstoppable curling shot, out of the blue, stuns us into a silence, even the Parisian, who hasn't stopped yapping since she took those lines, is muted by the Argentine's wonder goal. I have visions of Francesca while her compatriot celebrates in front of the North bank.

Fuck! Its only just gone seven and I am not an alcoholic yet, so I pass on the scotch Patrick has poured me, even though Chelsea are getting more and more into the game, and I fear that Hasselbaink (the annual tormentor of Arsenal) will send a 25 yard thunderbolt passed Lehmann.

After the break Arsenal are running the show. Bergkamp, who has replaced the ineffective Wiltord is linking up well with the other two Gaelic stars- Henry and Pires, who is having a great game. That goal at Anfield seems to have given the maverick Frenchman a new lease of life.

The young French model is engulfed in the atmosphere of the tense London derby and with the nervous tension Patrick and I are generating.

Ester moved here from Paris. She is only in LA for a fortnight, as she is based in New York with the Elite Model agency. She, like the rest of us, is begging for an Arsenal winner as the game moves into its last quarter. And of course it's two of her compatriots who combine to get it.

Pires flies down the right but his low cross goes straight into the arms of Chelsea keeper. However, luck is on our side as Cudicini makes a complete hash of it and lets the ball run through his arms and legs. The ball hits the on rushing Henry and then the back of net. 2-1 Arsenal, it finishes.

We sing a song that we're more accustomed to when playing Chelsea; *'One Team in London, There's only One team in London'* Ester learns the words and joins in.

SAN DIEGO,
19 October 2003

Manchester, Patrick and I, minus Pretty Boy who stayed behind in LA with Nigel's ex girlfriend, take the Greyhound bus for the three-hour trip down Interstate 5 to San Diego.

We want to be by the sea, so after a quick browse through the Lonely Planet we decide to stay at The Banana Beach Bungalow on Mission Beach. An Irish bird with fit legs and beautiful eyes, but a hanging, stretch-marked gut that flops over her jean mini skirt stands at reception with a Staffordshire bullterrier sitting at her side.

"How long are you guys staying?" she asks in a throaty, Dublin accent.

"Probably five nights," I reply.

"I bet you $20 you're here longer that," she replies, looking at our passports.

"OK you're on."

"If you that confident, why not make it a hundred?" she jokes.

Our room is a bit of a dump in all honesty, and it's nowhere near as clean as the rooms its sister hostel, the Orbit on Melrose. The only things they have in common are the metal bed frames. It has three bunk beds so that means we have to share with a few strangers. Patrick is above Manchester and I am bunked above an English girl, who looks like a real life version of the cartoon character, Pippi Long Stockings. Her name is Peggy; from somewhere in Wiltshire. She is one of those annoying travellers you meet who have been to everywhere you have been and beyond.

This hostel may be a shit-hole but it's in a great location; there's a deck that backs onto Mission Beach and Hooters is next door, where we are now having lunch.

"I'm leaving by Friday, I'm not giving fatty $20," says Patrick, polishing off a burger.

"She not that fat," I reply in her defence.

"Yea I suppose it's just that gut," he murmurs. "I guess some girls are bigger than others." That calls for some music. It's time to put some music on.

The jukebox selection isn't as grand as the one in Monterey, which instantly reminds me of Pamela. Shit, I better call her, see if she is all right.

There is still no answer on her mobile and I'm starting to get those visions of her lying on her kitchen floor, hacked to pieces by Creole and his hit men again.

I rejoin the others at our table; Peggy has now joined us for our lunch, and as I thought, she has taken a liking to Patrick.

Patrick's insulting style is like that of the Millwall Boys and it is irresistible to Peggy, who laughs at the onslaught of jokes and friendly abuse aimed in her direction.

Manchester is drum tapping his way through the songs that precede the tunes I have chosen (a commercial collection of Bon Jovi and Bryan Adams songs). He has been in an up beat mood since he spent the night that Malaysian bird he left with at that party in the Hyatt. Unfortunately for him though, there are not as many Asian birds here as there are in LA and a lot less than San Francisco.

"Fuck, she had soft skin, man," Manchester says reminiscing about his night with the Malaysian. "She was well supple too man." He says flicking his fingers Manchester and Caribbean style.

Thank fuck that those of Bon-Jovi and Bryan Adams tunes are over, they were doing my nut in.

The first song I have put on is *"All Along The Watch Tower"* by Jimmi Hendrix. I love Bob Dillon, he is a poetic genius, but this rendition of the song, absolutely smoked Dillon's slower paced, friendlier, original version. I am a supporter of the adage 'if it's not broken then, don't try and fix it, but Hendrix fixes it and a then some.

The music and Manchester's love-struck mood inspire me to call Francesca.

"Hey baby!" she answers, happy to hear my voice.

I grin like the Cheshire cat from Alice in Wonderland. "I was just calling to see how you're doing and where you are," I say, trying to play it cool.

"I'm so glad you called. I'm still in Palm Springs, finishing up some stuff here. I'll be in San Diego next Saturday, staying at a hotel downtown. Do you have a new girlfriend yet?" she asks coquettishly.

"Nah, we only just got here and haven't had time to get into trouble," I tell her, still smiling.

"Well, enjoy the sights and I'll see you next weekend," she says laughing as we hang up. I join the others back at our table.

"Walk This Way" by Run DMC is another cover but this one actually contains the vocals and the riffs from Aerosmith. In fact there isn't much to choose between this and Aerosmiths 1976 effort.

The last song of my selection is not a remake or hasn't been covered, as far as I know. It's Hendrix again, *"The Wind Cries Mary."* I would like to have mixed it up a bit, but this juke box isn't the best, besides it beats Bon Jovi and Bryan Adams any day of the week. The Hendrix ballad sends me into a daydream.

I dream of meeting Francesca, wearing those tight Bananrama pedal pushers she wore in San Francisco and a shirt elevated by her perky breasts. You definitely would see the happiness walking down the street.

We all leave before my last song comes on, *"Rotterdam"* by the Beautiful South. I break from the others and go for a short refreshing, walk alone along Mission Beach before getting back to the hostel. I'm glad to walk back alone so that I can collect my thoughts. I need sanctuary to reflect on this erratic journey, the unpredictable Francesca and Arsenals forthcoming fixtures which include a very tricky Champion's league tie in Kiev, and the North London Derby at Highbury.

I take in the sites and sounds of this beautiful beach community as I stroll back to the Hostel.

I meet with Patrick and Manchester on the deck of the Banana Bungalow, which faces Mission Beach. Peggy is still hovering, and boring us to death with her tales of backpacking through Australia and New Zealand. Thank fuck my trip there a few years back wasn't that boring.

We are sitting on the deck people watching. It's a different ball game down here compared to Venice Beach. Not many freaks and weirdo's down here. It has a more conservative, laid back feel to it, with surf dudes, sporting six-packs and gorgeous girls, looking faultless in their bikinis. The people here are blonde and beautiful, but the more you see them they become dull and dutiful.

We spend the early part of the evening playing pool at The Open Bar on Mission Boulevard just a stone's throw from the Banana bungalow. Two girls from the hostel have joined us; an Italian American from Brooklyn named Rita and a freckle-faced, mousey blonde with a boyish figure from St Louis, named Kathy. Her figure looks even straighter when standing next to Rita, who has those Italian child bearing hips.

I am playing pool against Rita, in what is my first game in over five years. She is giving me a pasting. I still have six balls on the table to her one. So in desperation, I snooker her by softly placing the white behind one of my balls. "You son of bitch," exclaims Rita, playfully pushing me. "You can't do that!"

"Of course I can," looking at the table.

"That's playing dirty, man," she accuses, grabbing the white ball off the table. "You can't shoot pool like that, man"

"What do you mean? It's a snooker," I say defensively, holding out my hand for the ball.

"A what?" she says, wrinkling her face, handing back the ball.

It's funny, all over London, never mind the world, there always seems to be different rules for the game of pool. However, these rules normally only differ when shooting for the black, or on a foul shot. However, I have never had anyone call foul play on me for snookering them.

Rita is so disgusted with my shot, that she returns the white ball to the spot it was before I took my shot that snookered her and orders me to retake my shot.

After a few more games, I notice that the bar is filling up and the music is getting louder. Monday night is Hip Hop night at the Open Bar, and this has brought a mixed crowd of baggy clothed African-Americans and Caucasians.

The Hip Hop music here is to my liking; the DJ is spinning old school tunes from the late eighties and early nineties. Music from Run DMC, Public Enemy, Beastie Boys, LL Cool J and Erick B and Rakim- the Def Jam era; what a great time that was for Hip Hop! I believe that these artists (the first real Rap superstars) shaped the Hip Hop genre for the impending lucrative Rap generation that followed.

Patrick, Manchester and I are grooving on the dance floor, singing every song word for word. I'm surprised Manchester knows all this stuff. He tells me that Mosside, Longsite and Salford had a great Hip Hop scenes back in the day.

Erik B and Rakim's *"Paid in Full"* is followed by *"California Love,"* which gets us off the packed dance floor and to the bar for a well-deserved drink. Manchester buys a round of double Sambucas and tequilas all around.

Peggy has now joined the fold, but looks slightly out of place with her pale skin and hippy clothes. I buy her a drink all the same and try to make small talk with her, but can't seem to keep a simple conversation going for longer than two questions, as she is hell bent on telling me about her travels in Asia and just starts nattering on about it out of the blue. Peggy now sees me as her best friend since she is being completely ignored by Patrick, who is chatting up Barbie dolls with Manchester as his wing command.

Thankfully, Peggy and I are joined by Rita and Kathy. The two met at the Banana Bungalow a fortnight ago and have both handed over $20 to the fat Irish bird who's on the hostel reception.

I fancy my chances with any of the three, but I think Kathy from St. Louis, is the one to go for. Rita would the obvious choice with her voluptuous curves and full breasts, but her attitude is not right. She is too aggressively opinionated for my liking.

Kathy is slimmer and straighter than the birds I would normally go for, but she has a pretty face, sparkling eyes, and has this cute mild stutter, that makes her eyes close when she has a word block. Once the word comes out, her sparkling eyes open again. I ask Kathy about her life in St. Louis and what has made her travel.

"My ex-boyfriend had a secret," she stutters lightly. "He invited me to be his guest on the Ricki Lake Show."

"Shit, tell me more," I encourage her, leaning in for the story.

"Well, I enter the stage joining him and Ricki. When I sit down, he grabs my hand and tells me that he loves me, you know the normal thing," she pauses to take a drink. "Have you ever seen that show?"

"Err yeah sure, now and then, like," I say, wanting her to continue.

"Yea, then Ricki encourages my boyfriend to spit it out so he turns to me, still holding my hand

and tells me that he is having an affair with my mom and dad."

"Mum and Dad!?" I yell, jolting backwards "Fuck off that's got to be bullshit!"

"Yea, my dad liked to watch and jerk off while my ex screwed my mom. Pretty weird, huh?" she says nonchalantly.

"Yea just a bit," I reply shaking my head in disbelief. "It's fucking unbelievable," I utter, wondering what the Millwall Boys would think of this.

"Look, I gotta go to the bathroom," she says, suddenly tearful. As soon as Kathy leaves, Peggy starts blathering on about her travels in Southeast Asia again. I welcome back Kathy before Peggy gets to the part where she left the floating market of Bangkok, and offer to buy her a drink.

I hand Kathy her Corona and as she squeezes the quarter lime into the bottle she looks at me and smiles, "I was just kidding about that story, hey."

"So it was all a load of bullshit?"

"Not exactly," she slowly says, smiling. "What I didn't tell you was that they asked me to join in."

"Nooooo, come on," I utter, as my jaw drops then she throws her head back laughing.

"No, it's all a joke," she says giggling. I join in with a chuckle, but I'm still a bit shocked. I have a great sense of humour, but I have never heard of a girl joke about her family in such a way.

Manchester and Patrick return empty handed from their "Blonde Ambition" tour. Patrick is unaware that I have plans for Kathy and immediately hits on her. Fair enough. Manchester is giving Rita from Brooklyn a lesson in Northern and showing her some magic tricks he knows. That leaves me with Peggy. I sigh, but I may as well give her stories a chance. I get myself a double scotch first.

I down the scotch pull Peggy to the dance floor to save myself from her story about having a quiet night in on full moon party night in Koh Panang.

The DJ is playing a set of West Coast Hip Hop classics. *"Nothing but a G thang"* by Dre and Snoop Dog is one of my favourite tunes of that era. I can't control my feet and I get my groove on. As expected, Peggy is an even worse dancer than the kangaroo hopping, Cindy Lauper look-alike at Club Rah in Vegas. No feet, no hips, no shoulders, no rhythm. To save face, I offer to buy her a drink in order to get her off the dance floor.

"Oh great," she says. "I'll be right here," and continues with some sort of hippy flowing arm movements.

"Ahh no," I say, grabbing one of her hands out of the air, "Come with me and tell about that night in Koh Panang" I demand pulling her towards the bar. "Okay cool," she says stumbling after me. "In this small village where our huts were they had this dog, right, that would chase its own tail, I tell you it was so funny." I look at her, give her a fake smile and then look over at the dance floor where

Patrick and Manchester are tonguing Kathy and Rita, respectively, showing their intentions. Great! The foursome soon join us at the bar. "Why don't we all go down to the beach?" Manchester suggests.

> **The Open Bar**
> 4302 Mission Blvd.
> San Diego,
> CA 92109
> (858) 270-3221
> You can't get snookered behind the black, but you can have more than two shots of whatever you want.

"Cool but we'll go back and get our guitars first," says Rita. We all head out of the Open Bar and back to the Banana Bungalow for the beach essentials.

The all-American girls get their guitars and Manchester brings some of the drinks we have amassed over the few weeks of hostel hopping. The six of us sit in a semi-circle, each with a beer as Patrick cracks a few jokes. Manchester opens a bottle of tequila, which we all take a swig of, and then chase it with a beer. Maybe when the tequila is finished we can play spin the bottle, then I can be paired with one of the Americans and get rid of Peggy.

Rita finishes her beer and plays the chords to *'No Women No Cry'* and sings with Kathy. They have great voices and we are all impressed.

"Hey man, you guys would have made great backing singers for "The Metamorphosis," says Manchester, putting his arm around Rita.

"The Metamorphosis? What's that?" she asks, snatching the tequila from him.

"Isn't that something to do with plants and stuff?" inquires Kathy.

"No that's photosynthesis," states Peggy informatively "Metamorphosis is a biological process by which an animal physically develops after birth or hatching, inv…"

"Ok Peggy, well done," I say interrupting the swotty geek, putting my hand on her shoulder. "The Metamorphosis that was our band in LA," Manchester says proudly.

"Hey you guys were a band?" Kathy asks, looking at Patrick. "No way!"

"Hey can you guys play a song?" Rita asks, holding the guitar out to anyone of us who is willing take it.

"No, our singer isn't here," says Patrick, while taking a fag out of his mouth. "He split the band up, cause of his slag of a bird, the fucking wanker"

"So what did you play?" Kathy asks him.

"The horns, you know sax and trombone," he replies modestly.

"Very sexy," purrs Kathy, as she kisses him.

"What about you Manchester?" Rita enquires, looking at him. "You look like a mad drummer."

"Yea that's right, I was the master banger, I can bang all night me." While the group laugh at Manchester's obvious pun. I pick up one of the guitars. Sticking with the Bob Marley theme, I play the bass chords of *"Redemption Song."*

"So you're the bass player of the group I take it," says Rita, strumming the guitar riff to the song. After the fourth bar, Kathy sings the opening verse.

The scene couldn't be better; three Englishmen with two American birds and one English, rag-doll looking traveller, sitting in a semi-circle performing an unplugged version of Bob Marley's *"Redemption Song,"* while the waves crash onto a moonlit Pacific Beach.

It's a warm night for this time of year, even for southern California. Patrick and Manchester take advantage of the climate and the cool moment that just past and lead Kathy and Rita to a far part of the beach, beyond an over-turned dingy. That leaves me with Peggy and her audio travel memoirs.

"So I was telling you about that dog in that village on Koh-Panang," Peggy immediately starts babbling, killing the moment.

I feel as though I've been somewhat short-changed by the whole affair. Patrick and Manchester are rolling around in the Californian sand with two young American backpackers, while I'm stuck with a plain, swotty geek from Wiltshire.

"So we were getting a bit bored with this dog, chasing its own tale," continues Peggy, oblivious to the fact that I'm not even paying attention to her. "So we threw it a few magic mushrooms. You should have seen the way it was tripping man, it was hilarious." This conversation is getting a whole lot better as Peggy is out drinking me two to one.

"The village also had this cat right, that was as big as the dog. It was so big we called it 'Dog'. It was fucking funny because the dog was getting frisky with the cat. The dog was a male and the cat was a female, I think."

That last part breaks a chuckle out of me. The image of a randy dog mounting a pissed off cat floods my mind while I crack open another two Budweiser's and hand one of them to Peggy. She continues with the now very quite interesting, transcending story.

"A guy from the camp had some Viagra he bought from a couple of locals in Hat Rin," she slurs, taking a long swig of beer. "We had already given the big cat a couple of magic mushrooms. Then we slipped the dog the Viagra pill cunningly encapsulated inside a chunk of chicken. Then! I tell you, this was the funniest thing I've ever seen." She stops suddenly, pointing at me, "Have you ever seen a dog with an erection?"

Haven't we all seen a dog with a boner, or a couple of dogs shagging in the park and then getting stuck together?

"Yea, it's pink," I reply, "and looks like a savaloy, doesn't it?"

"Ha ha haaaa! Yea something like that, but this dog had an enormous prick, due to the Viagra. And he was rampant!" she says laughing. "It was so funny! The dog kept trying to mount the cat but kept falling off it and everything." Peggy and

I are rolling on the sand in our drunken states, laughing uncontrollably, trying not to spill our beers.

When our giggles subside, she continues, "The cat eventually ran off in fear of getting rodgered to death by that big pink thing." This set us off in another volley of laughter.

"The dog gave up the chase, because the cat was too fast for him," she says, taking off her glasses and wiping her eyes, "And then, don't laugh, the dog collapsed! Ha Haaa!" she laughs hysterically. "The fucking thing dropped dead right in front of us. It was so funny."

I should stop laughing, as the story has a bit of a sad ending, but being drunk I can't help myself.

"Wasn't that a funny story?" asks Peggy, looking for adulation. She leans closer trying to kiss me but I avoid her advances by turning around and grabbing two beers that are behind me. When I hand her a beer she attempts to kiss me again. This time she succeeds and we are kissing. Although she looks like a cross between Jemima from playschool and Pippi Long Stockings, Peggy has a hell of a body buried under her baggy hippy clothes. She must have obtained this sporty body while playing hockey for her public school or horse riding in the Wiltshire countryside.

The next thing I know I am lying on the sand with Peggy looking at me lecherously.

"Hey Rich, did you have sweet dreams?" she asks, smiling at me seductively.

"Huh! What, What happened?" I sit up quickly.

"Ahh, you just fell asleep that's all, darling," she says cunningly. Fell asleep?! Darling?! What the fuck happened? Don't tell me Peggy and I... no way! Surely I would have remembered.

I don't think I should ask whether we did or not. That is the last thing a guy should say to girl or vice versa. I slyly feel my dick. It doesn't seem like I have had sex. I look over at Peggy who is sitting there with nothing but a T-shirt on. She has no reservations about exposing her pussy to me. Her cunt is the hairiest thing I have ever seen, never been shaved it would seem. I am not a massive fan of these hairy muffs, the kind that you would normally associate with a German bird in a seventies Porno flick.

Peggy gets up to light herself a cigarette. I get up to get myself together and head back to the hostel. As I do, I start to feel an uncomfortable, ticklish feeling at the back of my throat. I start to cough and cannot stop. Peggy hands me a beer. After a few mouthfuls, the coughing fit has stopped but I can still feel something stuck at the back of my throat.

"Ahh you poor thing, are you ok?" Peggy asks, downing her beer in one. That must have been one beer too many for her. "Oh shit, I think I'm going to be sick," she slurs, bending over and falling into the sand. I put down the beers and help her up. She looks at me with a half-closed eye, slack-jaw drunk stare that you get when you have had too much to drink and are about to puke.

"You're a right fit bloke, you are," she slurs, then turns around and vomits onto the sand. I catch her as she drops to her knees and continues to puke. Lovely, I think to myself as I do the gentleman thing and hold her hair. Surprisingly, she doesn't cry or carry on like most people do when their guts are turning inside out. Instead, after she finishes, she cracks open a another beer, takes a long swig, strips off her t-shirt and runs towards the Pacific. "Are you coming to join me Richard?"

"Ahh no thanks Peg, I'm not the best swimmer" I say in shock as I watch her pale body head towards the ocean.

I hear Patrick and Manchester fucking the two young American birds behind the upended boat, in the distance while I'm waiting for Peggy to come back. My thoughts turn to Francesca, and I look at the night sky wishing that we were together somewhere. Only a few more days now, I think to myself while I watch Peggy making her way back towards me.

The next morning, I dismount from my bunk at around 11am. A partially dressed Peggy sprawled out on her bed; star shaped is the only other person in the room. I walk quietly to the bathroom, so that she is not woken. That foreign body is still trapped at the back of my throat. I sneak back into the dorm in order to borrow some of Peggy's Oraldene mouthwash.

In the communion bathroom, I gargle with vigour, not once but twice. But still no sign of whatever it is at the back of my throat coming out. It feels a bit like a pubic hair has tangled itself around my tonsils. No it can't be. I didn't, did I? Or did I? Oh fuck!

Fucking hairy muffs, the fucking things should be outlawed. If I ruled the world or if I were at least the Health Secretary, I would make a Brazilian wax free on the NHS. Then if that didn't work I would make it compulsory.

My plan is to head to an Irish bar down town that shows English football, as Arsenal are playing in Kiev this morning. First, I stop off at a coffee house called The Seaside Cantina. I could have gone to Starbucks, but I remember Kathy telling me something about fair-trade in Latin America last night and that I must boycott Starbucks.

I order a freshly baked cinnamon roll and a large latte. I take it to a table outside, in order to watch the ocean while in the foreground locals jog, rollerblade, and skateboard in front of me. In the meantime I think of Francesca and what she is doing.

My thoughts then switch to Pamela. I try to call her. There's still no answer on Pamela's phone so I leave yet another message. My concerns for her well-being are increasing. I then call Francesca, who tells me that she will definitely be in San

Diego in two days. That means tonight will have to be a mad one!

The pub that I need to get to is called the Shakespeare. Its downtown, which means I will have to get to a bus in order to see if Arsenal can gain a much needed Champions win against Dynamo Kiev.

I ask the young overweight, Hispanic waitress where I can catch the bus downtown.

"It's very easy," she tells me, putting a hand on one of her large hips. "Take either the Number 2 or Number 5 bus, I think, on Mission Boulevard, next block." She points the direction I'm supposed to go.

"I need to get to the Shakespeare Pub, do you know it?"

"No I don't, I'm sorry," she smiles. "But I'm sure you will find it downtown."

"Are you gonna watch the soccer, man?" asks a masculine, croaky voice behind me.

Seaside Cantina
(formerly The Mission
2 Cafe)
4111 Ocean Blvd. (the
boardwalk)
Pacific Beach
San Diego, CA 92109
858-273-0775
Fair-trade coffee.

"Yea, I want to watch the Arsenal game," I say, turning around. The voice belongs to a grey, bearded guy in his sixties who looks like a retired Art teacher.

"Hey you should go to a bar called Costa Brava. They show all the soccer games there."

"Cool, how far is that?" I ask eagerly.

"It just five or six blocks up Garret Ave, you can walk," he says, turning back to his coffee and paper.

More like 10 blocks, fucking hippy! I finally get there and join fifteen or so Spaniards and Mexicans watching the Real Madrid game. Fucking hell. What chance do I have of turning the channel to watch the Arsenal game in Spanish restaurant full of Latinos? None.

Desperate, I ask the bartender if there is another TV, where I can watch the Arsenal game. The answer is no. So, I am forced to watch Real's game against Partizan Belgrade and spend over $40 on tapas and drinks in the process. I hope those fucking flash, over paid Galactico cunts of Real Madrid lose.

Before I've poured myself a glass of sangria, a goal flash reveals that Maksim Shatskikh has put Kiev ahead. I down it, and quickly pour myself a second one. Then to make matters worse, Raul puts Real Madrid one up. The Spaniards go wild and the bar erupts. Oh well, at least the Tortilla España here isn't bad.

There are no further goals in Madrid or in Kiev as half time approaches. I try calling Pamela again, but still no answer. If she has been killed by Creole, then surely her phone would have turned itself off by now. Or is it just ringing her service provider? Alternatively, does Creole or the police have the cell and are tracking every call?

"Did you just use the phone, señor?" asks the waiter, coming over to my table.

"Er yes, why?" I ask, ready to bolt for the door at the first sign of trouble.

"Well there is somebody on the phone who wants to speak to you señor."

I nervously walk toward the phone not knowing what to expect.

"Hello?" I say sheepishly

"Hello, who is this?" Pamela's familiar voice asks. "You just called my cell?"

"PAMELA!" I yell, relief washing over me.

"Richard?"

"Thank God your, OK!" I gush.

"Why wouldn't I be?" she asks, laughing at my enthusiasm.

"No, it's just that I have been trying to call you for weeks," I say slightly embarrassed.

"I was in Chicago, checking on some property. But the question is when are you coming to see me, baby?"

"I would see you now, but hey, I'm in San Diego," I reply casually.

"That's a shame. But hey, If you come back to LA, I can make an excuse to come down to Santa Barbara," she says keeping things open. That sounds very tempting; I had a great time with her in Monterey and then on the Sur, she was a hell of a woman, but hey, Francesca is coming tomorrow.

To celebrate Francesca impending arrival, Pamela's well-being and to drown my sorrows over yet another disappointing night in Europe for Arsenal, I order a bottle of Segura Viuda Heredad Reserva, a sparkling Spanish Cava with a full delicate taste. It has *"power, character and delicacy,"* apparently. At least, that's what it says on the menu.

I am thankfully completely pissed as an unwelcome goal flash pops up on the bottom of the TV screen and reads that Bialkevich has put Kiev two to the good. I grab my bottle of Cava and walk out. The Real Madrid game was boring anyway; the camera was constantly on the hair flicking Beckham.

"Fucking Arsenal, bunch of wankers," I curse as I leave.

"Hey senor, you can not take bottle outside," the bartender says blocking the exit. Fair enough, I still have half a bottle left, nevertheless I polish it off in three minutes. As I hand the waiter the empty bottle and burp loudly, another goal flash reveals that Henry has pulled one back, but

Costa Brava
1653 Garnet Ave
San Diego, CA 92109
858-273-1218
www.costabravasd.com
Great place to watch football, but only if you support a Spanish team.

it's too little too late for the perennial Euro flops and the game ends in a 2-1 defeat for us. In an annoyed drunken state, I manage to get a taxi back to the hostel and pass out on my bunk for the rest of the day.

I awake from a dream. Cybil Shepherd and Kathleen Turner are having a catfight in the centre circle at Highbury, all because our love triangle has come to a head. It must be around 1986 as they are both in their prime and I'm standing on the North Bank Terrace, just like I would have done in the mid eighties. Suddenly Creole enters the pitch from the East stand player's tunnel, pulls out a revolver and shoots them both.

I am awoken by the distinctive voice of Manchester at around 6:00pm.

"Guess who's here," he says, as he walks into the dorm.

"Who?" I ask, rolling over to face him.

"Wait for it...drum roll...here he is!" Manchester steps to one side, and reveals Pretty Boy. The Plastic Cockney comes over to me and gives me a hug.

"What happened to you and Nigel's bird?" I ask patting his back.

"Ahhh, she was doing my head in after a while. She's used to the finer things in life, you know what I mean, the high life. That fucking cunt Nigel gave her everything she wanted and she wasn't getting fuck all from me, you know what I mean," he says, putting his back pack down.

"Didn't you even take her out, you tight bastard?" asks Manchester.

"Fuck that! All I had to offer was in my pants," He says grabbing his package.

"And that's not much" I joke.

Pretty Boy is not alone. He has travelled down from LA with a camp looking American, aptly named Kelly, who he met at the Orbit hostel in Hollywood.

Kelly, who is as gay as Tottenham are underachievers, fancies Pretty Boy something chronic. Pretty Boy is almost broke after blowing away most of his band money on booze, coke and probably on Nigel's girlfriend, despite what he says. Therefore, Kelly has funded the whole trip, but at what price I ask myself. If I didn't know him, I would say that Pretty Boy would be rent boy material and Kelly probably sucked Pretty Boy's little dick from downtown LA to Mission Beach.

Kelly is one of those queers who want the whole world to know about his sexual preference. He should save that for someone who gives a shit. I'm not a homo, obviously, nor am I homophobic, but I can't stand it when gay guys over publicise their homosexuality for effect, like the numerous pink-clad, cocker spaniel owning faggots in Sydney. I like the gays in London or New York, who are comfortable with their gay status, and just live their lives like the rest of the community.

"I've heard all about you bad boys," says Kelly in typical camp fashion, "being in a band and everything"

"Can you sing, Kelly?" I ask.

"Yea I'm a diva, can't you tell?" he says, jutting a hip.

"Well, we don't want any girls in our band, mate," Patrick says jokingly.

"Very funny," Kelly reacts sarcastically.

"We ain't gonna start that band again, are we?" asks Pretty Boy.

"In my dreams! Where the fuck are we gonna get the instruments? The Metamorphosis are over mate," I reply, jumping off my bunk.

"But it was fun while it lasted, wasn't it?" laughs Manchester, giving me a hi-five.

"Well you never know, maybe in México, eh."

Pretty Boy and Kelly, who are starving suggest that we go and get a feed. We take a short walk up Mission Boulevard to The Pacific Beach Bar & Grill. Tuesday is taco day at the Grill and they are on offer for $2. Together with the beer at happy hour prices, this makes for a great afternoon.

I fill Patrick in on the latest Arsenal Champion's league disappointment. He in turn fills me on the night he and Manchester had with Kathy and Rita on the beach. They were fucking them on the beach, and then Richard got his bag of MDMA out. They then paid for a room at a hooker motel across the street and shagged them all the way through to a late check out.

Fucking great, while he was sorting out the freckled, cute Yank, I was watching Arsenal being stuffed like chickens in Kiev.

While we are eating our cheap but tasty tacos the friendly muscle-bound, tanned bartender suggests we come back tonight. Pretty Boy agrees. "It's the best midweek night out in San Diego," he says assertively. I had forgotten about Pretty Boy and his unofficial travel guide.

"There's gonna be fanny everywhere!" he continues excitedly.

"Maybe there'll be some cock for me," says Kelly, looking flirtatiously at Pretty Boy.

A few hours later, we are in the queue about to re-enter the Grill. Pretty Boy's guide was spot on; there is fanny everywhere. Hundreds of what must be the best-looking girls I have ever seen surround us. Even Patrick, who is the most confident person around, is getting nervous.

"Shit! I can't believe this!" he exclaims, mesmerised by a stunning brunette who has just joined the queue.

He shouldn't be too overawed by the occasion otherwise he will be beaten before he enters the joint.

It's a bit like when a lesser team like West Ham or Fulham go to places like Old Trafford or Anfield. You have to go there full of confidence, believing that you can actually win; otherwise you get beaten and beaten badly. But go there with a bit of self-belief, and you could come away with something.

Patrick reaches in his pocket pulls out a cellophane bag that contains a dozen or so pills.

"Bumbles all round," he says, shaking the bag in our direction.

"What?" asks Kelly.

"Bumble bees."

"Bumble bees?" Kelly repeats bemusedly.

"Oh for fuck sake! Bumble bees! Es! You knob, Ecstasy pills!" Patrick clarifies. "Come on, sweetheart, get with it."

"I see," says Kelly, rolling his eyes. "Cool, I'm game."

The Pacific Bar & Grill on a night like this isn't the kind of place one would drop a pill; however Patrick sees this as the last opportunity to get rid of them. We will be crossing the border very soon, and taking pills into México is not an option. This is the last of Patrick's stash as he, Manchester and the all American Girls polished off the MDMA last night and his coke was all but finished at that model party at the Hyatt in LA.

I give Patrick an apprehensive look as he hands me a pill.

"Come on Rich. If I had coke I would have offered that out, but this is all I've got mate," he says putting a pill on the palm of my hand. "I tell ya, I gotta be on something tonight. Have you seen the birds around here?"

I am looking at the pill on the palm of my hand with slight disdain, when we leave the queue and walk to 7-eleven to get a couple bottles of water. Patrick's bag is now empty. I do not know how many E's the other guys have each taken, but I will only be having the one.

Last time I took a pill was about five years ago at Bagleys, this dive of a rave club in the back streets of Kings Cross. I ended up hitching a ride with these guys I didn't know from Adam to fucking Northampton! For no reason! I didn't get back to London until 11:00 pm the following evening.

This is my last night as an honorary singleton in California before Francesca arrives tomorrow and I intend to make it count. As I'm sure Francesca is getting a good send off from some rich cunt in Palm Springs.

Straight to the bar, Patrick buys the first round; a Budweiser and a shot of tequila each. The shot has gone straight to my libido aided by the E.

A healthy looking, sturdy, short brunette is giving me the eye, so I approach her with Pretty Boy in support. I give her a few quick lines that consist of a few compliments and few light insults (Millwall Style), which results in a tonguing session. I don't stay with sturdy girl much longer, as all she wants to do is shake her arse to shitty, commercial R&B. Fuck that!

That charming man, Pretty Boy, who can more or less get any girl he talks to, has made short work of her friend, and has left with her. Kelly looks on and is not best pleased; he storms off in tears. The pills have made him even more emotionally insecure than he already was. I guess that's the last we will see of him.

Patrick and Manchester are working on a set of very tall blondes, and doing well.

I get myself another drink, a double Jim Beam and diet coke and a glass of water, as I am starting to sweat profusely from the effects of the pill. I down the water and take a look around. As I take a sip of my short I see a familiar-looking Latino hombre approach the bar just a few feet away. I can't quite place his face then remember the night with Francesca and Gabrielle in San Francisco. It's Creole!

Grabbing my drink, I head off in the opposite direction, looking out for the boys. Maybe he hasn't seen me and hopefully he doesn't recognize me, although Francesca is sure he will.

Hold on a minute, maybe I am hallucinating. These are Patrick's pills after all; fuck knows what could be in them.

I take another look to where Creole is. He isn't there. I am relieved but feeling a bit edgy and sweating more than ever. I definitely shouldn't have taken that pill.

The Grill has a small dance floor behind the bar. I head there, and dance to the thumping bass tunes, in order to take my mind off things.

I think momentarily about Francesca and what the fuck she would do if Creole was here for real. I should finish my drink quickly and run back to the hostel, but the scotch and tequila has pulled rank over the pill, so I stay.

Out of nowhere, a classic Hip Hop tune comes on, *"So What Ya Saying"* by EPMD. I start to shake my arse on the dance floor. A stunner with an unusual bob hairdo is impressed with my moves. We dance for the rest of the song, while I keep an eye out for more images of Creole. Before the next song comes on, Patrick and Manchester join us with their tall birds. None of the girls we have met are Californian, despite their electric blonde hair and extra white teeth. My admirer, René, is from Nebraska, the other two are part of California's biggest ethnic group; they are from Wisconsin.

The mid-west and small town America is an unknown quantity to most Americans, let alone us drunken, high Englishmen. It is never in the movies, on MTV or featured on any cop show. The only time we ever hear the name of a town in the mid-west is in times of tragedy; *"Crazed lonely teenager walks into a school and guns down a dozen kids, and then himself,"* or in disaster; *"killer Kansas Tornado takes everything with it as it passes through Hoisington."*

To a girl from very small town Nebraska, meeting a guy from London is for her pretty much the same as meeting a guy from New York or LA; completely foreign. Mid-westerners seldom travel out of their state, never mind out of their country. So it should have been no great surprise to us when that waitress in Las Vegas couldn't differentiate between London, France and Europe.

The ultra-persuasive Patrick has organised a party for six at the Wisconsin birds' apartment. René, the Nebraskan has accepted the invitation. It's music to my ears! My head is filled with paranoia and doubt as a result of that pill. We get one more round of drinks in before we head for their apartment.

Pacific Bar and Grill
860 Garnet Ave.
San Diego,
CA 92109
858-272-4745
Set your stall out early,
get a good start and
you can enter and leave
before you have paid to
get in.

We have been at the bar for no more than an hour and all of us, with the exception of Kelly, have exceeded our expectations for the night. The six of us leave the Grill and jump into two cabs. It is not yet eleven and the bar has not started its cover charge.

The students' apartment is like a plush flat in Chelsea or the Docklands, with its wooden floors, flash funiture and all mod-cons.

The last student accomodation I went to was in Manchester.

When I met this slapper at a bar in Deans Gate the night before Arsenals semi-final victory over Sheffield UTD at Old Trafford last season. We ended up in her damp, shit hole of a house. There must have been at least six scummy, unwashed students living in the three-bedroom terrace. Here in San Diego, three students share this delightful three bedroom apartment containing a balcony with views.

I am feeling a lot more level-headed now as the effects of the ecsatcy pill is being flushed out of my system by drinking shit loads of water and constantly pissing. The other two are fine as they are seasoned drug takers, and the two pills they have taken would not have scratched the surface of their heavily contaminated bodies.

We all end up in the living area. One of the girls cracks open a bottle of red wine, while another puts some music on- *Dookie* a half decent Green Day album.

"Awe, not fucking Green Day!" shouts Patrick. He can't stand them. He thinks they are poor excuse for the Clash or any British punk band of that era and I agree.

"What's wrong with Green Day, man? I love them!" replies one of the giant Wisconsin girls.

"They're a Californian plastic punk band!" says Patrick.

The giant Wiscounsin jokingly squares up to Patrick. "Hey Buster, if you have a problem with Green Day, then you have a problem with me." Their noses almost touch.

"Well let's step outside and settle this dispute," suggests Patrick.

"Ok let's" she replies leading Patrick to her room.

Patrick was right; there are so many Californian punk bands that have emerged over the last fifteen years or so. I've always thought that punk music was about, frustration and rebellion. The Clash and The Pistols emerged from run down parts of urban London in a time of social, economic and racial turmoil in London. I just can't see what these Californian bands living in their Pleasantville Beach towns have got to be frustrated and angry about. Maybe they are frustrated that they are from clean cut beach towns and not inner city London slums, and have nothing to complain about.

Manchester continues with the musical conversation. "These fucking American bands are nothing man, nothing, compared to the greats of Manchester."

I love Manchester, everytime he gets drunk he has to talk proudly about his hometown. "So who are your greatest of the greats of Manchester?" I ask curiously.

"My favs," he starts, profoundly, "Are The Stone Roses, followed by The Monday's, and then The Charlatans man."

"What about the Smiths or Oasis?"

"The Smiths are legends, of course man, but Oasis are fucking dick-heads, man. At that audition, when their first drummer left, I fucking nailed the the audition, man, fucking nailed it, I did. I practiced my sequence for weeks. Nobody could've been better than me, nobody."

"Ahh, it just wasn't meant to be," says the remaining giant Wisconsin chick, trying to console the big Manc.

"Wasn't meant to be, my arse. I was the best and then to rub salt into the wound, they gave the spot to this fucking flash, Cockney bastard. Fucking joke man, they are supposed to be a bloody Manchester band," he says throwing his hands in the air. "So there's your answer, Richard, Oasis aren't even a Manchester band."

Manchester, obviously still bitter from his failed Oasis audition, slumps to the sofa with his head in his hands. Manchester maybe a seasoned drug taker but these pills must have found a way to fuck with the big man's emotions.

The friendly Wisconsin giant consoles him then escorts the dejected Manc to her room. Very forward, are these girls from the mid west. That leaves me alone with René.

René from Nebraska is clueless, she hasn't heard of any of the Manchester bands, that includes Oasis! But what she lacks in musical knowledge, she makes for in looks and sex appeal. A young Susan Sarandon with a crazy bob is the best way to describe her. I top up her glass with the red wine that remains.

René is a medical student who likes to surf. I love the sea but I am no surfer, however I do have an admiration for surfers. There's no better sight than watching a surfer glide through a tubular crest.

I can hear Manchester and Patrick going to town on their respective Wisconsin birds. It's something about hearing other people having sex that turns on whoever hears the noise, women, even more so. Rene is red-faced, but I can see that she is turned on by those screams straight out of the mid-west. I have been in this situation before, so I know what's going down, and what's going on down between her legs.

I take a step toward her and take the glass of wine from her hand. "There's no need to be embarrassed," I utter softly

"Who says I'm embarrassed?" she purrs caressing my face slowly and confidently with the back of her hand. I grab her fingers as they brush along my lips and kiss/suck them.

The groans from the rest of the apartment are getting louder and sounding, I guess more pleasurable. A mass onslaught of seduction is not required. I kiss Rene's full lips, this time harder and passionately, then rip her skimpy, sluttish looking top off. She tries to do the same to me, but these Lyle & Scott polo tops are quality, hand made and built to last. I take it off myself.

I put the handful of tit that she has into my mouth and suck with gusto. Then grab a handful of her hair and yank her head back, spinning her around. I behave like Michael Douglas in *Basic Instinct,* when the ageing, self-confessed sex addicts character rapidly fucks that psychologist up against the wall.

With one hand I grab and twist her hair, while the other is cupped over her vagina.

Patrick burst out of the bedroom in his boxers, dripping with sweat. He likes the look of what I'm doing and gets hard instantly.

Patrick doesn't give a shit about anyone or anything and pulls out his 12 incher, which almost chokes René when he sticks it in her mouth. She takes to it and licks it like a stick of Blackpool rock.

I can see that Patrick wants to swap positions, in our spit roast setting. René is willing so I make way for him. I take a leaf out of Patrick's book. I don't bother with putting my cock into Rene's mouth. Instead, I enter the room Patrick came out of, where a blond Amazonian from Wisconsin awaits. She is shocked as I am confident, but she soon gets the picture when she hears Patrick jack hammering René.

She yanks the covers open to revel her massive, naked frame. Her feet are almost hanging off the end of the bed. This is a massive turn-on for me, as I have never shagged a bird taller than 5ft 9" and have always wanted to fuck a female giant. She orders me to put a new condom on, and jump on. I obey orders and give it to her missionary, while pinning her down, to impose my authority. The Amazonian soon spins me over and gains the upper hand. She pins me to the mattress and rides the bollocks off me.

I awake the next morning with a thirst, squashed between the Amazonian's arm and body. I break free to get a drink of water from the kitchen. I get into the living room area, and find that neither Patrick or René are there. I quietly open the room where Manchester ended up; he is still there fast asleep with his 6ft Wisconsin giant. My presence wakes him. I signal with my head, to get him to join me in outside. In the kitchen, I fix him a glass of water and I tell him that I'm going to leave quietly.

"Hey don't leave me here, you Cockney bastard."

"What you talking about? If you stay you can fuck both of them," I say, trying to present a promising situation.

"Nah, I can't be arsed man. I've got a surf lesson on Mission Beach at noon."

I quickly get dressed, as my clothes are still on the sofa in the front room. But Manchester has to go back into the bedroom. He leaves the door slightly ajar and I can see him trying to get dressed quietly.

"Hey where are you going, baby?" the Wisconsin giant ask him, waking up.

"Oh, Richard and I thought that it would be a great idea if we went and got us some breakfast," he says, tucking his shirt into his pants.

"Oh that's so sweet of you. You English boys are great," she says drowsily falling back to sleep.

Back at the Hostel there is no sign of Patrick or Pretty Boy. I get some more sleep while Manchester puts on his full wet suit and heads for his maiden surf lesson.

Two hours later he wakes me up, by dripping his wet hair over me. In the two hours that have passed, Pretty Boy and Patrick have returned and are resting on their bunks.

Since I have known Pretty boy and Manchester, I haven't exactly been waxing lyrical about Francesca and they really have no idea how she makes me feel. After we share stories and jokes about last nights shenanigans, I give them a brief summary of the Richard and Francesca story thus far and then tell them that I will be staying with Francesca for about a week down town.

"I don't think I'm gonna stay around here much longer anyway," says Manchester.

"I haven't been here long and I'm thinking of moving on too," says, Pretty Boy.

"I'm looking to cross the border," adds Manchester, "maybe in a few days."

"I'm not sure when I will be in México , but I reckon it will be in no more than two weeks," I state.

"Hey what about New Order and Joy Division?" asks Patrick, returning from the communal showers.

"What!?" we all say in unison, staring at him bewildered.

"Last night I heard you lot having a discussion about who's the greatest ever band from Manchester."

"What, you were listening to us while you were shagging?" asks Manchester.

"Yea, you silly cunts were putting me off."

"I got to agree with him," I say looking in Manchester's direction. "Joy Division and New Order would be in my top three."

Manchester gives me and then the dripping Patrick a high five for the knowledge of his beloved hometown bands.

"So what about you Pat, what are you doing? Going to México, or are you staying here with me for a while?" I ask him.

"I'm going to stay here for a while. That René was georgeous. I'm going to hang about with her for a while," he says towelling off.

"Rene! Really?" I say, putting him on the back foot. "That Nebraskan Bird?"

"Yeah, you don't mind, do ya?" I don't give a fuck. Who am I to deny him? Besides it will be great having him close by, while I'm sorting out things with Francesca, especially now that I'm having hallucinogenic thoughts of being stalked by Creole.

The four of us conclude our plans; Manchester and Pretty Boy will cross the border tomorrow with the all American girls (Rita and Kathy) who are also enroute to México, Patrick and I will meet them in Ensenada in around a week or so.

I meet with Francesca at her downtown hotel, The Westgate, in the vibrant Gaslamp Quarter.

The Argentinian is looking gorgeous as ever, wearing tight jeans and a fitted white shirt. We are delighted to see each other. She gives me a run down of her tales in Palm Springs; she was hustling a real estate tycoon. She tells me how she took the geezer to the cleaners and sent the rich fucker back to his wife and kids almost insolvent. I don't quite know how to react to the Argentines hustling ways, but I don't pay it too much mind as I am very relieved to see her.

We don't shag each others brains out, as you would expect a couple would after not seeing each other for so long. Which suprises me, as I would have expected the Argy to go down like the Belgrano and make me come quicker than you can say 'GOTCHA'[1]. Instead we just lie on the hotel bed all afternoon and talk about what's gone before and what is going to happen next.

Creole and Mehmet are still hot on her heels, according to a source of hers in San Fran, Creole has followed Francesca trail all the way to Mehmet the Turks condo and they have now teamed up and are in LA looking for more clues that could lead them to the Argentine.

They have even been to Vegas looking for her. And are now on their way to plam Springs. Francesca is confident they will not get here before

---

[1] Please note that this is just word play. I am in no way glorifying the sinking of the ARA General Belgrano and I profusely apologise to anyone who takes offence, especially to the families of those who lost their lives. – JJ Williams

she has left, but according to my hallucinogenic self, Creole is already here. I definitely don't mention that sighting of Creole at the Grill, as Francesca would freak and I am now sure that I was only seeing things in my drunken high state of mind. It was all just dramatized paranoia. My mind maybe playing tricks on me and it's all my own doing of course, but my fucked up mind still has a state of conscience to tell me to leave her and her problems right now, and head for México and join Manchester and Pretty Boy and take Patrick with me.

Apparently Creole couldn't trace the coke back to Pamela, but rumours have got around that Francesca sold a few grams in Long Beach to some desperados and to a few to few gang bangers in East LA. Silly bitch.

At least I don't have to worry about Pamela anymore. That's a relief, I wouldn't have wanted anything to happening to her, she didn't deserve that shit.

"Why haven't you left for México already?" I ask her.

"I can't right now," she says, swinging her legs over the edge of the bed. "I have to lay low here in Diego for a few days and wait for one of my connections in LA to bring down some of my personals."

"Fuck that!" I tell her, sitting up. "Don't you know what kind of mess you're in? You're in danger for fuck's sake! We gotta to get the fuck out of here"

"Danger? Don't make me laugh." She dismisses my paranoia. "Creole is, as you English say, a 'Wanker,' harmless. All he wants is the coke or the money. And that fucking Turkish son of a bitch is nothing but a rich mamma's boy. Anyway a friend of mine in LA is bringing my passport, and without that, I can't go anywhere."

That night Francesca and I meet with Patrick, who has been dumped by René. When Francesca asks what happend, he smiles at me and says, "Aw, I got a hotel room for us, and offered her some pills that I bought of this surfer geezer at Mission.

At first she wasn't havin' any of it, but after a few shots of tequila, she dropped a couple and started getting all kinky. After about half an hour, there was a knock on the door. I had asked this gorgeous pro in her 50's to join us earlier, and when René clued in to what was happening, she shot off sharpish."

I start laughing, while Francesca looks from me to Patrick shaking her head in disbelief. Patrick joins in with my laughter, "Yea, I guess she wasn't into a bit of manage a trois with an older woman." Francesca punches Patrick's arm.

"I don't know what her problem was," he says, grabbing his arm in mock pain.

"Well maybe you should have got a younger prositute." Says Francesca sarcastically.

"Yea thats what I would have done" I add. This time Francesca punches me on the arm.

We end up at a bar in The Gas Lamp called The Casabah. Its a local joint where up and coming bands show off their jamming skills to a clued up, alternative crowd.

The band currently playing are a pile of shit. They play lame Green Day and Offspring covers and to top it off, the bass player can't keep rhythm with the exceptionally good drummer. Francesca urges us to stay for a few sets, but Patrick and I have other ideas and other things to worry about. Tonight is Derby Day in North London. Yes Arsenal are playing the Scum, the Filth, the Yids, the Spurs, the wanky Tottenham Hotspur.

A stunning Henry free kick got us a deserved draw against Charlton at the Valley. That was followed by a fine display of attacking football at Ellend Road, where we cruised to an emphatic 4-1 victory against a hapless Leeds UTD side, who six months ago, all but ended our title defence at Highbury. Henry 2, Pires, and Gilberto the scorers.

Our good form turned into good fortune in the Champions League on Tuesday night. Ashley Cole's last gasp injury time winner in our home game agaist dynamo Kiev means we live to fight another day in Europe. This has set us up nicely for the visit of our under-achieving arch rivals from N17.

The question is where the hell are we going to watch it. I'm not going back to that Spanish gaff, whatever it was called. Those bastards will probably be watching some Real Madrid or Barcelona game.

An option we do have is watching it in Francesca's room, as I'm sure that she has FOX Sports. The only thing is getting her to leave this club and go straight back to the hotel at closing time, and not go to a party she has been invited to.

Francesca asks us if we would like to go to this party. Even if we weren't playing the scum I still wouldn't have gone. The party will be full of pot smoking airheads, and

> The Casabah
> 2501 Kettner Blvd.
> San Diego,
> CA 92101
> Decent club with a shit band on the night. Saying that, Nirvana, The Smashing Pumpkins, and The Lemonheads, have all played there. I just hope the band playing tonight are not the best up and coming band San Diego has to offer, if so I weep for the future of Southern Californian guitar bands.

most of them will be guys. Not that I'm on the pull of course. We decline telling her that Patrick has had one too many and will make a tit of himself. Francesca falls for it and gives us the key to her room. We can hardly contain ourselves as we head for the hotel.

Patrick and I are sitting in Francesca's luxurious room at the hotel drinking a few beers we picked up on the way from an Armenian 24-hour shop. We paid double the price we would have normally paid, but watching the game would not be the same without some sort of alcohol, especially this one.

I am always very nervous before a home game against the Scum, because the thought of them beating us at Highbury would be too much to take. The last time I had such a feeling was in 1987, a Littlewoods Cup semi-final first leg. Clive Allen gave Tottenham a first-leg advantage at Highbury. I can remember feeling sick after that, so much so, I couldn't go to school the next day. Not only had the Scumbags beaten us at home, but they had almost certainly knocked us out of the competition and reached the final.

However, an amazing turnaround saw Arsenal come through the tie in an exhilarating reply at the "Shit Hole" (White Hart Lane). David "Rocky" Rocastle will never be forgotten for scoring the late winner that lead to the creation of the fanzine; "*one nil down, two one up.*" For the record, Spurs did beat us at Highbury in 1993, but that does not count because we sent the reserves out in an act of precaution for the FA cup final a few days later.

A huge meat pizza has arrived to soak up the beer. We are in heaven.

Spurs have sent out a very defensive line up with King and Konchesky, (both defenders) in midfield. However Patrick and I are both super confident that we will break them down eventually. But with only five minutes gone, we and 35,000 Gooners at Highbury are stunned into a silence as "Sicknote" Darren Anderton has somehow got on the end of a defected pass and slipped the ball past Lehmann. For fuck sake!

Now I need a drink. We have drunk all six beers come half time as we are still one nil down, at home to the Scum, and we can hear the Spurs fans in the Clock End making the most of their rear lead at Highbury. I cannot blame them I suppose, as you are more likely to see a blow up doll have an orgasm than see Tottenham lead at Highbury.

I just hope it is not going to one of those days where the unthinkable happens, surely not.

It's good timing as Francesca calls during the interval to see if everything is okay, and to see if we wanted to anything brought back from the party, as she is about to jump a cab and return to the hotel. I tell her everything is not OK, as we are one nil down at home to Tottenham. I ask her to bring back a bottle of scotch, brandy or rum. Something hard. I think we're going to need it if the Scum hang on to their lead.

Francesca returns with a bottle of Jack Daniels she has also brought us some nachos with a salsa dip and all. What a girl!

"That party sucked man," she tells us, fixing us some drinks. "Full of wankers."

Francesca has picked up on the tense, nail-biting atmosphere of the hotel room. The three of us are on the edge of the bed nervously munching nachos and washing them down with very strong

JD and diet cokes, as Arsenal still cannot break down the scum's resilience.

"We can't lose to these cunts surely, they're a fucking shit Spurs side," says Patrick walking around the room aimlessly waving his arms.

I just sit there in silence on the edge of the bed drowning myself in JD. We are nearly into the 70th minute, the Highbury faithful are even quieter than what they normally are (if that's possible) and Keller in the Tottenham goal is playing a blinder.

Suddenly Henry burst down the right, his shot has brought another fine save from Keller, but this time man-of-the-moment, Pires is on hand to slot the ball home. Relief! I feel as if a block of cement has jumped out of my body, while the three of us leap onto the king sized bed for joy! In the midst of the excitement, the bed collapses making a thunderous noise. But we don't care, as Arsenal have equalised.

"Now for kill, let's finish off these cunts!" shouts Patrick frantically.

Francesca pours us some more drinks as the last ones went flying when Bobby Pires scored that equaliser. A draw is better than a loss to Spurs. But at home, I would expect us to beat this second rate Tottenham side.

Some nice build up play between Bergkamp and Kanu finds Lyungberg in space, who cuts in from the right and lets fly. The shot deflects off Stephen "Wan" Carr and loops over the despairing Keller and into the back of the net.

The three of us go mental again and the bed gets the same treatment. One nil down, two one up; its 1987 all over again, that one was for you Rocky.

The game ends 2-1 and keeps us top of the table, still unbeaten!

"We beat the Scum, 2-1!" Patrick and I sing, as Francesca looks horny as ever, drunkenly laughing on the dishevelled, broken bed.

Patrick gets on the phone to London to celebrate with some mates who were at Highbury. While he does, I take Francesca to the bathroom and fuck her in the standing position, underneath the power shower. We do not even bother to take our clothes off. What a way to celebrate beating the Scum.

The next day Patrick decides to leave San Diego and join, Manchester, Pretty Boy and the all American girls who are now in Ensenada a small, touristy port 100 kilometres south of Tijuana. I tell him I'm going to stay with Francesca for another week; her papers are due to arrive on Saturday. She insists that I spend the next week in the hotel with her. Brilliant! I can now get my stuff from that shit hole, The Banana Beach Bungalow.

"I should also charge you an extra $20," says the Irish receptionist when I'm checking out.

"What! What for?" I ask, surprised.

"I bet you that if you stayed longer than five days you would give me $20 remember" she says, giving me an all-knowing look.

"Shit, oh yea, I forgot about that" I reply, relieved I don't have to pay for a hidden charge or something.

"I tell you what, I'm going to the Open Bar tonight, so if you're around, come and buy me a drink," she says handing me my receipt.

"A $20 drink?"

"No a $5 drink. I'll cash the other $15 on something else," she says with a wink and a smile.

"Maybe I'll see you tonight, then." Great sense of humour, these Irish birds. If Francesca wasn't around, I might have taken her up on that drink, and I reckon I would have given her good value for that $15.

> The Banana Beach
> Bungalows
> 707 Reed Ave
> Pacific Beach, San Diego
> CA 92109
> 858 273 3060
> Great location, great birds, great price, friendly Staffordshire Bull terrier but an absolute shit hole.

I am sitting on a table outside in a Mexican restaurant called 'Su Casa', in La Jolla, a lavish northern beach suburb of San Diego. It is Thursday, November 20, just two days left of my last week in California. I was meant to be spending most of this week with Francesca but she has been going crazy trying to sort out her papers and money. To be honest it's doing my nut in.

I was sitting in her hotel room for three days doing fuck all; flicking through the TV channels and being resigned to watching self-improvement shows hosted by Dr. Phil or Anthony Robbins.

I wanted to get to a Californian beach one more time, I give Mission and Pacific beaches a miss, as I don't want to run into the likes of Peggy or any of those other Muppets from the hostel. Besides, seeing a different beach would be nice on this, my penultimate day in the Golden State.

Nice spot this, La Jolla Cove. I wish I spent more time here; it a bit more sophisticated than Mission or Pacific Beach, and not a scrubby backpacker in sight. I have nothing against my fellow backpackers, but it is great to get away from the musky smell, the bed bugs and the meaningless small talk from time to time.

Feeling peckish, I wander into the first restaurant I come across. It is an authentic Mexican restaurant. I guess I will be eating shit loads of Mexican food in the coming weeks, so I had better become accustomed to it. I order a Tostadas Grande Special, and wash it down with a Sol beer then a shot of tequila.

There are no tables in the shade to protect me from the uncompromising sun so I pay for the meal and leave as the sun is killing me, and I'm

Su Casa
6738 La Jolla Blvd.
La Jolla, CA
858-454-0369
Su casa means 'your house' in Spanish. Your house, bollocks! Where was a parasol when I needed one, saying that the meal was lovely, as was the price.

sweating like a cunt. However sweating is a good thing, for one, it is ridding my body of all the alcohol and other shit it has had to endure, especially in the past few weeks; secondly it shows that my kidneys and liver are still functioning. I would be more worried if I wasn't perspiration in conditions like this after some of the nights I've had.

Across the road from the restaurant, there is a hairdressing salon called Sun's Barber & Beauty Salon. The sight of this salon and the sweat pouring down my face has made me realise that I am in need of a much-needed haircut. Inside, an attractive, slim, blonde hairdresser is having a conversation on a cordless phone. "Be with you in a second, honey," she says to me, in a high-pitched voice, "I'm nearly done here. Just gimme five minutes, okay sweetie. Take a seat."

I wait patiently, wiping my sweaty forehead, flicking through magazines. I should have really given that beer and tequila a wide berth, as it's not doing me any favours in this heat. The sweat continues to pour. Ten minutes later, I am still sitting in the waiting area while the hairdresser continues to gossip on the phone about another woman's cheating husband.

When she eventually hangs up the phone, I put down the December 2003 edition of *Cosmopolitan* I was reading and stand up to greet the hairdresser.

"Hey I'm Carla, I own this salon," she introduces herself with a soft whiny Californian accent. "What can I do you for sir?"

"Do you cut men's hair?" I ask.

"Sure, it's a unisex salon. That will be no bother at all, man."

"In that case, I'll have a number one, please."

Carla has the physique of a yoga teacher. Her skinny but muscular arms are pumped as she runs the clippers over my skull.

"Nice little salon you have here," I say, making light conversation.

"Oh yeah thank you sweetie. I started out in 92. God that was a long time ago, huh! It was so quiet then, just had one customer, that was little old Stacey from the Travelodge reception," she tells me, gesturing to some place behind us. "Now I have a full diary every week and even had to expand the business last year. I got me a little helper on Saturdays."

I cannot get a word in edgeways, as Carla waffles on proudly about her precious little salon. I sit there in silence looking at the man in mirror reflecting on my journey thus far. I only get as far as the cable car to Fisherman's Wharf and seeing Francesca for the first time.

"That's it honey. How does that suit ya?" Carla asks, interrupting her own babbling conversation and my daydream.

It looks good actually; a clean shaved head. That should ease the suffering from the heat.

"That will be $15 for you sweetie."

"Cheap at half the price!" I reply.

"Sorry, what's that sweetie?"

"Cheap at half the price."

"What does that mean?"

"Nothing really, it's just an English idiom, you know, like a saying, it kind of means I should have paid more."

"Cheap at half the price. Hey, I've never heard that before, it almost sound as if that haircut was too expensive for you honey."

"Yea I suppose it should be - cheap at double the price."

"So what brings you to La Jolla with that accent?" she says as I am walking out the salon door, I lie to her, and tell her that I am on leave from the British army, and I have just left Iraq.

"What! Why didn't you tell me?" she exclaims, following me to the door. "A British soldier? No way, man! You should have told me! You were sitting there all quiet and stuff. I guess that's an army thing, huh?"

I would have told her but she did not shut the fuck up for the duration of the whole haircut.

> **Sun's Barber and**
> **Beauty Salon**
> 6784 La Jolla Blvd
> La Jolla, CA
> 858 454 1082
> **Great salon, great**
> **haircut, great host, great**
> **conversation.**

"Have you got a cap, soldier boy? You better put one on or you will get sunstroke on that freshly shaved head of yours," she scolds me, generously handing me one of hers. "And I can smell that liquor on your breath, so you'd better take this" she adds, handing me a bottle of water to re-hydrate myself.

I spend the rest of the afternoon on the beach perving at bikini clad blondes and Latin chicas on La Jolla beach.

When I get back to Francesca's hotel room around six, she isn't there, but has left a note on the freshly made bed. It reads:

'Hey baby! Everything is sorted. The passport and the money is in order. I will be leaving San Diego tomorrow. I will be at a restaurant called The Dakota Grill on 5th Avenue, meet me there at eight.'

I guess that means I'm leaving tomorrow too. After a refreshing shower and half an hour of watching teenage dating shows on MTV, I take a stroll in search of the restaurant and the expectant Francesca.

She leaps in the air and gives me a very warm, tight hug. It is the happiest I have ever seen her. All her shit is sorted. One of her mates is meeting her at the border with her passport and other things she left behind in San Fran when she departed hastily in order to avoid Creole.

"My English *papi*," she says with her natural Latino accent, then switching back to her adopted American accent "Richie, sit down and have anything you want on the menu. My treat, ok?" she smiles and winks at me.

Fucking, thieving Argentine! Ok, generous she may be, but the cash she is splashing out on me is either drug money or money she has hustled out

The waiter has to check with his boss to see if indeed we can buy spirits by the bottle. But in California money can get you anything you want.

In her excitement, she barely touches the food, but the bottle of vodka is nearly half empty and has made her speak freely about how she played all these men and scammed fortunes off of them. She puts the bottle of vodka and her glass down on the table and looks at me seductively.

"Hey baby," she whispers, "take me home, and make love to me." She pays for the meal and we jump in a cab for the short ride back to the hotel.

I would love to fuck Francesca or make love to her like she suggested, but as soon as she slumps on the bed, she passes out. That leaves me with a bottle of single malt scotch, a big screen TV and a king size bed. Just as it was on my first night in California.

I am awoken the following morning by Francesca, who is licking my balls and shaft. I have a boner but I can bearly move a muscle due to the hangover I have just realised I have. My current state suggests that this is not going to be a action-packed sex session, so I leave her to it. Francesca is in a league of her own in the art of sucking dick, and as a result, I am soon flooding her mouth. Just as I am finishing my orgasm, she jumps up off the bed nonchalantly and takes a shower. I am just as unmoved as Francesca is unflappable about what has just taken place, this is due to the minging hangover I have. I fall back to sleep in order to get rid of it.

> **The Westin Horton Plaza**
> 910 Broadway Circle
> San Diego,
> California 92101
> Phone: (619) 239-2200
> The beds just aren't strong enough!

Two hours later, I'm again woken up, this time by a young, stocky Mexican chamber maid. She has come to set up the room for the next guest. Franseca has paid, checked out of the room, and left me with lying on the bed with my pants down.

The chamber maid looks at me with wide eyes. In my dreams she would have stripped off, sucked me off and then ridden me with those Mexican, thunder thighs. But instead all I get, "Sorry, señor," and the door is shut.

Today is Saturday, 22nd November, 2003, my last day in California. It's also a day when we can finally see a team of English sportsmen crowned as world champions on a field of play. I am of course, talking about the Rugby World Cup final; England versus our old nemeses the Aussies. To many an Englishman, whether in South London, Sydney or of course San Diego, it is a day to saviour.

I, of course, missed the match due to the time difference.

When Johnny Wilkinson dropped kicked through the sticks in Sydney to send us to world cup glory, this Englishman was getting a good old cock sucking from an Argentine.

It's great to see an English team become world champions, whatever the sport, wherever you are, and it's always good to put one over those fucking arrogant Aussie cunts.

However, there is a football game taking place in Birmingham today, which for me, and to millions of other Arsenal fans around the globe, is a lot more important than the England rugby team beating the Aussies in their own back yard and becoming the world champions. This, despite the fact I can collect my winnings of $1,000 from the Kiwi owner of the Venice Whaler, and another grand from that huge Canadian I met Pier 23 in San Francisco. With all this cash, I will be able to travel through Central and South America all the way to Buenos Aires.

Arsenal's game today against a Birmingham City side, who have made a surprisingly good start to the season, will keep us unbeaten at the top of the table, should we win.

Still slightly hung over from last night's scotch drinking, I attempt to get dressed, but am all of a sudden overcome with a bout of tiredness, which make my limbs stop functioning. I flop back onto the bed and turn on the TV.

I search frantically through the six thousand channels and finally get to Fox Sports where Arsenal have kicked off with a Fred bare, depleted team: Gilberto- jetlagged, The Man UTD four; (Vieira, Keown, Parlour and Lauren) are all suspended and Wiltord is injured. Pires and Cole join Edu in a midfield that must have Savage and co, rubbing their hands with the expectancy of a home banker of an upset. However, since we are Arsenal, and no matter whom we play outside of the top four, we are expected to win, whoever is in our midfield.

The Arsenal hater/referee for the day is the strawberry blonde Paul Durkin of Dorset, who in all honesty is a wanker, and probably supports Man Utd.

True to form Durkin, the ginger twat, gives us nothing in the opening exchanges and allows the Birmingham midfield trio of Savage, Cisse and Spurs, Daddy Boy reject Clemence, to kick the shit out of our flair players.

I am already getting pissed off and yelling abuse at the TV, in the direction of Gerkin, as he gives Forsell a free kick on the edge of our box for climbing and then falling over Cygan, who is in for Toure at centre half. Toure, our best player so far this season, is playing at right back. Fuck! A makeshift defence to go with the already makeshift midfield! Away from home, with Durkin refereeing. Where's that bottle of scotch?

Before I can find it, Bergkamp, who is skipper for the day finds Henry with a slick pass, he then slides through an inch perfect, telepathic through ball to Ljungberg, who he knows by now, would be running into gaping the hole between our old boy, Upson and Cunningham. Freddie slips it under the onrushing Taylor to make it 1-0 with only five minutes gone.

That is such an important goal for us and for me. It has settled our nerves in this hostile Brummy cauldron, aided by an Arsenal hating, cheating ref. As for me, it probably prevented me from becoming a rubber stamped alcoholic.

While the shaven-headed Ljungberg celebrates, the phone rings. It is Francesca. She tells me that she has paid for another night, and that I can stay as long as I want, just so long as I am at the Mexican border at three o'clock. She predicts that I'm watching football and asks what the score is.

Birmingham are stunned into action, as their passionate fans demand more from them, whether they are playing the Champions elect or not. Campbell, Cygan and Toure, who has gone a little narrower from his right back position, are stifling the waves of the Blues aerial bombardment. Nevertheless, Birmingham are soon inevitably aided. Durkin, the fat ginger cunt, shows Toure a needless yellow, when he slipped on the greasy surface and clipped Forssell.

Durkin's biased adjudicating has left Toure edgy and made me pour myself a Macullum with a diet coke I got from the mini bar.

Savage, now spurred on by the crowd, has gone berserk. He is kicking his way through our stylish midfield. A player, who is more dangerous without the ball than with it, is the Welsh international, now assisted by Durkin who has given him the freedom of the park and to our midfielder's shins.

Nevertheless, we hold onto our slight advantage at the break.

The American "soccer" pundits are not worth listening to, so I mute the TV set during the interval.

That's one thing, I do miss about watching the football back home. You cannot beat a bit of Lineker and Hansen on *Match of the Day* or Keyes and Gray on Sky Sports.

The second half begins just as the first ended, with us under the cosh and me pouring myself a Macullum and diet coke. We are not offering much up front; Henry and Bergkamp are not getting much service from the midfield and are not getting sufficient support from Pires or Ljungberg.

It is going to be traditional Arsenal performance, where we try and grind out a 1-0 win. Wenger will then put on a defensive player with about 15 minutes left which will consequently invite more pressure, and will then result in us getting hit with a late sucker punch that will send the home fans delirious.

That happened all too often in our failed title defence last season.

Feeling a bit tipsy, I am hailing more abuse at the TV, calling Wenger a cunt for being negative by inviting Birmingham pressure. However after 80 long minutes, Bergkamp races onto a Henry through ball leaving Upson and Cunningham in his wake, he coolly lifts the ball over the advancing Taylor and wheels away with glee. He celebrates Ian Wright style, in front of the travelling Gooners, by pointing at the captain's armband he so proudly wears on his left arm. At last, a two-goal cushion, I can now relax. My nerves are settled but I still pour myself another single malt to celebrate.

Very late on, Henry is the provider again, this time for my man Pires who finishes neatly making it 3-0 and rounding off a very high-quality away team performance.

It is going to be a long journey crossing that border and then somehow getting to Ensenada, so to supplement the trip, I stock up my backpack with miniature scotches, bourbons, rums and brandy from the mini bar. Francesca has already paid for the room so what the fuck.

It's only an hour and a half until I meet Francesca. There are many ways to get to the border, but I elect for the trolley, it takes about 45 minutes and only cost $2. I hop on and listen to some old school Jamaican Ska tracks on my Sony

Discman. I got to get myself one of those MP3 players. Carrying around all these disk just isn't practical anymore, I've got to get with the times and live in the future.

The trolley is full to capacity mainly with Mexican men with legit visas bringing home a minimum wage salary to feed their wife and kids, whom they haven't seen all week. It's all quite sad really, but listening to songs like *"Skinhead Moonstomp"* by Symarip and *"54-46 Was My Number"* by the Maytals, takes my mind off of the plight of many a Mexican worker in the US.

I get to San Ysidro, the stop at the border. It's still early, so I enter McDonalds and grab a Big Mac, fries and diet coke to sort me out. I grab a table by the window in order to see when Francesca arrives.

As I gaze at a mother feeding a Happy Meal to her young daughter, I reflect on my three months in California, a montage of this unpredictable journey from San Francisco to San Diego. I have had many great moments with many great people; Pamela along the Big Sur, Ian and Derek in LA and Vegas, forming the band in LA with Manchester, Pretty Boy and then being joined by my mate Patrick, the lovely Jessica, Katrina the Israeli, The Hollywood bender, that night we all had at the Pacific Bar & Grill and those giant birds from Wisconsin. I even think of Peggy and then of course Francesca and seeing her for the first time at that tram stop in San Francisco.

We will be saying good-byes until we see each other again in about six months or so. While she is sorting herself out in Buenos Aires, I will be having the time of my life with Manchester, Pretty Boy and Patrick travelling through Mexico and Central America.

It is a quarter past three and still no sign of her. I order a coffee and continue to wait. Twenty minutes later still no sign of her. In my frustration and impatience, I pop open a miniature Johnny Walker and pour it into the diet coke. Oh well, I guess I'll be seeing her in Argentina, maybe. Maybe she was never coming here at all, and just fed me this story to make me feel good and she already has her passport and has flown straight home.

My insecurities and worries are not necessary, as the beautiful Argentine bursts into the restaurant and gives me a tight hug. She is so happy to see me and her complexion has an effervescent glow that illuminates the dull, McDonald's restaurant.

"Oh Richard," she says, catching her breath, "I'm going to miss you so much when I go to Buenos Aires." Tears are already streaming down her face, as she gives me a beautiful smile.

"I'm going to miss you too," I admit, feeling a lump in my throat.

"Come with me, Richard," she urges, pulling on my arm. "Come with me to Argentina. I realised while I was away from you this morning

315

that I have so many feelings for you and maybe I love you."

"Love me?" I repeat, staring at her in disbelief.

"I'm going to the bathroom," she announces. "Think about it." As she wheels away, I watch that faultless arse of hers all the way then head back to my table.

Hmm, flying straight to Buenos Aires with Francesca would be good, so long as her hustling, rich-man-robbing days are over. But I would miss out on travelling Central America with the lads. It's not going happen.

As she comes out of the bathroom, I see a familiar face walk into the restaurant. It's Gabrielle, her Argy mate. She is carrying a few bags; it must be Francesca's stuff.

"Gabby!" shouts Francesca, excitedly when she comes out of the bathroom. "You're here Gabby! Right on time." She goes to hug Gabrielle, then suddenly stops in her tracks, with her smile fading.

"And so am I," says another familiar face, who appears from behind Gabrielle. It's Creole!

Francesca backs up looking like a rabbit in headlights. Creole stands beside Gabrielle, who glares cryptically at Francesca.

"Hello Francesca," he says slowly.

"Gabby," she shrieks! "Wha... what the hell are you doing? What the hell are you doing with him? You're my friend!"

Gabby smiles, "Was your friend, bitch." She takes a step closer and continues, "You've had this coming to you for months."

I'm sitting back at the table, inconspicuous to all of them, but hide my head behind my McDonalds paper bag just to make sure they don't see me.

Creole hands Gabby a nine millimetre pistol.

"Gabby! Please no!" pleads Francesca with her hands out in front of her. She turns to look at me, as Gabby pulls the trigger. The bullet hits its target. Francesca flies back towards the bathroom door from the impact. Creole and Gabby holding the smoking gun leave instantly.

Chaos ensues as people scream and run frantically to the door at the rear of the restaurant. The mother beside me shrieks, picks up her crying daughter and hits the floor. I can't see Francesca anymore amidst the mayhem.

Shocked, confused and thinking that Francesca is dead; I grab my bags and leave with everyone else.

LOS ANGELES,
23 November 2003

I am sitting at LAX waiting for a 2:00 pm flight to Tijuana, listening to *The Smith's Greatest Hits* on my Discman.

It turns out Francesca wasn't only ripping off ex-boyfriends and fat old rich men. She also secretly shafted her best mate, Gabby out of $5000. Gabby found out through Creole, who she has been shagging for the past month. She has since become besotted with him. So, when Creole asked her to kill Francesca, she did not hesitate.

However, kill Francesca, she did not. The bullet hit her in the shoulder, missing all vital organs. Gabby and Creole left the scene immediately. I slipped out the back door before the police and the paramedics arrived. Too shaken by the ordeal to cross the border, I jumped on a Greyhound and headed back to LA.

As soon as I got back, I rang the Sharp Coronado Hospital in San Diego to enquire about Francesca's well being. They told me that she was alive and in a stable condition. The police will be detaining her in San Diego for further questioning when she is well enough to give an interview.

of rich, deceitful, married men on golfing trips in Palm Springs.

We order appetizers and chit chat about what we are going to do in México while we enjoy them.

Francesca, as usual, looks stunning, wearing a low cut, satin-looking, loose-fitting, zebra top, which just shows a hint of cleavage. Her elaborate dark eye makeup and pulled back hair are complimentary of the top, giving her this wild look. The glossed lipstick she wears doesn't quite suit the outfit but makes her mouth stand out and look delicious.

"Why don't you order a bottle of your beloved scotch?" Francesca suggests, when the waiter comes around to take our dinner orders.

"A bottle!" I reply.

"Yea well bring it back to the hotel and finish it there" Both Francesca and I order the same; grilled steak salsa fresca, charred scallions, green beans accompanied with garlic mashed potatoes. Normally a bottle of Merlot would be the order of the day, but at Francesca's request, I order a bottle of scotch; Macullum Twelve. Twelve, because they didn't have Eighteen. Franseca orders bottle of Vodka to wash down her meal.

> **Dakota Grill Restaurant**
> 901 5th Avenue
> San Diego
> CA 92101
> 1-866-839-1606
> Name your price and you can buy alcohol by the bottle but not Macullum Eighteen?

I also came to LA, because I needed extra cash for my trip. When I got back here I collected my winnings from the Rugby World Cup. The Kiwi owner of the Venice Whaler was shocked to see me, but more than happy to hand over the cash and now we now have a bet going on the 2007 Rugby world cup in France. I also emailed that huge Canadian and asked for my winnings to be wired into my HSBC account.

I'm just relieved not to be hurt, killed or in a police cell being questioned. I will email Francesca in about six weeks when the dust settles. For now, I can't wait to meet up with Patrick, Pretty Boy and Manchester in Ensenada.

I reflect on the past 24 hours as I board the Mexicana flight to Tijuana while Morrissey poetically whines in my ears, *"But still I'll leap in front of a flying bullet for you"* – would I fuck?

Featured Games

2001/02
Aston Villa 1 (Dublin) **Arsenal 2** (Edu, Pires)

2003/04
Man City 1 (Lauren og) **Arsenal 2** (Wiltord, Ljungberg)
Arsenal 1 (Henry pen) **Portsmouth 1** (Sheringham)
Arsenal 0 Inter Milan 3 (Cruz, Van de Meyde, Martins)
Man UTD 0 Arsenal 0
Arsenal 3 (Henry 2, Gilberto) **Newcastle 2** (Robert, Bernard)
Lokomotiv Moscow 0 Arsenal 0
Liverpool 1(Kewell) **Arsenal 2** (Edu, Pires)
Arsenal 2 (Edu, Henry) **Chelsea 1** (Crespo)
Dynamo Kyiv 2 (Shatskikh, Bialkevich) **Arsenal 1** (Henry)
Charlton Athletic 1 (Di Canio. pen) **Arsenal 1** (Henry)
Leeds United 1 (Smith) **Arsenal 4** (Henry 2, Pirez, Gilberto)
Arsenal 1 (Cole) **Dynamo Kiev 0**
Arsenal 2 (Pires, Ljungberg) **Tottenham 1** (Anderton)
Birmingham City 0 Arsenal 3 (Ljungberg, Bergkamp, Pires)

Barclays Premier League, 22nd November 2003

	Pld	W	L	D	F	A	GD	Pts
Arsenal	13	10	0	3	27	7	18	33
Chelsea	13	10	2	1	27	9	18	32
Man Utd	13	10	1	2	25	8	17	31
Charlton	13	6	4	3	20	16	4	22
Birmingham	13	5	5	3	11	11	0	22
Newcastle	13	5	4	4	19	18	1	19
Man City	13	5	3	5	22	18	4	18
Fulham	12	5	3	4	22	18	4	18
Liverpool	13	5	3	5	18	14	4	18
Southampton	13	4	5	4	10	8	2	17
Portsmouth	12	4	3	5	17	16	1	15
Middlesbrough	13	4	3	6	11	15	-4	15
Bolton	13	3	6	4	11	19	-8	15
Everton	13	3	4	6	15	17	-2	13
Leicester	13	3	3	7	20	22	-2	12
Tottenham	12	3	3	6	11	16	-5	12
Blackburn	13	3	2	8	18	24	-6	11
Aston Villa	12	2	5	5	9	15	-6	11
Wolves	13	2	4	7	8	26	-18	10
Leeds	13	2	2	9	11	33	-22	8

Printed in the United Kingdom
by Lightning Source UK Ltd.
125288UK00001BA/2/A